THE WHITE DRESS

THE WHITE DRESS

Mignon G. Eberhart

FIVE STAR
Unity, Maine

Five Star Romance.
Published in conjunction with
Brandt & Brandt Literary Agents, Inc.

Cover photograph by Tom Knobloch

October 1997
Standard Print Hardcover Edition.

Five Star Standard Print Romance Series.

The text of this edition is unabridged.

Set in 11 pt. Plantin by Minnie B. Raven.

Printed in the United States on permanent paper.

Library of Congress Cataloging in Publication Data

Eberhart, Mignon Good, 1899–
    The white dress / Mignon G. Eberhart.
        p.   cm.
    ISBN 0-7862-1131-8 (hc : alk. paper)
    I. Title.
PS3509.B453W46   1997
813'.52—dc21   97-14521

78294

To
Helen Perce
who reads them
forward and backward

CHAPTER I

At six they landed at Miami and Judith and Winnie met them.

As always, the sweet, moist tropical air, falling on them like a perfume as they walked down the runway, marked the distance they had come. Only that morning they had been in the modern, civilized skyscraper world of New York City. Now, with a few hours intervening, they were in the tropics, three hundred miles south of Cairo, actually. New York had been hot and lazy with summer, but this was different; the sky had a softer blue, the palms moved with a whispering grace against it; a dusty cloud of smoke drifted from a fire somewhere in the Everglades, as if reminding them of the strange, savage world that lay outside, still untamed and unconquered. There was a world which, at night, seemed to creep nearer, stealthily, as if in an everlasting attempt to reclaim its own.

She faced an unexpected and obscurely frightening thought; it was nonsense and yet it had a certain authority strong enough for Marny to pause a second, her hand on the railing, caught by an absurd compulsion to retreat, to turn around, re-enter the plane, go back to New York, go anywhere, but go. It was exactly as if she were afraid of something, as if some vague and unaccountable uneasiness, unrealized or, at least, certainly not acknowledged, had crystallized that moment and become fear.

Fear? But fear had to have an object and there was none. It was as baseless as the balmy, humid air. Tim was already ahead and she was holding up the other passengers.

She followed Tim as he bounced down the runway.

Tim Wales quite naturally was the first passenger off the plane, although he had sat in the choice single seat on the right, away up ahead. His promptness in getting back to the door and out of the plane first was not, however, because he was

7

president of the Wales Airlines, which spanned the globe like silver threads, making a shining web over the planet with Tim Wales in its center. Nobody stood back for him in deference; the plane was one of the company's regular passenger air liners, but probably no one on it except Marny and Andre (and of course the crew) knew he was the great Tim Wales. He got to the runway first merely because it was in Tim's nature to beat anybody to the draw, whether it was a contract for a foreign air base or getting off a plane.

This time Winnie, his daughter, and Judith, his young and beautiful second wife, were waiting. Marny knew him perhaps better than anyone except Judith and Winnie but she was never quite certain of what to expect from him. Except for his eyes (granite eyes with sparks of cold light in them) he looked rather like a fat, shiny, slightly bald but very rosy and healthy child. He was incredibly energetic, always buoyant and coupled swift-leaping imagination with a cold, acute business sense.

He took off his hat and waved it furiously. Winnie was standing inside the gate, waving too, laughing, and so exactly like the first Mrs. Wales that it was always a little astonishing to see her. Except, of course, she was young and attractive with her neat brown hair in a bun on her neck, her fresh high color, her lipsticked red mouth and even white teeth, her tanned, bare legs. She had slimmed down since Marny had last seen her, in the winter, just before Winnie and Judith left for the Florida house and the stay which had been lengthened, by degrees, for so many weeks. By nature rather on the stocky side, Winnie was now reasonably slender, and it was becoming to her. Her wholesome, laughing face showed very attractive lines; her bones were large and now that she had lost some of the extra flesh that had padded them, were visibly well shaped.

Tim kissed his daughter enthusiastically, and passed her on to Marny. "Darling," she said, embracing Marny and wafting a new and very successful perfume around her. "Judith's in the car. How are you, Father? Marny, you always look marvelous. Andre . . ."

Andre Durant had followed Marny. Winnie embraced him with hearty cordiality as she had Marny; he kissed her and

8

pulled her arm through his. Marny saw it, naturally; but rather unnaturally she looked quickly away. Andre's dark head bent like that over Winnie!

But everybody always kissed everybody else on arrival anywhere. It didn't mean anything, and even if it did it was nothing to her. Andre Durant was only a man she'd known (because Judith sent him to Tim Wales in New York with a letter of introduction) for exactly a week. They had lunched, dined, gone to some musicals, done the night clubs, danced. Because Tim asked her to go about with him, because Andre was a friend of Judith's, because Tim wanted him to enjoy New York. If she wasn't going to like it when she saw Andre kiss somebody else, even lightly on the cheek, like that, then she was in for a bad time because Andre would probably kiss everybody all his life.

Which was an irrelevant and silly thought and had nothing to do with her. But she listened, all the same. He said, "Winnie, dear! It's grand to see you. How was the tennis match? How are you? How's Judith?"

"Come along, come along," fussed Tim, bouncing ahead again and through the building, letting Marny and Andre and Winnie follow him to the long, shining car, chauffeur-driven, in which Judith sat waiting for them.

"Darlings," she said. Her voice was low and husky and beautiful. "How wonderful! Winnie, did you see to their baggage? Tim, my precious, you look too marvelous. Sit by me, Marny. Andre, how did you like New York?"

Winnie had seemed smart and pretty with her wholesome, fresh face and her white sports dress, pearls at her throat and in her ears, her new comparative slimness and new perfume, until they saw Judith. Judith was so lovely, so sleek, so streamlined and smart and groomed down to the last fine detail that, by comparison, she made Winnie lapse into the thick, rather awkward girl of teen age that she had actually been. Marny got into the car beside Judith and felt Judith's slender, cool cheek press her own in the only gesture of affectionate greeting Judith allowed herself and wondered if she, beside Judith's perfection, slipped back to the gangling, uncertain, awkward little-girl state. But she liked Judith; everybody liked her: Winnie, who might have been expected to dislike the beautiful young woman who had slipped into her mother's place and who instead had loved, mimicked, run errands for and adored her from the beginning; Tim, who'd fallen in love with her at what amounted to first sight. The business staff, the servants, trained by the first Mrs. Wales, resenting and fearing the advent of the new and young Mrs. Wales, had at once succumbed to her beauty and friendliness — as had Marny herself.

When she first heard of the projected marriage, two years ago, she'd been skeptical, mainly because of Judith's youth and Tim's money. She knew little of Judith, only what Tim had told her. Judith was young, she was a widow, Tim had met her during a trip to Buenos Aires and married her as soon as she arrived in New York. Marny's slight skepticism did not survive her first interview with Judith.

She looked at Judith now, as the porter finished stowing the bags in the back and the big car moved smoothly away. Judith looked remarkably well. She was only lightly tanned, as if she knew that a certain pallor was becoming to her. Her black hair was done with a long, straight white part in the middle and a kind of fan on her neck, so smoothly and so neatly that you felt there was not a hair out of place. She wore white, too, simple and straight, with a green belt and green sandals and an emerald Tim had given her as an anniversary present, glowing on her long, lovely hand. She was wearing mother-of-pearl nail polish, instead of red or pink. There was no detail of dress too small to engage Judith's lively and experimental attention. Tim had her other hand in his own. She turned to smile at him, but he was leaning out, in order to watch ahead through the space between Andre and Winnie who sat on the folding seats, and drive mentally with the chauffeur. He did not return Judith's smile and, in fact, except for clasping his young wife's hand, looked rather preoccupied and grim. The lines showed sharply around his eyes and mouth as they did when he was intent upon some urgent business problem and something he intended to settle promptly and in any way he could employ to settle it. Tim was always within the law but was not too scrupulous about the finer points of human relationship when he wanted his way. He'd been distrait, Marny reflected briefly, for several days. Probably some business deal was brewing and seething in his active mind and he was simply not ready to tell her about it yet. It was always like that. Yet he depended upon her, in an odd way, too.

Winnie was talking rapidly, about the week's tennis match in which, it developed as Andre questioned her, she had won a cup; about some recent changes in the house, about their trip, and the weather in New York, and how nice it was to have them there. Winnie was always dependable socially; Judith rarely. Tim peered ahead at the traffic. Judith smiled and listened.

They turned along Biscayne Boulevard and the smell of the sea came through the open windows of the car. Winnie said, "We had no idea you were planning to come, Father. Did you come on business or just to see us?"

For an instant Tim said nothing. Judith's lovely face was very still. Everyone, suddenly, in the car seemed to listen. Winnie turned, surprise in her candid face, and repeated, "Why did you come?"

"Wanted to," said Tim. "Glad to see me?"

"But of course," cried Winnie. Judith said nothing. Winnie chartered on: "Charlie Ingram is here too. Staying at his place on Silver Point. He's coming to dinner."

Marny remembered and liked Charlie Ingram, a perennial bachelor of fifty-odd, of vaguely English background, who lived on an inherited income and flitted in and about society with the greatest good nature, kindliness and popularity.

"He's taken up tennis again," went on Winnie. "He's developed a really good backhand drive. He's one of Judith's admirers this summer." She laughed, but admiringly, at Judith. "He's underfoot all the time."

Marny thought suddenly and rather sharply: Why exactly *had* they come to Florida?

It had been Tim's decision and a sudden one.

This was Monday. Sunday about noon he had announced they were going to Florida, he and Marny and Andre Durant

11

and that was all. At nine-thirty Monday they had been ushered (with some ceremony and welcome) into one of his own passenger planes.

For Andre, of course, it was returning; it was in Miami Beach that he'd met Judith. But Tim had added no word to his announcement of the impending journey. Usually he explained trips to Marny, telling her why, telling her what he intended to accomplish, outlining her own duties. He'd had time to tell her all that on the plane and hadn't.

She hadn't, however, given it any particular thought until then. Certainly, whatever the reason was, it was a perfectly matter-of-fact and sensible one.

The plane trip had been monotonous yet tiring. That and the sharply unwelcome notion of something inexorable and rather frightening in the steady encroachment of the tropical night plucked a little at Marny's nerves. Unbidden and unexpected and certainly unwelcome, another thought entered her mind: had Tim failed to tell her the reason for their trip because it was a personal one? Had it anything to do with Judith?

She glanced at them again; Judith's lovely hand in Tim's fat, shiny, strong one; Tim's preoccupied, uncommunicative face. Had Judith tired of that marriage?

That was unfair; merely a thought with no rhyme and reason for it. Judith and Tim were exactly as they'd always been, happy and in love, in spite of the difference in their ages, in spite of Judith's look of glamour and sophistication and the romantic atmosphere that somehow surrounded her wherever she went.

So far as Marny knew, and she would certainly have known otherwise, without any justification for it. If Judith had had lovers, Winnie would have known it; Marny would have known it.

Moreover, Tim Wales, with his shrewdness, his intuition, his great sensitiveness to people's feelings would probably have known it first.

No, the reason for their trip had nothing to do with Judith, not, at least, in that sense. As Marny thought that, Judith turned her exquisite, triangular face with its pointed chin and high cheekbones, its wide, soft dark eyes and arched, shining eyebrows and smiled at her. The uneasy question, almost, again, the fear (but of nothing certainly) was instantly made the absurdity it actually had to be. Marny felt her heart warming toward Judith as she always did when Judith smiled like that. In a queer way Judith and Andre Durant were alike; both of them had the most extraordinary, apparently unstudied and unconscious charm.

Winnie turned, putting her large, fair forearm across the back of the folding seat. "You are very quiet, Marny," she said. "Tired? We'll soon be at the house. We've done wonders with it this year, Judith and I. Of course, we never stayed in Florida long enough to do anything, other seasons. But it's really awfully nice in the summer, you know. We like it better, honestly, than the winter tourist season. There's always a breeze and . . . Here we turn off." She leaned forward and poked the chauffeur efficiently. "Turn here, then right across the bridge."

"New chauffeur?" asked Tim.

"We've had him a week," said Judith lazily. "He can't drive but don't be nervous, darling. We'll be home in a minute or two. It's so hard to get any help now. But Winnie finds them, I don't know how. Winnie is wonderful."

They were on the causeway, with Miami glittering in the setting sun behind them now, strung with a few early lights as if they were jewels, and ahead of them Miami Beach stretching to the right and left beyond the bay, green and white and beautiful. Islands like emeralds dotted the bay. Presently they would turn, and turn again, cross a bridge and reach Shadow Island, which Tim had bought several years before.

Andre seemed to be going to the island with them; it appeared to be taken for granted. Perhaps he'd been staying at Shadow Island before Judith sent him to New York with the letter to Tim. It was odd, thought Marny, that in all her conversation with Andre during that week, she didn't happen to know that.

She didn't, and if it came to that, she did not know very much about him. She had an impression that Judith had asked Tim to give him a job; if so, however, Tim had not mentioned it to her. She knew that he was young, good company and vouched for by Judith. There was something vaguely foreign about him. She knew he had lived in France and in various Caribbean islands and had traveled considerably. He had gone to school, briefly, he'd said once, in England, but he spoke American with only a touch of any sort of accent and that was, if anything, French. He was good at swimming, tennis, dancing, and knew odd bits of information on many and varied subjects. He was attractive — too attractive? — gay, handsome in a rather casual, careless way. She knew how he'd laughed, she knew he liked a rumba and danced with an easy Latin rhythm, she knew — well, that was enough. Why should she catalogue the virtues of Andre Durant, whose black head was bent near Winnie's as they both leaned near the open window to watch the jewel-like lights of Miami?

They turned off the causeway and crossed a bridge. It was the only approach to the island by road. During the previous summers when the house had been closed, the bridge was closed off by a chain. The car went through coral gates, and along a winding avenue set so beautifully and so thickly with tropical flowering shrubs that it blazed with scarlet and red and purple.

It was by that time growing dusk, so the shadows along the driveway were soft and thick. Another turn and they approached the house, long, white, Spanish in effect, with grilled iron, lacy and painted white, along the balconies, and lights glowing inside.

It was a beautiful house. It suited the palms, the thick, rustling bamboos, the bougainvillaea and poinciana, and the blue waters of the bay as perfectly as if it had grown there. Its modern, stylized lines were in complete and beautiful harmony with the brilliant, bold colors of the tropical setting. On the south, directly below it, lay the bay, blue now in the dusk. On the north was a swimming pool, tiled in blue. They caught a glimpse of it through thick shrubbery.

It looked cool and inviting. A quick swim before dinner was exactly what she needed, thought Marny. Something was wrong with her, something that the tropic twilight, the lush

14

greens, the bright scarlets, the sweet, humid air had sharpened, rather than lulled. It was like a bud, that small hidden sense of uneasiness, forced by the tropical air into swift, full — and rather sinister — bloom.

CHAPTER II

It was, however, an imaginary bloom; something she could not see or touch or account for in any way and she'd have to hurry for her swim.

Winnie took charge as the car stopped and moved things along briskly; dinner would be at eight, drinks on the terrace above the bay, now or at any time.

Under Winnie's brisk direction and bustling there was no chance for further talk. Before she realized it, Marny found herself in one of the guest rooms — a charming room — all modern blond wood and thick beige rugs and pale-pink cushions. An open door led to a balcony, from which winding iron steps, painted white and laden with purple flowering bougainvillaea led down to the strip of lawn and the bay. Winnie had painstakingly decorated the house and it made a perfect background for Judith's own perfection.

A small colored maid, neatly aproned and capped, appeared to unpack Marny's bags and see to the towels in the sea-green and scarlet bathroom adjoining.

The quiet was soothing after the steady, strong drone of the airplane engines.

It would be even quieter in the pool.

She searched out the white two-piece bathing suit she had packed hurriedly the night before and got into it, quickly. Her small midriff looked rather white, but a few days of Florida sunshine would cure that. She slid her tanned feet into scarlet sandals, twisted her dark hair into a bathroom knot on top of her head and fastened it with combs, considered and rejected the hot stickiness of a bathing cap, and went to the pool.

She knew the house rather uncertainly. She could cross the balcony, go down the twisting iron stairway, and around either end of the house, but probably there were people on the wide porch for which the balcony just there formed a roof.

She took the back way, narrow back stairs and a hall which ran past the kitchen door. She met no one on the way; there were only the clatter of dishes and smell of cooking from the kitchen.

She went quietly across the driveway leading toward the garage. Once beyond the hibiscus hedge, flaming outwardly with scarlet yet deep blue in the shadows below, she felt singularly removed from the house.

The pool was an even deeper blue; she sat on the flagstone border around it and took off her sandals thoughtfully.

She glanced back toward the high-enclosing hedge, and the green-shuttered windows of the house. Would Andre see her? And would he come to swim with her — the two of them, alone, in the cool blue water with the dusky, tranquil sky above them?

She broke off that train of thought abruptly. She slid into the water, turned over on her back and floated, barely using her hands, deliberately aware only of the slight movement of her slim body and the coolness of the water.

She wouldn't think of Andre Durant, and she'd conquer the abruptly flowering sense of something that was so like — well, like fear!

All right, then, face it and analyze it, she told herself, half in earnest and half in self-derision. Fear of what? Certainly nothing definable, nothing she could analyze or even identify; merely this was an uneasiness that surrounded her as softly, as intangibly and as inexorably as the deepening tropic shadow.

Well, then, forget it.

She swam and floated again. Usually it was easy to float like that, for a few moments, away from the job and the façade she had, perhaps unconsciously, perhaps in self-defense, built for herself, back to plain Marny Sanderson who didn't have to worry about keeping her feet on the rung she'd got to on a steep ladder.

How easily she could slip off that rung! Due to ill luck, due to a wrong decision, due to being a woman! Due to Andre.

There she was back to Andre again and glancing again toward the green hedge between her and the house.

She gave herself a violent push, turning so she could not see the house. Her body glided through the water; everything was quiet and cool and there was no one anywhere — especially no Andre — and nothing but the water and the darkening sky, and the lush, protecting lines of hibiscus all around.

She never knew how long the man at the rim of the pool had stood there watching her. She never knew how she knew that she was being watched, or what made her catch herself and lift her head and look toward the end of the pool, opposite to the house, not far from the driveway. She did so, however, with sudden expectancy as if someone had spoken to her.

He was quite near; she had floated almost to the end of the pool. He was looking across the strip of clear water directly into her eyes.

He was in uniform. He carried a cap in his hand. Seen from the water, there was an extraordinary strength and solidity about him, as if he had planted himself there and could not possibly be removed, except by his own will. He was, for a rather shocked instant, a part of the dream into which she had drifted, a figure coming from nowhere, silently adding itself to the fantasy.

Then she realized that several seconds had passed and they were still looking directly into each other's eyes. Directly and very intently, almost as if they had known each other or were going to know each other.

But she couldn't have known him; she'd have remembered him. In any case she must move, break that silence, and that locked and seeking look. The white, short skirt of her bathing suit lay on top of the water. She whirled over so quickly that she got salt water in her eyes and soaked her hair. She pushed the wet hair back and said, "Who are you? What do you want?"

It was not in her office voice — that pleasant, cool voice she had learned and tried to use, although with only a modicum of success. The hard, fast, thrilling, taut, adventurous, slightly piratical, altogether exciting world of the aviation industry was not one to induce coolness and calm at all times. But her voice

18

now was uneven and slightly breathless.

He said, "Are you Marny Sanderson?" And even in whirling over in the water, it flashed across her bemused, yet somehow shocked and startled consciousness that when he asked the question he hoped she would say no.

She swam toward him. The splash of her brown hands with their scarlet tips sounded loud and clear. The man at the end of the pool moved as she approached and put down a hand for her. It was sun-tanned and square with his academy ring on the third finger, and unexpectedly strong, for he hauled her up out of the water and onto the flagstones so swiftly and neatly and easily that again she was caught by a sense of surprise and breathlessness. She felt very small, standing now, looking up at him. She must look like a wet cat, with her hair hanging in dripping strands around her face. He was considerably taller than she and still had that squarely planted look of solidity he had had when she looked up at him from the water. She wished for her usual high heels, pulled down the wet and sticking skirt of her bathing suit, silently cursed her wet hair, and said aloud, "Thank you."

"You *are* Miss Sanderson?" he said again, looking down at her, and again she had the notion that he wanted her to say no.

"Yes."

Definitely there was something disapproving in his narrow, cool, gray-blue eyes. His mouth was rather tight, she thought — a Scotch mouth. His face was brown; his hair was black and looked shiny, as if he'd used copious water in making the neat part in it, and not very long ago. It was, as a matter of fact, rather disarming, as if it gave her a glimpse of a boy, square and straight-eyed and innately conventional, doing the things he'd been told to do, because reasonably and conventionally he accepted them. Not that there was anything boyish about the man, in the green uniform of a Navy flier, who stood there, so solidly and substantially before her. He said, "I thought so. They said at the house that you were down here. I'd better explain that I have no appointment. I learned that you and Mr. Wales were here so I took the chance of coming

19

out in the hope that you would see me. I'm sorry I disturbed you."

The flicker of dislike (Dislike? But he'd never seen her before!) in his eyes made her reply brusque. "I'd finished my swim. But Mr. Wales has just arrived. He prefers not to see people down here."

Everybody who knew of Tim Wales knew that he saw people anywhere he chose to see them. The man before her obviously knew that too; his face stiffened.

She continued quickly, "If you'll phone tomorrow and make an appointment . . ."

There was a short silence. The Navy flier looked angry; a slow flush crept up over his cheekbones and his eyes were so cold and gray that she lowered her own gaze. There was a row of little bright ribbons above his left pocket, a double row, as a matter of fact.

It was very quiet; the water was a shade darker, reflecting the deeper blue of the sky. The thick hedge all around them was like a wall of green. In the house a light showed in a window.

She thought swiftly of taking him to Tim and rejected it. Certainly this man who knew her name and had come to Shadow Island in the hope of seeing Tim wanted something. Everybody wanted something of Tim. Part of her job was to get rid of the people who wanted things. So she'd better say something.

She said, "I didn't mean to be rude; if you'll tell me something of your reason for . . ."

He interrupted. His face was still hard and angry, but he spoke evenly. "We seem to have got off on the wrong — that is, made a bad start. I — my name is Cameron, Bill Cameron, I'm in the Navy; that is, I'm on leave."

There were three black stripes on the sleeve of his green coat. That would be Commander Bill Cameron, then. She said, "Did you say you want to see me? Or Mr. Wales?"

"I — well, as a matter of fact, I want to see you. It's important."

Again there was a look in his eyes that seemed to disapprove, as if he wished she were someone else. She felt small because of his height and her flat-heeled sandals; she wished for her office desk and that her hair wasn't plastered wetly to her head and her bathing suit to her body. She said, before she could stop herself, stung in an odd small way by that look in his face, "Important to you, you mean?"

His face didn't change but the pupils of his eyes grew very dark. "Yes. Important to me. Important to everybody who's fought in this war and who doesn't want to fight in another."

Tim Wales hated cranks. He had, indeed, a swift and highly unpleasant manner of dealing with anyone whom he suspected even remotely of falling into that category. She knew that, usually, the cranks were going to make over the world, only it usually developed that they were going to make it over by means of some invention which they quite honestly (and sometimes with rather heartbreaking earnestness) begged Tim Wales to introduce — and finance.

Yet there was an effect of urgency and truth and, more than anything, of common sense in the face and voice of the man before her. She said slowly, "Perhaps you'd better tell me specifically just what you mean."

"Look here, Miss Sanderson. I'm no diplomat. What I've come for is really big and really important. And I — somehow I've got to convince you and Tim Wales."

"I have nothing to do with any decision of Mr. Wales. I am only . . ."

He interrupted, "I don't know exactly the title they've given you now, head of Public Relations or some such thing. Actually you are the nearest thing to a partner that a man of Tim Wales' stature could accept."

"Don't be ridiculous . . ."

"They'll make you a vice-president next year probably. You're at the top. I know. I've looked you up. I've asked. I had to know. You see . . ." He paused then, and said very slowly and deliberately, "You see, I don't want another war in another twenty years. Or ten years, or five years. I want you to stop it. You, Marny Sanderson. It *can* be up to you to stop the whole bloody business."

He *was* a crank! In spite of his steady eyes, in spite of his sensible, firm chin, in spite of the air of urgency and truth. She thought that, and he said instantly as if she'd spoken it, "I'm not crazy. Did you ever read the *Night Mail*? No, of course it was before your time. Anyway, it's all come true. Only it's come true now instead of in the year 2000. From now on the people who make planes make planets. Air power makes or breaks peace. Listen, Miss Sanderson, I saw this war. I don't want another. I'm speaking, too, for a lot of men who can't speak for themselves, ever again."

She did not believe him; she did believe him; she could not help listening. She said slowly, "Why do you come to me?"

"Because you're Marny Sanderson; because Tim Wales will listen to you. Because you are a woman. Because it's up to Tim Wales and a few other people to prevent another war."

"A few other people!" Other airlines, competitors, rivals? Had he come from them? Why? To entrap Tim Wales somehow with all those noble-sounding generalities. Suspicion shot through her involuntary, growing belief in his sincerity. His reply confirmed it.

"The others can't do it without Tim Wales. He's a czar. He . . ."

"You mean he has what they want, those others! You've come from them! They sent you, the other American lines? Or was it the foreign ones? And you thought I'd help you pull the wool over Mr. Wales' eyes for them. Who sent you here? Exactly who?"

She was angry at herself for listening, at Bill Cameron for coming to her like that, for catching her at a disadvantage, for inducing her to listen, for making her, almost, believe in his sincerity and then proving to be, probably in so many words, an emissary from an enemy camp.

She was not prepared for his reply, for he said simply, "You won't believe this, but it's true. I was sent by persons of the highest authority . . ."

"*What!*"

22

"Nationally and internationally important."

"*Who?*"

"I can't tell you," he said simply again.

"But what . . . I don't believe you. . . ."

Then someone quite near said lazily, "Am I interrupting?"

She whirled around. It was Andre Durant, in swimming trunks with a towel over his shoulder, a cigarette in one hand. She had been so caught, in spite of herself, by the things Bill Cameron had said that she had not seen Andre emerge from the hedge and come across the flagstones toward them. He said, eyeing Commander Cameron, "A friend of yours, Marny?"

She said automatically, "This is Commander Cameron — Mr. Durant . . ."

Andre put out a hand which Commander Cameron did not appear to see. Andre shrugged and said, "Is this an international conference? I thought I heard something about people of importance."

Bill Cameron, his eyes and mouth hard, said, "You don't believe me, Miss Sanderson? You are saying to yourself, if this is true he'd have letters of introduction, people would have telephoned, the way would have been paved in advance."

It was of course exactly what would have happened. But he wasn't a phony. He was merely, and in spite of that reasonable, sturdy Scottish face, a crank. Tim would make short work of him; it would be better and kinder if it came to that, to send him on his way without seeing Tim. She said, "Mr. Wales is here for a vacation. I don't know exactly how long we'll be here, but I really think it would be better to . . ."

He was angry again. He said, ". . . to get the hell out of here."

"Now really, Commander," said Andre. "Here . . ." he held his cigarette case, a gold case, set with sardonyx, ornate but handsome, toward the Navy flier. "Do have a cigarette. Let's talk this over peaceably, whatever it is you want!"

Bill Cameron turned toward Andre suddenly and swiftly. "Are you interested in the Wales Airlines?"

"My dear fellow, no. I merely thought . . ."

23

"Then I'll thank you to keep out of this."

Andre's eyebrows went up. He gave a small deprecating shrug. "No need to get worked up about things, Commander. Are you dining here? How about a swim before dinner?"

"I don't want a swim," said Bill Cameron. He turned to Marny. "I haven't got credentials, if that is what you want. I hoped to be able to make you understand. I thought you might be human. You looked that way — in the water. I thought you were a woman. I was wrong . . ."

"That has nothing to do with my job."

"No," he said. "I can see that now. I can see a lot of things." There were hard, dark pupils in his eyes. Unexpectedly, he took her hands, both of them, in his hard clasp and looked at them for an instant or two, and said, "You look like a little girl, a rather nice, pretty little girl with your hair down like that and your white bathing suit. Your hands are nice, too — slim and brown and quite pretty, really. And you'll not lift one little finger to stop this bloody business from happening all over again."

He dropped her hands with a gesture of something like contempt and turned away. Andre said quickly, "Now really, my dear fellow, I can't let you talk to my — to Miss Sanderson like this." He put his hand on Marny's wrist in a proprietary and protecting manner. "You'd better apologize, Cameron, and quickly."

Commander Cameron swung around, his eyes suddenly blazing, his hand doubled into a fist. Then abruptly he walked away.

There was a strip of grass and, further down, an opening through the green hedge upon the driveway. Marny watched the solid green-clad figure approach that opening and disappear within the blank and shadowy wall of deeper green. There was a brief sound of hard, angry footsteps on the gravel and then nothing. Suddenly Marny looked down at her brown hands, holding them out, turning them slowly, as if compelled to search the pink palms. It was darker; she could scarcely see the lines in her hands. The thick heavy foliage all around seemed nearer, as if it had moved in, closer, with the night.

Andre's voice came lazily through the dusk. "Pleasant fellow," he said. "Nice manners. Thought for a moment he was going to hit me. Who is he and what is it all about?"

CHAPTER III

"I don't know," she said slowly. "That is, yes, I do."

"Marny, darling, pull yourself together. This isn't like you."

She pulled down the wet skirt of her bathing suit again, and gave a little twist to the wet knot of hair. She'd been taken by surprise, and at a disadvantage by a man who was — well, who must be a crank. Talking of persons of high authority and stopping wars and all that. She'd looked very silly, probably, floating on top of the water with practically nothing on. Like a little girl, indeed, she thought angrily. She could feel her cheeks growing rather hot and flushed.

Andre saw it and laughed. "You're blushing. What did the fellow say to you? Who is he?"

"His name is Bill Cameron, Commander."

"Yes, I know. But what's the idea? What did he want you to do?"

"I don't know exactly. Mainly he wants to get at Tim."

"Oh, I see. Of course. Through you. And when he couldn't he got mad and left." Andre shrugged. "Don't give him another thought. He's a crank. Obviously. Probably touched by the war. Forget him. Let's have a swim."

She was listening for the sound of Commander Cameron's departing car along the driveway; he must have left it parked down near the gate. "I've been," she said absently, giving her hair another twist.

"I saw you from my room," said Andre. He put out his cigarette. "I thought, what a good idea. So I came down as soon as I could. Come on. There's plenty of time." He went to the rim of the pool and dropped his towel on the flag-stones.

She still did not hear the sound of Commander Cameron's

26

car. She said absently again to Andre, "It's all right to dive; that's the deep end."

He flashed her a rather odd glance. His eyes were dark and vivid but it was not easy to know what he was thinking about. He stood for a moment, poised on the rim of the pool, tall, deeply browned by the Florida sun, neither too muscular nor too flabby. He said then, "Yes, I know. Coming?"

Obviously, Commander Cameron had walked in from the causeway; in any case it didn't matter. She went to the pool and Andre made a long, easy dive. She waited until his head came up, shining and wet and black. He shook the water out of his eyes. "Cool," he said. "Come on in. I'll catch you." Her hair was already soaked; she might as well dive. That was due to Bill Cameron's unexpected appearance!

She had an odd feeling just as she dived that Bill Cameron had come back to the opening of the hedge and was looking at her, a mistaken one, for when she came up and Andre caught her, laughing, in his arms, she glanced back toward the hedge and no one was there.

"A good dive," said Andre. "What are you looking for?"

"I thought somebody was there."

He looked too, letting his hands slip down her arms to her wrists.

"I don't see anybody. Who did you think it was? Your sailor friend or somebody else?"

"I thought . . ." She'd thought of Commander Bill Cameron. For no reason, however, she did not say so. Instead she said, "I didn't see anyone. It was only an idea that someone was there. Nothing, really."

"Oh," said Andre, treading water and watching the thick green hedge. She glanced that way, too, again, but again the opening of the hedge showed merely a white strip of driveway. "Nobody's there now," said Andre, and dived again.

But both of them had been wrong, for someone said, "Good dive, old chap."

It was Charlie Ingram. He had come, however, from the hedge entrance near the house, for he stood at that end of the pool, hatless, browned, his white silk sport shirt open at the throat, wearing white slacks and tennis shoes and carrying a racket. He beamed at Marny. "Hello, my dear, hello."

"Hello, Charlie." As he walked around the pool, Marny swam to the side and hoisted herself up to the brim. He shook her wet hand heartily, his monocle falling from his pocket and swinging madly as he bent to greet her.

"Glad to see you, my dear. Glad to see you." He glanced at Andre swimming lazily across the pool. His face seemed to change slightly, but he said with even greater heartiness, "Have a nice time in New York, Durant?"

"Great," said Andre, swimming. "How's your tennis?"

"Very fine, old chap, splendid! Jolly good." He looked down at Marny. The forced heartiness in his voice changed to Charlie's naturally friendly tones. "Having a good swim? Must be nice after your trip today. Well, I must run along." He swung the tennis racket he carried. "Only walked over to pick up a racket Winnie had restrung for me. Have to go back now and change. 'Bye, my dear. See you at dinner. I want to hear all the news." He waved the racket cheerily and went toward the path through the hedge which Bill Cameron had taken. Halfway along he appeared to remember Andre, turned around, hesitated, said painstakingly, "See you, too, Durant," hesitated again and went abruptly on.

"Oh, by all means," replied Andre, fishing a large hibiscus leaf out of the pool where it had fallen and swimming to the edge to drop it over the curb. He didn't look at Marny, and they swam lazily for a while, saying nothing. The pool was quiet and cool, reflecting the sky so that it seemed light; there was no sound from the house. The thick hibiscus hedge seemed to wall them off from everyone.

She'd better tell Tim about Bill Cameron and the preposterous things he'd said, Marny decided presently. Tim disliked being bothered with anything that seemed to him unimportant, but she'd tell him, nevertheless. She tried a crawl and a dive and came up near Andre, who had turned on his back and was floating, his smooth brown face with its rather blunt, straight nose and chin, clipped black mustache, and unfathomable dark eyes turned upward to the sky.

Andre swam well and easily, the way he walked or danced, with an extraordinary, apparently effortless grace and ease. It was, it suddenly struck her, rather like the instinctive, perfect coordination of an extraordinarily slender and graceful animal. Actually, however, he was almost as extraordinarily poised and sophisticated and, she suspected, worldly.

Rather like an animal again, he knew instinctively she was looking at him and thinking about him, for he turned and looked at her quickly across the few feet of clear, pale water between them. He smiled, so his face flashed into vivacity and liveliness, although his eyes remained, as always, enigmatic.

"Do you approve?"

"Approve?"

"Of me, of course."

He saw too much. She said lightly, "Why not?"

He floated a moment, watching her, a rather speculative look in his face, and said abruptly, "You are — I don't know how to say it — different tonight."

"Different!"

"As if you'd forgotten the Wales Airlines and filing cabinets, for one thing."

Definitely he saw too much. He added lazily, his voice carrying over the quiet water, "You've always put the Wales Airlines first, haven't you?"

"That's my job."

"Oh, naturally." There was an effect of a shrug in his voice. He turned over with a lithe slow movement. "But don't you ever think of anything else? Men, for instance?"

If he knew how much she'd been thinking of him! But perhaps he did know it. She said, a shade too lightly, "I think of nothing else."

He swam nearer her. Occasionally he became for a moment very literal. It was, like his faint accent, suggestive of something foreign, un-American, even though he spoke the American idiom with ease and fluency. With a flash of that literalness, he said, "You are joking."

"Not at all. I like men."

He came up beside her. "We've seen a lot of each other

29

this week in New York. I know you better than you think I do. I might even know some things about you that you don't know yourself." He paused, his eyes laughing, and then said abruptly, "I'll race you to the end of the pool."

He won by a large margin and was sitting on the edge of the pool when she reached it. She climbed up to sit beside him. She caught her breath and tried to arrange her wet hair again.

"We'd better go in," she said. "I've got to do something civilized about my hair before dinner."

"It's only a little after seven," he said. "The butler was putting drinks on the porch when I came down the balcony stairs. Nobody else was around yet."

He got up nevertheless. "Want your sandals? Here they are."

She got up too and reached for the sandals, but he had them in his hands. "Put out your foot," he said, bending and holding a sandal for her. She did so, a little unsteadily, and he laughed softly and said, "Hold onto me." She put her hand on his wet, brown shoulder for balance. "Now the other one. All right." It seemed to her that he lingered a little over the laced tie. Then he got up briskly and went to get the towel he had left at the other end of the pool and came back, towel slung over one shoulder, while she waited. Obviously he knew his way around on the island. He knew the varying depths of the pool; he knew the balcony stairway; probably his room, which overlooked the pool and thus was on the opposite side of the house from her own, also had a good view to the balcony which, at different levels owing to the irregularly charming architecture of the house, encircled three sides of it. She said, when he reached her, "You've stayed here before?"

Again he gave her rather an odd glance. "You mean at the Island? Of course. Didn't Judith tell you?"

"She didn't write to me. Her letter was to Tim, naturally."

They strolled across the strip of grass toward the hedge.

"I was stopping at a hotel," explained Andre. "A rather shabby little dump, as a matter of fact, when Judith took pity on me and invited me here. Marny, I've been wondering, has

Tim said anything to you about a job for me?"

She couldn't have told him if Tim had discussed it with her, but he hadn't. "No."

"Oh," said Andre, after a moment. They reached the hedge. "Well, it's all right. I don't know exactly what talents I have to offer the Wales Airlines, but Judith thought there might be something."

It was like Judith; she could be aloof and bored, or impulsive and generous.

"Tim hasn't said anything of it," she said. "But he might not. He may have something planned for you."

"I doubt it," said Andre. He didn't seem particularly cast down, however; he said it indeed rather lightly and contentedly.

As they reached the hedge, he added, "Let's get through here. It's simpler than to go around to the path." He held back branches; one slipped from his hand and slapped back gently against Marny's face; she drew back sharply and involuntarily and was suddenly in Andre's arms. Close and hard and warm. He held her for a moment, and then moved her face with his own so his mouth came down upon hers and held her like that.

They were so close to the hedge that the soft shadow seemed to envelop them. Andre kissed her and held her and kissed her again.

Only all at once it didn't seem to be Andre holding her like that. By the most extraordinary alchemy it was Commander Bill Cameron standing there in the soft dusk with her, his green uniform against her bare shoulder instead of the rough towel, his mouth pressed down upon her own. That straight, hard, Scottish mouth.

She tried to move. "Andre . . ."

"Don't pull away like that. . . ."

"But I . . ."

"Be quiet." He kissed her again long and hard. She pulled away from him then, and he laughed a little, his handsome dark face vivid against the soft greens. "Don't be a child. I'm not asking you for anything. But it's silly to pretend you can run away from love."

31

"I'm not in love. At least I . . ." She was trying to escape his arms, she was pushing her wet hair back, she was altogether ineffectual and shaken and breathless.

He said, "You don't know a thing about it," and, half-laughing, kissed her again. He released her and stood for a moment, looking down at her. Then he said suddenly, "You've been in love with me from the moment we met. I've been in love with you. We've been pretending it isn't so. It's silly to do that. Life is short. You have to take love if it happens. Don't try to run away from it."

"I'm not. I — we've got to go in." Had Bill Cameron really gone? For another absurd, fleeting second she had an impression that his solid, green-clad figure had returned to stand in the opening of the hedge farther down. It was fleeting enough, that sense of surveillance, but strong enough, too, so she glanced swiftly that way. There was no one. And Andre unexpectedly and very gracefully gave in.

"All right. I expect you're right. But you're wrong about love. You'll learn that you can't always run away from it."

He held the branches for her and she slipped quickly through them. The house immediately overlooked them, windows light, balcony making a rim of shadow. The hedge had made a perfect screen, she thought, and it was just as well.

Andre said nothing as they walked across the drive, skirted the back entrance of the house again, and this time walked round it on the bay side and toward the balcony stairway which came down at the end of the porch. There was no one on the porch, but a tray of glasses and ice and bottles stood there, and lights came from the open French windows of the drawing room beyond. It was still light, however, outside; only the clustering massed shrubbery held shadows; the sky had the clear light of sunset and the water of the bay reflected it. They went quietly up the winding, grilled-iron stairway and paused for an instant on the balcony with its vine-hung railing and widely separated line of French windows.

Most of the bedrooms probably gave upon the balcony. Andre said, "It's confusing, isn't it? You have to count. But I think yours is the third from the front. Judith's is the first and then there's a couple of guest rooms."

The third door was open. The maid had opened it. Marny glanced into the room and could see her own traveling clock on the bed table. Andre said, low, "Remember what I said. You can't run away from love, ever." He took her hand for an instant and put it against his face, lightly, so her palm touched his cheek, laughed a little and turned away. "See you for a drink," he said and walked along the balcony toward the other end of the house, slinging his towel across his brown shoulders.

She went into her room, closing the screened door behind her. Suppose Andre was right.

Her scarlet sandals made vivid points of color against the beige rug at her feet. She remembered Andre's stooping to put them on and her hand on his shoulder and the sense — or hope? — that he was doing it slowly, rather deliberately, prolonging the small intimacy.

She'd better get off her wet bathing suit. She moved toward the bathroom and paused again, involuntarily, before the mirror. Her hair was wet and plastered to her head; her eyes were very bright in the semi-shadow in the room, and her mouth very red. She wished rather oddly that the Navy flier could have seen her then, rather than earlier, floating in the pool, her face probably a complete, regular blank. But it was Andre who was important, not the intrusive Navy flier, who had intruded even, in an annoying and subtle way, upon Andre and herself, there by the hibiscus hedge, quite as if he were present.

She turned abruptly toward the bathroom as Judith knocked on the door and called in her low, rather husky voice, "Marny, may I come in?"

She opened the door, and Judith, in pale yellow satin, which dripped lace at the wide long sleeves and trailed along the floor and left Judith's beautiful white throat bare, came into the room. She was smoking, her hair was thrust back with combs, and her face without make-up was as creamy white as a magnolia. She wore emerald green satin mules. Any other woman in yellow satin and lace would have looked theatrical in the extreme. Judith only looked perfectly beautiful and perfectly

33

self-possessed and normal. She closed the door and said, "I saw you come up the stairs. Did you have a good swim?"

"Yes, of course."

Judith sat down on the bed and shook ashes into the tray on the bed table. "You'd better get out of that wet bathing suit."

"I was just going to. Wait a second." Marny went on into the bright, gaily decorated bathroom and took off her bathing suit; the cool, soft silk fabric clung to her. She hung the brassiere and skirt over the shower railing, and Judith, ever practical, appeared at the door with her white dressing gown. "Here," said Judith. "There's lots of time before dinner. Winnie is seeing to the table. Tim's showering frantically by the sound from his bathroom. Nobody's dressed yet. I wanted to talk to you a minute."

"All right." She put on the dressing gown and twisted a towel around her dripping hair.

"Makes a good turban. Very becoming to you," said Judith, and surveyed her rather thoughtfully. "You look awfully well, Marny."

Marny secured the end of the towel and followed Judith back into the bedroom. "It's nice to be here."

"That's not what I mean," said Judith coolly, sitting down again in graceful folds of yellow satin, her dark eyes still rather thoughtful. "As a matter of fact," said Judith coolly, "you look as if a man had been kissing you."

"A . . ." Marny looked around the room. "Oh, here they are," she said, and took a cigarette, lighting it slowly.

A little glitter came into Judith's eyes. "You knew the cigarettes were there all the time, darling. And it doesn't take a full sixty seconds to light a cigarette. Never mind. I don't think you've been luring Tim on to indiscreet embraces."

"Tim . . . !" Marny choked on smoke and Judith chuckled.

"Really, darling, something's wrong with you! Pull yourself together."

Andre had said that, too, thought Marny sharply. Judith was laughing gently. "Whatever it is, darling, it's good for you. I've often thought you paid too much attention to public

34

relations for the Wales Airlines and not enough to human relations for yourself. Specifically," said Judith dryly, "men." She took a long breath of smoke and said, "How did you like Andre?"

Marny, too, took a long breath before she replied with what she hoped was the right mixture of interest and disinterest. "Very much. He was there a week, you know."

"Yes, I know. He was staying here. Have a good time with him?"

Was there anything too interested, or again too disinterested in Judith's voice? She tested it, swiftly and instinctively, as she had tested her own voice, before she replied, "Yes. Tim rather turned him over to me to entertain."

Judith had long, very dark eyelashes; they lowered a little which, oddly, made her eyes more thoughtful and more penetrating. She said, "Andre isn't difficult to entertain. On the contrary."

"Who is he, exactly?"

"Didn't he tell you all about himself?"

"No. That is . . . Oh, he mentioned few things — not much."

Judith's eyelashes still shaded her eyes, but her gaze didn't shift from Marny. She said slowly, "Oh, he's all right. Charming. Pleasant company. French, I think. Related, distantly, I fancy, to some minor nobility. Arrived at Miami Beach by way of Jamaica and Cuba. He's lived here and there. Everywhere. I rather like him. I . . . ." Judith put out her cigarette, half-smoked, and in the same gesture took up another cigarette and lighted it and said, looking now at the cigarette, "Andre is out of money. He needs a job. I thought Tim might give him one."

"Oh," said Marny, which was safe. Judith's luminous dark eyes flashed across at her. "Did he?" she asked directly.

"I don't know."

Judith waited a moment. Finally she said, "I thought Tim would tell you."

"He didn't mention it. I got a sort of impression that it was in the air. That's all."

"Oh," said Judith in her turn. There was a short silence.

Then Judith put out another barely lighted cigarette and rose, the pale yellow satin outlining her figure in gleaming high lights. Judith was a little too smart, a little too thin, a little too fine-drawn — and altogether enchanting when she chose to be. She turned to Marny and the enchantment flashed out again as she smiled. "I only wondered," she said, and somehow a warmth seemed to flow from her voice, her eyes, her very presence. It was Judith's gift, yet to do her justice it never seemed to Marny that she employed that gift consciously or with motives. She yawned a little. "I'd better go and get some clothes on and let you dress. Oh, by the way, somebody else is coming to dinner."

"Who?"

"I don't know. Some man who knows somebody Winnie knows. Turned up unexpectedly. Heard Winnie talking to him in the hall, but I didn't hear his name. Gives us an extra man." Judith tied the yellow satin belt more closely around her lovely, small waist. "Always a good idea," she said, yawning slightly again. "I'll see you. . . . 'Bye, darling."

She opened the door and trailed languidly away, leaving the room remarkably empty, as Judith's departure was likely to do, and a scent of lilies which she liked.

But the yawn, thought Marny, hadn't been quite natural. Had it? And if Judith wanted to know whether or not Tim had given Andre a job why didn't she go to Tim's room and ask him?

A shadow glided lightly across the closed door, passed briefly along the bed table and was gone before it had really, actually existed. Someone, thought Marny absently, must have gone along the balcony, although she had been so engrossed in thought that she had heard no footsteps. She looked at the small clock on her bed table, with the initials M.S. outlined in small diamonds below the face of the clock. Tim, in one of his expansive moments, had selected it and he and Judith had given it to her the previous Christmas. It seemed surprising that it was only a quarter after seven; she must hurry nevertheless. And she must dress very carefully; Judith was so beautiful.

Had Andre lingered on in that house because of Judith? That was nonsense. Or was it jealousy? Was she, then, in love with Andre? She thought again, suppose Andre is right. Suppose she had, actually, fallen in love with him a week ago, when they had met. It happened like that, suddenly and unexpectedly. So unexpectedly that it wasn't immediately recognizable.

It was twenty minutes after seven when she went to the bathroom, rinsed the salt water out of her hair and combed and pushed it into shape. Winnie had the room luxuriously stocked with salts and cologne and powder and bath oils and Marny lay back in the fragrant water, pretending not to think, and thinking in spite of herself, of Andre and the things he had said.

Later it seemed to her that she must have heard a door open or close. If so, however, she was not really conscious of it, and roused herself merely with a feeling that much more time had passed than she meant to let pass, and got out of the tub. She slid into her long, white robe and went into the bedroom. And stopped.

A girl stood there — a very, young girl, eighteen perhaps. She was small and gentle-looking with misty light hair in a halo about her young face, and enormously large eyes, very bright and dark with blue shadows under them. Her mouth was lipsticked, hurriedly, for it was smeared and red.

She had something clutched tightly in both hands. Marny could not see what it was. And she looked at Marny out of those enormous shadowed eyes and said, whispering, her badly painted mouth trembling, "You are lovelier even than he said."

Marny had never seen the girl in her life before. She put her hand on the chair beside her. And the girl said jerkily, "You're so pretty. I knew that. I knew you'd be pretty. . . ."

"You knew . . ."

"He doesn't like women unless they're pretty."

"He . . ."

"Andre, of course."

"Andre . . ."

"I'm his wife," said the child, and stood there as still as a little white marble statue.

37

CHAPTER IV

There was the murmur of water still running out of the tub in the bathroom. The door was open upon the balcony and off in the distance somewhere a motor boat droned softly. There was a radio going somewhere too, not loud, so Marny could barely hear a masculine voice, a news commentator probably. The air was fragrant with bath salts. Nothing like this could be happening, thought Marny numbly, and stared at the thin, white child. She said, "His wife . . ."

The girl nodded. There was pride and defiance and a childish, strange wistfulness in her look. "He married me. A year ago. I'm Cecily. Laideau brought me here. I've talked to Andre. He told me about you. I knew something had happened; he was different. But he'd have told me even if I hadn't asked him. He likes to hurt me. He'll hurt you. Only he'll not have a chance. Because I can't let you take him from me."

"Cecily . . ." said Marny, and was stopped by the grain of damning truth in the girl's words. Andre *had* made love to her, briefly and only that night, but it had happened, she *had* let him, she *had* considered whether or not she was in love with him and she had implied, within herself, a consent.

She said, "I didn't know about you. . . ."

Cecily said very quietly, "You see, there's only one thing for me to do," and lifted her thin, young hands and pointed a revolver straight at Marny.

She had held it, clutched in both hands, concealed. Her hands were trembling, her eyes resolute with desperation.

The girl was mad.

Young, frantic, mad — and heartbreaking. Marny looked at the revolver. How had she got it? She'd have to take it away from her. Or she could shout for help, of course, but that was

38

silly. Everyone would hear. Everyone would have to know the explanation, and the explanation, put in its best and truest facts was not, now that she knew of Cecily's existence, a very pleasant one. Nor was it, really, very convincing. Phrases rushed through her mind. Yes, I thought I might have fallen in love with him. But I didn't know about Cecily. . . . No, it wouldn't do. She'd have to get the revolver away from the child and then induce her to listen to the truth. And Cecily was strung to a nervous pitch which would make any move more or less dangerous.

Definitely dangerous! She was hysterical, desperately determined and too far away for Marny to snatch the revolver from her hands. She couldn't reason with her — not in that state. There wasn't anything to do, and she had to do something.

And the child was going to faint! No face could be so white, so drained of color, so thin and tragic and dreadful.

"Cecily," cried Marny, "you're sick. . . ." and ran as the girl swayed and caught her in her arms. She pushed her dinner dress, which the maid had laid out on the bed, onto the floor and let the slight figure down gently on the pillows. She reached for the water carafe on the bed table and poured some quickly into her hands and rubbed that stone-white, small face.

She must have help. The girl looked as if she were going to die. She couldn't leave her.

She glanced frantically around the room. There was nothing of course — no smelling salts, no ammonia. The bell was across the room beside the door. If she shouted everyone would hear and have to know all about it. Cecily's enormous eyes opened and looked straight up at her.

"Better?"

Cecily's small head went up and down.

"I'll get a towel. I've soaked your dress."

"No . . ." whispered Cecily.

"But . . ."

"Please stay here." Her hand caught at Marny's imploringly.

The whole situation was suddenly perfectly normal and simple and straightforward. In an instant it had shaken away from a nightmare. The revolver was on the bed and Marny picked it up as casually as if it had been a book and put it on the table. Cecily said, "I made a scene."

"Believe me, Cecily, I didn't know about you. Nothing has happened, really."

"He's in love with you."

"No."

"Yes. Yes, he told me. I talked to him. I asked him, I had to know. He's through with me. He told me."

"He . . ." Marny swallowed. "He didn't mean it, Cecily, believe me."

The girl moved her fair head hopelessly on the pillow, her eyes never leaving Marny's. "Oh, yes, he meant it. I know. Laideau knows it too. He's known him so long. Longer than I've known him. Longer than anybody . . ."

"Who is Laideau?"

A look of faint perplexity crossed Cecily's face. "But you must know — everybody who knows Andre knows Laideau. They've always been together. Ever since Andre was a little boy. Laideau took care of him and then they left France and went to Haiti and then to Puerto Rico and then to Jamaica. But you know all that. Andre has told you."

"Listen, Cecily, Andre hasn't told me anything. You are altogether mistaken."

A look came into the child's eyes that was adult and wise and more tragic than Marny had ever seen in anything before. She said, "He made love to you."

"A little," said Marny, hating herself. "But that's all, Cecily. It didn't mean a thing. Believe me. I'm telling you the truth. And I didn't know about you."

Cecily frowned. She had fine, light eyebrows. She said, "I don't understand. He said he wants to marry you. He said he was going to get a divorce."

"Cecily, that isn't true! There isn't anything between us. I've only known him a week. I didn't know about you. . . ."

Cecily said suddenly, "I'm all right now. I'm going home."

"No, you can't. You're not well."

"Yes, I'm going." She pushed away Marny's hand and slid upward and off the bed. She was white. She was so thin that

40

Marny could almost see her quick heartbeats under the thin blue dress she wore.

"But I can't let you, Cecily. Let's straighten this thing out. Let me call Andre. . . ."

"No, no!" It was a repressed scream. Cecily caught herself and put her hand over her mouth and looked at the door into the hall. After a moment she whispered, "I didn't mean . . . I'm sorry . . . I've got to go."

"I'm going with you then. Where is home?"

"No, you can't. Laideau will take me. Laideau is here. We came in a boat. We . . . No, you can't go. . . ."

"Yes, I . . ."

"No!" cried Cecily and whirled around the room, like a little frightened animal seeking a way out of a trap. Then she saw the door open upon the balcony and ran toward it and slid out.

"Cecily," cried Marny and ran after her. By the time she reached the balcony the girl had gone. She looked up and down; each end of the narrow balcony was hung with heavy vines. Then she heard a light swift sound of motion and ran to the railing and looked down. Cecily was running down the winding, grilled-iron stairway that led directly to the strip of green lawn. Her thin figure seemed scarcely to touch the step, her hand over the railing was like the soft flutter of a bird's wing. She was again infinitely childish, infinitely pathetic with her trembling, badly painted mouth hidden and her fair hair falling over her face. "Cecily . . ." cried Marny softly, but the girl did not look up. Marny started after her, and as she reached the top of the stairs the girl flashed out of sight in the thick shrubbery across the lawn and at an angle of the shore line of the island. Marny stopped. Somewhere she heard the sound of oarlocks.

It was a steady creak, creak which suddenly stopped. She clutched her white dressing gown around her and ran halfway down the winding steps and paused again to listen. She could see most of the sea wall, the thick clump of bamboos behind which the girl had disappeared. And then clearly through the twilight the sound of oars began again. As she waited, staring

41

at the blue water, after a moment, a rowboat came gradually into sight heading away from the island and toward the strip of lights and buildings, blue and gold in the light of the setting sun, which was Miami Beach. A man was rowing. Cecily was sitting with her small light-clad back turned toward Shadow Island. The man rowing was thick and swarthy with gleaming black hair. He bent over the oars with thick, powerful shoulders and sent the boat rapidly into the dusk.

She didn't know what to do. A hundred things occurred to her, standing there on the stairs, watching the boat grow smaller and farther away. Call Andre, call Tim, call Winnie. Do something.

But what exactly?

She went a step or two farther down the winding, vine-hung stairway. The curve of the stairway brought into view below the wide, open porch, with its bright cushions and rugs and brilliant flowers, and tray of glasses. She could see again the lights in the drawing room and bookshelves and white fur rugs. The porch itself was shadowy now, although it was still fairly light on the water. She stopped, with her hand on the iron railing, to look after Cecily again. The rowboat was approaching a curve of the island where there were thick, green Casuarina trees. Neither Cecily nor the man bending over the oars appeared to have changed position. As she watched, the boat rounded the curve and disappeared completely behind the fringy green curtain.

And at that instant someone walked across the porch and said, "Miss Sanderson."

She looked down sharply. Commander Bill Cameron stood there looking up at her. He was in Navy whites now instead of green. His face was partially in the shadow, but it was Bill Cameron.

He said, "I didn't mean to startle you. I meant . . . I thought I'd better tell you. . . . That is, I . . ."

"What are you doing here?"

His face stiffened; he made a formal brief bow. "I was trying to apologize, Miss Sanderson. I seem to have been wrong again."

Already the reaction of the meeting with Cecily was beginning. His words and his stiff, angry Scottish face seemed to crystallize her confused and shaken emotions into a single one which was anger. She said, "Don't apologize. Answer my question. What are you doing here?"

Her tone drew a spark of anger into his own eye. He answered, however, with a calm politeness which in itself was infuriating. "I've come to dinner."

"But you . . ." She paused and thought swiftly. "Who invited you? Does Tim Wales know?"

"I rarely go to dinner without an invitation," he said with a spark of laughter in his eyes.

"But you don't know Tim!"

He made a sketchy bow. "Miss Wales and I have mutual friends."

"Miss Wales!" This then was the man Judith had mentioned — the extra man, always welcome. Well, he wouldn't be welcomed by Tim.

He said, "This is all rather childish. I meant . . . Well, when I left you I came to the house and asked for Miss Wales. I gave her a note from a friend of hers and mine. She asked me to dinner, I accepted and drove back to my hotel, changed and returned. That's all. If it's any business of yours," he added with a sudden twinkle.

She whirled around on the step and he reached up suddenly and caught her wrist so hard that it turned her around again facing him. "Where are you going? Are you going to tell Tim Wales about me and get me thrown out?"

"Is it any business of yours?" she snapped irresistibly.

"That's childish, too," he said. He went on, all at once very sober. "Look here, Miss Sanderson. Everything's gone wrong between us. It's been my fault. But I . . . You must believe me, I *am* serious. I have a real and urgent reason for seeing you and seeing Tim Wales. I think you should give me a hearing. You were taken at a disadvantage this evening. I saw that; I don't blame you for being annoyed. I'm not much of a diplomat. But I — there were reasons for the things I said. I'm sorry I lost my temper. But that wasn't why I left. I didn't see

43

any point in talking in front of that — of the fellow who joined us. I . . . Won't you let bygones be bygones? I ask you to be fair and not hold any prejudice against me."

An inner and uneasy feeling that she might not have been quite fair seemed to link itself up with another less definable but even less creditable impulse of opposition. She told herself quickly that the fact that he was right didn't make him any less of a crank and a nuisance. He said abruptly, "You're very stubborn, aren't you?"

"Will you let go my hand?"

"I'm a fool," said Bill Cameron. "Well, I've done everything I can do. I suppose I spoke to you again at the wrong time."

She had forgotten Cecily. Naturally he had seen the girl run down the stairs, and had seen Marny following. She glanced swiftly out toward the point of the Casuarina trees but the boat was not in sight anywhere.

It was very quiet; whoever had turned on a radio had apparently turned it off again. It seemed to her suddenly that she could hear again the regular creak of oars.

CHAPTER V

Was the boat returning?

But Cecily would not return to the island. Why should she? Marny watched and listened for a moment and the boat did not reappear. It was darker. The water of the bay still reflected what light was left in the sky, but the shadows were thick and heavy under the trees and vines. The man standing below her said suddenly, in a different voice, "You look — so pretty. I thought you might listen. . . ."

She glanced down at her white robe and bare feet, jerked her hand away from his, clutched the negligee about her and ran up the steps.

She thought he started to call after her and stopped. She didn't look back. She reached the balcony and looked out across the bay and still could not see the rowboat with Cecily's slim figure in it, and now did not hear — or did not imagine that she heard — the sound of oars.

She went into her room.

She was angrily conscious of the way she looked. Her bare feet, her thin white robe clutched tight around her. And of the way she had behaved; unintentionally, simply because there was something about Bill Cameron which roused her instant antagonism. She hadn't been entirely fair, and she had been stubborn.

She had let something about the personality of the Navy flier and her own personality clash and spark. It was wrong. Personalities had no place in business. Besides, it was not really important either way. He had managed to get an introduction to Winnie, and Winnie's first impulse always was one of hearty and lavish hospitality. He'd thus got himself invited to Shadow Island for dinner; now it was up to Tim to deal with the thing as he pleased. So that was that.

The main thing to decide was what to do about Cecily.

The red-and-white dinner dress which she'd flung to the floor to make room for Cecily still lay there. It was almost as if she needed that to convince her that Cecily had come and said the things she had said, and gone.

She picked it up and started mechanically to dress.

Where had Cecily gone? Where was home? Obviously Cecily was not staying in the house. She must have seen Andre, though, some time since their arrival, either before or after their swim, and talked to him. She couldn't have had a long talk with Andre but she had seen him, somehow. Otherwise Andre couldn't have said the incredible things Cecily had quoted him as saying.

But then he couldn't have said them anyway! Cecily was pathetic and young and tragic, really. But she was also obviously hysterical. Mad, Marny had thought her for a moment; not that she was that actually, but she was clearly not responsible just then for anything she said or did.

There were two sides to everything. How could she condemn Andre without a hearing? On the evidence of a pathetic but hysterical child who threatened to kill people and talked incoherently of Andre's cruelty? Andre, who was always gay and pleasant and even-tempered.

He hadn't told her of Cecily.

Well, perhaps there was a reason for that, too. Cecily was tragic, but conceivably, it was something like tragedy for Andre, too.

In any case the child ought to have a nurse. Was the rather sinister-looking man in the boat the only companion the girl had? Laideau — why had he brought her there?

She couldn't condemn Andre without a hearing.

But she wouldn't have listened to him at all if she had known about Cecily.

Someone downstairs turned on the radio again. The gay sound of dance music floated upward and through the still-open door from the balcony. It had grown so dark that she had turned on lights over the dressing table. There were voices

46

from below, too, so Judith and Winnie and Tim — and Commander Cameron and Andre and Charlie Ingram — were gathering for cocktails before dinner. Several motor boats passed the island as she dressed. Later she remembered having heard the accelerating and diminishing crescendo of their engines. Once an outboard went past with the sharp explosions of a machine gun. It seemed a long time before she had finished dressing. Usually she was not so slow and clumsy. She looked at herself carefully in the mirror. There was some reason why she must look particularly well tonight.

The red-and-white sheer chiffon clung to her waist and swirled about her feet; it looked cool and soft and feminine. Her mouth was red, too. Her eyes were dark blue and her face rather pale below the light tan. Then she remembered why she had wanted to look well that night.

It had been for Andre, so he would look at her and not at Judith. So he would ask her to stroll with him under the tropic night sky. Andre! Well, she wouldn't question the state of her heart any further on that subject! She turned quickly to the door. As she put her hand on the latch she glanced down at the bed table.

Something was wrong. The carafe of water was there, with the glass stopper still lying beside it. There was an ash tray and her clock. She paused for an instant puzzled, groping — and then realized with a blinding flash what was wrong.

The revolver was not there.

It had to be there. It had to be somewhere.

It was not. She looked rapidly around the room. She knelt and fumbled under the low bed and around the thick fringe of the rugs. She looked and searched and it was not there.

She got to her feet, stumbling in her long chiffon skirt.

So Cecily had taken it. Somehow under her very eyes, the girl had snatched it up and taken it away with her.

Her knees were shaking.

How could she have let the child take it? How could she have let a feeling of normality, of being in control of the situation so blind her?

Where had Cecily gone? How could she find her?

Had Cecily returned to the island?

She had heard the sound of oars returning. At least she thought she had heard it.

She was shivering, trembling as Cecily had trembled. She didn't know what she was doing. It was queer because she realized it and yet could not stop and think. She ran to the balcony. It was dark now and if Cecily had dropped the revolver upon the balcony she could not find it. She ran swiftly down the winding stairway, tripping, snatching up her swirling chiffon skirt, clutching the railing. It was a dark night, with clouds scudding across the sky and the water very black. The revolver couldn't be on the stairway. If Cecily had dropped it in her flight Marny would have seen it when she followed Cecily.

She stopped at the foot of the stairway. Lights streamed out from the French windows opening upon the porch. She could hear voices and Winnie's laughter and the dance music from the radio. She could see Judith on the sofa behind white calla lilies, and Andre standing beside her, a cocktail glass in his hand.

It was light enough, now that her eyes were adjusted to the night, to see the dark, thick clump of bamboos down at the water's edge, where Cecily had apparently got into the boat and gone, and then perhaps returned. She must find her and she must hurry; she was obsessed with a need to hurry. It was a compulsion, a command — put upon her from something outside herself. Marny ran across the lawn. The grass was cool below the thin soles of her slippers. Far away she could hear the murmur of surf; nearer, the lap of water against the low sea wall which rimmed the entire island. It grew louder as the sounds of voices and dance music grew fainter behind her.

She reached the clump of bamboo and the turf skirted it like a path with bamboos on one side, whispering and moving in the light wind, the low sea wall on her right. Clouds moved across the sky and stars shone down brilliantly all at once. The black water glittered, reflecting them. The strip of grass gave way to white sand. A small pier lay there, white and ghostly in the starlight. It was merely a platform over the water, with steps. Two or three boats lay moored below — rowboats and a cabin cruiser.

It was perfectly still except for the faint lapping of water and the distant sound of music. There was, of course, no revolver. She couldn't have found it, it was so dark, if it had been there. She'd lost her head and wasted time. She'd have to go back and tell them what had happened. Andre would know where Cecily had gone. They must reach her quickly. Before those unsteady hands could turn the revolver toward that broken, childish heart and pull the trigger. She turned toward the house. The bamboos rustled and whispered beside her. Someone had dropped a coat in the shadow of the nearest clump, on the strip of grass just at the edge of the white sand. She hadn't seen it when she passed, she hadn't . . .

It wasn't a coat.

She was on her knees.

It was something limp and white, flung down like a coat. It was Cecily Durant with her childish pretty face pressed down into the earth. It was Cecily Durant, and this time she had not fainted. She was dead and there was something dark and splotchy all across her back between her thin shoulders.

"Cecily — Cecily — Cecily . . ."

It was Marny's own voice and she knew it; yet she hadn't meant to sob like that; she hadn't meant to scream.

She knew too that someone was coming. She could hear footsteps on the turf path, rounding the clump of bamboos.

Someone reached her. Someone stopped and said something short and muffled and was down beside her, pushing her out of the way, bending over that limp, small figure.

It was Bill Cameron. He turned abruptly toward her. He was so close that even in the darkness she could see his face. He put his hand hard on her shoulder. "What happened? Who is it?" His voice was so rough and harsh it sounded as if it hurt. "For God's sake, what happened?"

She couldn't answer. She had no voice, no feeling, no power to move.

Clouds drifted again across the stars; a curtain of shadow dropped upon them. Water lapped against the pier somewhere in that soft darkness and the warm wind rattled the bamboos. Marny fought through something that caught at her throat as if it had hands and whispered, "Is she dead?"

"Yes. Where is the gun?"

"Gun?"

"Gun. What did you do with it?"

"She had it. That's why I came." Marny stared at the dimly white face of the man beside her. The clouds were heavy, and the bamboos rustled thinly together. She cried, jerkily, "She had the gun. I took it and she went away. She went in the boat. I . . . Then the gun was gone. So I came . . . I hurried . . ." She stopped and caught her breath so it hurt and she had to press her own hands against her throat, queerly, to relieve it. "Are you sure she's dead? Perhaps . . ."

"Yes."

"But isn't there — a doctor — anything? We must do something. She can't be dead!"

"She's dead." He waited a moment, kneeling there, his white uniform outlining his solid figure. "Yes," he said again, very quietly, "she's dead. I don't know what to do. We'll have to call the police, of course. Right away. And you . . ." He turned around and rose, taking her by the arms and pulling her up with him. He drew her away from little dead Cecily, there in the shadow. "You understand, they'll arrest you."

"Arrest . . ." He was saying something very important and very terrible and yet she could not fully comprehend it.

"Arrest you. On a murder charge." He waited a moment and seemed to watch her through the darkness. Then he said, "Quick. Tell me how it happened."

She was shaking, her words incoherent and jumbled. "But I . . . You see, she had the gun — I hurried . . ." His hands came down hard on her shoulders again. "Marny, for God's sake, think. Snap out of it. For God's sake, why did you kill her?"

50

CHAPTER VI

The grip of Bill Cameron's hands on her bare shoulders was so hard it hurt. It was real and its reality, for an instant, extended to everything. It roused her; it made her believe the unbelievable. Cecily — Andre's wife — lay dead, there in the starlight. Only it wasn't starlight now; thick black clouds like smoke were scudding across the sky and the wind was bending the Casuarina trees at the point of the little island just beyond. They made a black, moving mass. A rowboat had disappeared behind that black shadow, not far beyond the white-clad shoulder of the man before her who had said she would be arrested. For murder! Who had said, incredibly, "Why did you kill her?"

She cried, her mouth so stiff and dry that her words jumbled and tripped themselves, "*I didn't kill her!* She had the gun, and I took it. All at once everything seemed all right. I wouldn't have let her go, like that, if she hadn't seemed all right."

Bill Cameron held her rightly. "Go on."

"I — I followed her. Down the steps. But she went so fast and I didn't think about the gun. I didn't see her pick it up. He was waiting for her and they rowed away . . ."

"Who?"

"The man. Laideau, she said. Yes, Laideau. And then you were there and we talked and when I looked the boat was gone, behind those trees. I went to my room. I didn't think about the gun. It had been all so wrong, you see; that girl there, and the gun and the things she said. It was like a — like a bad play. I didn't believe it. Then when she fainted and I got her on the bed I — I don't know what happened, but it seemed all right. Not so — so unreal." She took a long, half-sobbing breath.

He said, "You went back to your room after you talked to

me. The girl had gone and she had left the gun on the table in your room? Is that right?"

"No, no. I put the gun on the table."

"Wait a minute. First she came to you and had a gun."

"Yes. Yes, that's right."

"Did she threaten you with that gun?"

"Yes. Yes, but she didn't mean it. She said things that couldn't have been true. She was a child. She was hysterical. She didn't know what she was doing."

"Marny, I'm trying to get this straight. For God's sake, help me. There's no time, understand. You do understand me?"

"Yes — yes . . ."

"You took the gun away from her?"

"No. She fainted, I told you. The gun dropped somewhere. I put it on the table. Then I came back to my room and dressed. When I looked down at the bed table the gun wasn't there. So I . . ."

"So you what? Tell me."

"I was afraid."

"Afraid she'd come back and kill you? Is that it? So you found her and shot her and are going to plead self-defense?"

"No! No! No!"

"You said you were afraid."

"How could I have let her take the revolver! I was watching. I thought I was watching. She seemed bewildered, and she ran to the door and then to the door upon the balcony, and somehow she got the gun and I didn't see it."

"Are you trying to say that she killed herself?"

"She didn't know what she was doing. She was hysterical. It's my fault. I ought to have stopped her. I ought to have seen her take the gun. The instant I saw it was gone I was afraid. Of . . ."

"Of what?"

"Of this," cried Marny and sobbed.

"Stop," he said, and put his arms around her. "Stop that. Listen. You've got to stop it, Marny. . . ."

He held her for a moment against him. There was something distantly and faintly familiar about it as if he had held her like that some other time. His arms were warm and tight and shut out horror and the thin rattle of the bamboos. But then he put her away from him and made her look at him.

"Who is she?"

"Cecily . . ."

"Yes, I heard you call her. But who . . ."

"Andre's wife."

"Andre? Oh, Your friend! Durant. Why did she threaten you with a gun?"

"Because . . ." Words stuck in her throat. That unexpected moment with Andre to have come to this!

"Go on."

"Because of Andre . . ." she whispered.

There was a silence that seemed long. Clouds moved swiftly above so there were flashes of clear starlight. One such came then, a clear, straight shaft of light. Bill Cameron's face looked white and stern and the water silver and the shadows very black. From the house, distantly, came the sound of the radio. It was as if it were the same dance tune. Probably very little time had passed; it seemed years; it seemed a great and terrible gulf in time. He said at last, "Oh, I see. Andre. I thought he seemed rather proprietary about you at the pool."

"No, no! She was wrong."

"Yes, you would say that."

"Don't, don't. You must believe me! I didn't know there was a Cecily. Besides . . ."

"Hi, there . . ." called a voice loudly from somewhere in the night. "Where are you?" There was the sound of footsteps beyond the bamboo hedge. A man rounded the path. It was Charlie Ingram, his thick figure clad in a white dinner jacket. He came up to them, saying in his high voice, "There you are! I say, don't you know dinner's ready? Judith sent me. I say . . ." He stopped abruptly. A swift path of starlight moved over them and sharply outlined his tall, stooped figure with its paunchy middle, his thin fair hair and small mustache, monocle on its black ribbon. He stared at them as if caught by their attitude. "I say, what's wrong?"

Bill Cameron's white-clad shoulders seemed to square

53

themselves. His hand was still on Marny's shoulder. He dropped it and said, "Something very terrible has happened, Ingram. We'd better call the police."

"What? What?" Charlie peered at Bill Cameron and at Marny, his monocle glittering with light. Bill Cameron said, "There . . ."

Marny was standing alone in the shaft of starlight, her slippers deep in the sand. Both men were bending over the strip of grass beside the clump of bamboo, talking, and she couldn't hear what they said. The water swished against the pier. The bamboos clattered in small slivers of sound and Charlie Ingram exclaimed in a loud, shocked voice, "Good God, she's been shot!"

Bill Cameron replied rapidly. They were beside Marny again, Charlie was taking her arm. Cameron said tersely, ". . . and let Mr. Wales know. I'll stay here with . . . I'll stay here."

She couldn't move. She had to make Bill Cameron understand exactly what had happened. She had to fight the knowledge of Cecily's death; she could not accept it. Perhaps she made some move toward the silent, small figure half-hidden now by a cloud shadow, mercifully hidden and gently. Bill Cameron caught her swiftly and said to Charlie Ingram, "Take her to the house."

They were moving along the turf path, Charlie's warm soft hand on her bare arm, thrusting her along with him, making her walk. Suddenly there were lights from the house; Charlie was talking in a high, repetitive jumble. ". . . dreadful, dreadful. What happened, do you know? Chap said she was Durant's wife. Didn't know he had a wife. Don't know him much, as a matter of fact. Can't see what Judith sees in the fellow. Dreadful . . . This way, now, mind the step . . ."

Lights streamed across the porch. Dance music from the radio was louder and incredibly gay as if it came from a bright world that had ceased to exist; nothing now was right, nothing had the same proportions. The door was flung open and a moth, dislodged from the screen, brushed past her cheek. Then Charlie Ingram had drawn her into the room beyond with its lights, its flowers, its music, the glitter of cocktail glasses, the beige and white rugs and cushions and the people. All moving. All getting suddenly to their feet. All staring. Charlie Ingram gasped, "Dreadful thing. Woman's dead. Shot. Here, take her . . . Got some whisky there, Judith? Good."

He had put Marny down in the deep softness of a sofa, and was shoving cushions behind her. Everybody was there. Judith in black chiffon was saying something quick and sharp and reaching for a great crystal decanter of whisky. Tim Wales in black and white snatched it from Judith's hand and splashed whisky into a glass. Winnie in a long blue dinner dress was there too — and Andre. A glass in his hand and a cigarette, and his face a shocked, rigid mask with brilliant eyes.

Everybody was talking. Tim's voice cut through it all sharply. "What woman? Where? What are you talking about, Charlie?"

Charlie Ingram straightened up from bending over Marny. His monocle dangled on the end of its ribbon, his face was red and his breath puffy. "Girl. Saw her. She — well, she's your wife, Durant. She . . ." He stopped, puffing, uneasy, searching for words. Blurting it out. "I'm sorry, old chap. Hate to shout it out like this. Only way. She's your wife. She's — she's dead. I — er — here . . ." He turned to the low glass table and poured a stiff drink into a glass and went to Andre. "Here, old chap — better than that thing you've got in your hand. Drink it."

"What do you mean?" said Andre.

He was standing beside the painted white piano, leaning back against it as if at bay. His face had not changed except it was very white, and his eyes were narrow dark points of light. One arm had gone backward, so he rested against the curve of the piano; the other still held his cigarette and the cocktail glass which Charlie Ingram was trying to remove from it.

Judith swirled around and sat down suddenly beside Marny. Charlie said, "Here, here now. A shock, of course. Sorry to break it like this. Drink it now." He pried Andre's rigid hand from the stemmed glass he held and put the glass of whisky into it. And Judith cried in a thin scream, "Cecily . . . oh, Andre, Cecily! She's dead, That's what he means. She's dead

. . ." Tim was beside Judith so quickly Marny hadn't seen him move. He had his hand over her mouth hard. *"Shut up! Stop that!"* He pushed Judith back against the pillow and held his hand tight over her mouth, which strangely, queerly, added to the nightmare. Tim always treated Judith as if she were glass and precious and might break. His eyes were like steel daggers bright and sharp. "Charlie, what in hell has happened?"

Charlie Ingram had made Andre bend his handsome black head and blazing white face and gulp the whisky. Winnie said, "Father . . . Father, don't . . ." and went across to Andre, her blue gown swishing gently. She took the glass from Andre's hand and put it down on the piano. Charlie said, "Girl's dead. Marny and the Navy chap found her."

"Did you say she was shot?" Tim's question snapped out like a whip.

"Yes. Horrible. Shot." Charlie Ingram looked at the table where the tray of glasses stood and left Andre, who still had not moved, who still stared fixedly out of a fixed white mask, and poured himself some whisky. He drank it quickly and shivered. "Horrible! I say, Tim, what does one do?"

Judith gave a little sigh and relaxed under Tim's hand and lay back against the cushions.

Marny's throat stung. Her eyes were no longer dazed and dazzled by the lights. Everything seemed all at once very sharp and clear like a photograph in colors which one could study at one's leisure, which one would always remember no matter how hard one tried to forget it. As one would never forget Cecily, under the starlight, her young face pressed down into the earth.

She drank more whisky. It made tears come to her eyes and was like a hot little sword in her throat. Winnie cried, "Oh, Father, you've frightened her," and ran to Judith.

Tim stood up. "Where is she? Come along, Charlie."

Tim led the way and Charlie Ingram followed him. The screened door banged and tiny insects rose in a cloud. They stepped off the porch and onto the lawn. Andre half turned as to follow them, gave a kind of groan and sat down in a sudden huddle on a footstool, and put his head in his hands. Judith had not fainted. She was leaning back against the pillows, Winnie fanning her desperately with a newspaper she had snatched. Judith opened her lovely dark eyes as soon as the footsteps left the porch and said to Winnie, "I'm all right. Let me alone. Andre!"

Andre seemed to bury his handsome head tighter in his hands. Judith said sharply, "Andre! Andre, you must listen. They'll get the police. If the girl is dead . . . Andre, what are you going to do?"

Winnie went across to Andre again and put her hand on his shoulder. "Andre, was it your wife? Is it true?"

He did not move. The great bowl of calla lilies beside Marny sent up a dizzying sweet fragrance. Judith's hand, still wearing the great emerald, was twisting and twisting the fringe on a cushion. The fresh, pretty color had gone from Winnie's face. She stood for a moment looking down at Andre's bowed black head, her hand steady on his shoulder. Then she knelt beside him, her blue dress outlining her large, firm figure. She tried to take his hands from his face and he would not let her and she said in her mother's voice, steady and comforting, in spite of the trouble in it, "Andre, Andre, you must get yourself together. Whatever she was . . ."

"Oh, she was his wife," said Judith suddenly. "And if the girl was shot . . ." A servant, a colored man, his black bow tie a sharp contrast to his white shirtfront, came into the doorway and stopped, his glance taking in the whole scene. Judith saw him and said, "Rilly, hold up dinner. Tell cook . . ."

He hesitated. He must have known something was terribly wrong. Then he said, "Yes, Madam . . ." and vanished from the arched doorway. Judith said in a whisper, "They heard . . . Oh, my God, this means police. It means an inquest."

Winnie slid her bare, fair arm through Andre's beseechingly. "They'll be back in a minute. Andre, answer me."

He put back his head as footsteps crossed the porch again swiftly. Charlie Ingram flung open the door and came in, puffing again and red. "Tim says to call the police."

"But you . . ." Winnie got up. "You'd better bring her in here."

57

"No, we can't," said Charlie. "Navy chap says we can't move her. Nothing we can do for her anyway. Horrible." He jerked the enormous, thin handkerchief from his breast pocket and wiped his face and polished his monocle. Bill Cameron came in followed by Tim, who crossed swiftly to the hall and they heard him at the telephone. "Operator, operator — get the police — I don't know what the hell the number is — get them. It's murder . . ."

This time nobody moved or spoke until Andre, slowly, as if he didn't know what he was doing, dropped his hands and turned his handsome black head and stared at Bill Cameron who stood just inside the room. Everybody was staring at Bill Cameron. Marny thought desperately, he'll tell them now. He'll tell them now. He hates me. He'll say I killed her. Andre's wife. Because I wanted Andre.

Tim was talking into the phone. ". . . Shadow Island. Yes, off the causeway — the Wales place. Right. No, there's no other house on the island — just follow the drive. Hurry. Name was Cecily Durant. Yes, she's been murdered; she was shot in the back."

Andre got up then, slowly, turning as if blindly toward the porch. It was horrible for him, thought Marny swiftly, to be told like that — brutally, bluntly, so there was nothing he could do for the girl who, no matter what had happened between them, had been his wife. Charlie Ingram caught Andre's arm. "Better not go down there, Durant. Leave it to us."

"Who killed her?" whispered Andre then, staring at Bill Cameron.

Bill Cameron stood perfectly still. He looked extraordinarily big and firm in that white Navy uniform with the little row of ribbons. He said, "She was your wife, then, Durant?"

Andre's lips moved. He whispered, "Yes . . . That is, I suppose so. If it is really Cecily."

Bill Cameron said, "I'm sorry. There was nothing we could do for her."

"Who killed her?" said Andre again.

"I don't know," said Bill Cameron. "She was shot in the

58

back and the gun is gone. We couldn't find it anywhere. I'm — sorry, Durant."

He did not look at Marny.

From the hall, Tim said, "No, of course we haven't touched anything. I don't know who killed her. Ten minutes? Okay. Don't miss the bridge. It's the only entrance to the island."

"How did you know it was Cecily?" asked Andre.

CHAPTER VII

Charlie Ingram hadn't known Cecily; he had said so. He hadn't known Andre had a wife. And Bill Cameron had barely known Andre's name. "Andre?" he'd said. "Oh, your friend Durant."

So there was only one way for Bill to know that it was Cecily and that was because Marny had told him. The whole story was going to come out now; there was no way to stop it.

But then it had to come out anyway, and she had to tell it. The police were on their way to investigate the suicide. . . .

But they had said murder! They had said that Cecily was shot in the back and the gun was not there.

Marny quite literally could not think. Cecily had come to see her, Marny, with a gun, because she thought that Marny wanted to take Andre. And then Cecily was shot. And Bill Cameron called it murder and said Marny would be arrested and charged with murder. Those were the facts but none of them seemed real.

It did occur to her that so far Bill Cameron had not told what he knew; so far he had not betrayed her; he had appeared, on the contrary, to protect her.

But that didn't matter, because she had to tell the police about Cecily and the gun.

In spite of the slowness with which she seemed to be groping her way about in a fog, in reality very little time had passed. Andre was still looking at Bill Cameron, waiting for an answer to his question and Tim Wales was returning from the telephone, his footsteps rapid and loud across the tiled floor of the hall.

She took a long breath and began, "Cecily . . ." and Bill Cameron's voice cut in rather loudly, "Miss Sanderson had seen her. She knew it was Cecily Durant."

He did not look at her. He opened a box of cigarettes on the table near him and took one, lighting it deliberately.

So she'd been wrong. He'd thrown her to the wolves, after all. He was not trying to protect her, but the reverse. Not that it mattered; she had to tell them everything she knew.

Andre had turned quickly to her, and Judith and Winnie both gave her startled, questioning looks. Tim Wales from the doorway said, "What's this? Did you know the girl, Marny?"

She tried to sit more erectly in the deep sofa, pushing the cushions behind her. "No. No, but she was here," she began again. How many times would she tell the police the story she was about to tell now? Police and reporters and — a jury. A jury! No, no, it couldn't have happened. Not to her. Not to Marny Sanderson. Not even to people one knew.

Tim said, "Yes, yes, go on. She wasn't staying here, was she, Judith?"

Judith shook her dark head once. She was watching Marny and scarcely seeming to breathe, so fixed was that quiet regard. And Bill Cameron crossed quickly to Marny and took the glass from her hand. "You've had enough of that," he said shortly, and turned to the others. "She told me when we found Mrs. Durant. It was this way. Mrs. Durant had come to the house and happened to meet Miss Sanderson. She told her who she was. So Miss Sanderson recognized her, of course."

"Cecily came *here?*" cried Judith, watching Marny.

"But she couldn't have . . . She was never here. . . . We didn't know there was such a person — we . . ." Winnie stopped as her father advanced heavily. His usual buoyancy had dropped away. He looked old and sagging and the fine lines around his eyes and mouth showed up sharply. His granite-gray eyes, however, were never brighter. He said, commanding the room instantly, "This is a bad business. I don't need to tell you. I've called the police; I did it as quickly as possible. We've got to be on the right side of the law. But before they come we've got to get some things clear. We're in for some ugly publicity, in any case. This girl was your wife, Andre?"

Andre looked at the black screened door, he looked at

61

Judith, he looked at the rug, he ran his hands through his black hair and said, "Yes."

Tim glanced at Judith. His look was sharp, cold, impersonal. It was his business look that Marny knew well. "Did you know the girl?"

"No," replied Judith composedly. "I knew she existed. I never saw her."

"How long has Andre been staying here? At Shadow Island?"

Judith's hands moved and the emerald flashed green fire. "I don't know exactly. A month perhaps."

Tim turned to Winnie. "Where did he come from?" He jerked his head toward Andre. "Why did you invite him here? How did you meet him?"

Winnie went to her father. Her stocky figure in its blue ruffled chiffon, her fresh, clean-looking face and neat brown hair, the gesture with which she put a soothing hand on her father's arm were all exactly like the first Mrs. Wales. "Now, Father," she said seriously, yet placatively, "don't take that tone, please. We invited Andre here because we met him and liked him, the same as we would invite any guest to stay in our home. This . . ." Winnie's calm seemed threatened for an instant, for her mouth trembled a little. She continued, however, "This is a terrible thing. But don't accuse . . ."

"I'm not accusing," said Tim sharply, but he looked quieter somehow, comforted as Winnie could always comfort him. He said, looking into his daughter's eyes directly, for they were almost the same height, "There's so little time before the police get here, Winnie. Give me the details. . . ."

"All right," said Winnie. "It's just as I told you. We met him first, I think, at Mrs. Hodge's — you know, Ella Hodge — and then several times at the Bath Club or at different parties. Then, I don't remember just how it happened . . ."

Judith was sitting perfectly still, watching Winnie and Tim, watching Marny, watching everybody with those lovely heavily made-up eyes. She said suddenly, "I'll tell you exactly. We were all swimming one day at the Beach Club and he said he was going to have to move because the hotel where he was staying had been sold and was being redecorated and everybody was to be turned out. So I said if he couldn't find a place before — oh, whatever day it was that he was to be turned out, he could come here and we'd put him up till he found a place. So he did. That's all. . . ."

Tim did not look at her. He seemed to be searching his daughter's eyes deeply, as if checking every detail of Judith's explanation. Winnie's bland, serious blue gaze, so like her mother's, did not waver. She nodded as Judith finished, her eyes steady upon her father's. "That's right," she said. "It's exactly what happened. And then after a week or so, I don't know . . ."

"He stayed on. With or without an invitation?"

"Darling, darling," said Winnie beseechingly. "*Please* — we asked him to stay. You're making Andre seem an — an impostor. He isn't. He was our guest. He still is our guest, and he is in trouble."

"But, Winnie . . ." Tim hesitated, blinked and said, "but what of his wife? Why wasn't she here?"

Andre cleared his throat, "I'll tell you that, sir," he said. "It is a painful thing but — the fact is my wife was not well."

There are two sides to everything, Marny had thought. And this was Andre's side, and he was right. She had seen tragic little Cecily and heard her. She leaned forward, listening. Tim said shortly, "If she was sick, your place was at her side."

Judith moved, crossing one knee over the other. Marny glanced at her and a faint smile touched Judith's painted mouth and was gone. It was a queer little shadow, half amusement, half derision, wholly Judith.

Andre said, his black head up now, his face grave and pale. "It was not that kind of sickness, sir."

"Are you meaning to imply that your wife was insane?"

"No," said Andre. "No. It might have been better if she had been, then she could have gone to a sanitarium and been properly treated. As it was we could do nothing."

"We?'

"Myself, I should have said."

"Where was she? Where did you leave her?"

63

Andre hesitated. He said, "She came with me from Havana some months ago. Her — illness developed alarmingly. She was not violent — oh, nothing like that. But she had fancies. One was, for a while, that she didn't wish me to be with her. We were stopping in a hotel. She made me leave and go to another hotel. It was all," said Andre unexpectedly, "very expensive."

Again Tim seemed to hesitate for an instant. Then he said, "Was she alone there? Had she any friends?"

"Laideau . . ." began Marny suddenly, intending to explain, intending to say that Laideau was with Cecily, that he had taken her away from the island after her talk with Andre, intending again, to tell all the things that must be told, and Bill Cameron said loudly, "We need some coffee before the police get here. It's likely to last forever — the inquiry, I mean. May I get it, Mrs. Wales? Will you show me the way, Marny . . . ?"

Tim had heard the name. Tim had ears like a cat's. He said, "What's that? Laideau, who is that?"

Judith said, "Of course, Commander Cameron. Tell the butler . . ."

Andre said, "Laideau is my friend. Cecily was fond of him; he took care of her. I'd trust him with my wife. I'm going to phone to him now."

Bill Cameron had taken Marny's arm and half lifted her from the soft depths of the sofa, and then slid her arm through his own. Winnie said quickly, "I'll go. Let me . . ."

"Thanks, I'll see to it," replied Bill Cameron briefly. "Come along, Marny . . ."

They were in the wide hall with its gay tiles and white and scarlet furniture, now brilliantly lighted. He steered her rapidly toward the dining room at the back — a lovely room with the candles lighted already on the table circling a great silver bowl which reflected them and the silver and glass glittering. Covers were laid, dinner time long past. He put her down in a high-backed chair.

"For God's sake, why did you drink all that?" he said angrily. "You haven't got the head of a kitten. I'd have stopped you if I'd known. Didn't you ever take a drink in your life before? Stay there." He went quickly to the swinging door into a pantry beyond and opened it. "Hey, there, Rilly. Coffee. Quick."

The door closed and he came back and stood, big and substantial and solid in his white uniform with its black shoulder boards. His face was grave; the breeze came in the open, black rectangles that were windows and sent the candles wavering, touching his high cheekbones, and straight nose, and chin with points of flickering light. He said, "You're tight. You're in a jam. The police will be here. It's murder. How quickly can you sober up?"

"I don't know. I'm not tight."

"You . . ." he stopped, shrugged and pulled a chair up near her suddenly and sat down close to her, making her look at him. "Listen. Do you understand me?"

"Of course."

"Well, then. I may be the fool of all the world but — I can't see any other way to play it. Not from here. I'm going to take a chance."

"Chance . . ."

His eyes were exasperated, worried, intent all at once. He said slowly, marking the words, "I'm going to tell you what to say to the police. Understand?"

She had already crossed the bridge — ugly and horrible and full of danger. Danger that couldn't have come upon her, Marny, and yet had done so. "I know," she said. "I've got to tell them about Cecily and the gun and . . ."

"You're going to do no such thing. Listen, for God's sake, and shut up." He glanced at the wide, open arch that led from the dining room into the hall. He lowered his voice. "You're going to say this. Word for word. Now pull yourself together, if you can, and listen. You'll say that you were in your room — upstairs there off that balcony. Cecily came along. She stopped and said she was — oh, what? — looking for Durant, of course. Had she talked to him?"

Marny sought back, trying to remember. "Yes, yes, she said she'd talked to him. She said . . ."

"Okay. She was looking for Durant. . . ."

"But she . . ."

". . . and you said something — How do you do? — anything. She said her name was Cecily Durant. And that's all . . ."

"But . . ."

"That is all."

"I've got to tell them. If she was murdered . . ."

"*That's why?* Can't you understand?"

She pushed her hands dazedly across her forehead. She could understand; she knew exactly what he meant. Police, reporters — and then a jury. An ugly triumvirate of inexorable fate.

She thought that and it sounded melodramatic and trite and yet was horribly true. And Bill Cameron said, "Have you thought of what will happen? Newspapers and . . ."

"*Yes.*"

"Then — Marny, they'll arrest you. I told you that. No matter who did it, there you are at hand, with a motive, with self-defense to use as a defense. You were in love with Andre . . ."

"No . . ."

"She threatened you with a gun. She was found a few minutes later, shot. You found her. If any of those facts get into the hands of the police . . ."

"But I didn't kill her."

"No," said Bill Cameron suddenly and very quietly. "Somehow I don't think you did."

The candles wavered gently again. The warm night breeze touched Marny's face. For a long moment she looked at Bill Cameron and he looked at her. It was, somehow, like a repeated experience. As if they had known each other, somewhere, very well.

Perhaps she *was* tight, she thought, confused; perhaps he was right.

Perhaps he was right, too, in what he told her. She said, "But Cecily . . . If she was murdered I've got to help them find whoever killed her. She — she was so young."

He didn't reply for a moment. There was the clatter of

china, soft and musical from somewhere beyond the pantry door. The breeze drifted through the room again. Then he said, "All right. Be noble, and brave and a martyr if you want to. Be a heroine. Go right ahead; don't let me stop you. Or good sense or anything. But has it occurred to you that your little story is going to put Andre on a very bad spot?"

"*Andre!*"

"Who else? She was his wife!" He shrugged. "Andre will automatically become their first and principal suspect: You'll see. Your story will present them with the thing they'll need most — a motive. He wanted to get rid of her to marry you."

"No, no, he didn't. He couldn't have . . ."

"Oh, for God's sake, *think*. I'm talking about the police. If you want to give them evidence against Andre that'll hang him or whatever capital punishment is in this state, go right ahead. But you . . ." He paused, looked at her for a moment, and said in a different, quieter way: "Time is the important thing just now. Don't do anything irrevocable until — we see something of the set-up. Don't throw yourself — or Andre — into a cell with a murder charge until — well, wait. Give yourself at least a chance to think. You can't defend Cecily now. You can't help her now. Believe me, this is right. For you — and certainly for Andre. And I ask you to let yourself be persuaded by me, at least until you've had time to think. Until — well, say until morning. Will you promise me that?"

"Why are you doing this?" she asked suddenly. "What does it matter . . ."

The nameless thing that had held their gaze linked like a chain broke and dropped away. He got up with a brusque motion. His profile, straight and hard, was clear against the candlelight. He said shortly, "I don't know why. I'm not trying to get something on you, if that's what you mean." He went to the door and met the colored butler coming out, a small silver tray in his hands. Bill Cameron took it and put it on the table beside her. He took the silver pot and began to pour coffee into a cup as the telephone in the hall rang sharply. They could hear a woman's voice answer it — Winnie's — capable, pleasant in spite of its undertones of gravity. "Yes, Edward . . .

67

Yes, it's quite all right. Let them come in. Oh, Edward, there's been some trouble at the house. Dinner is late; in fact, we've not had it at all. Rilly will be late bringing your supper over. But you'd better stay at the gate. Let me know if — if anyone tries to come in. Except Mr. Laideau . . . No, Laideau. *Lai-deau*. Well, that's near enough. He'll be here soon and we are expecting him, so let him come right up to the house. Thank you."

The telephone was put down. Winnie's firm footsteps came toward the dining room, nearer and nearer. Bill Cameron finished pouring the hot clear stream of coffee into the cup. As Winnie reached the doorway and came in, her blue dress rustling, her face pale in the candlelight but calm, Bill Cameron said nonchalantly to Marny, "Sugar? How much?"

Winnie came nearer. "Are you all right, Marny? I thought you looked sick." Winnie was worried; her thick, rather shapeless brown eyebrows were drawn together. "That was the man at the gate," she said. "He phoned to say that the police have come. I told him to send them up to the house."

Bill's brown hand paused, holding itself still over the coffee. He did not look up but said, "The man at the gate? Who . . . ?"

"Oh," said Winnie. "Edward, the chauffeur. We always have a man at the gate at night. Judith and I, living alone you see — and so many odd people drifting around these days and . . ."

"Do you mean that this man, Edward, is on guard at the gate?"

"At the bridge, really. There's a little house there, hidden by vines. I planted . . ."

"When did he go on duty?"

"Why, he always goes at dusk, about sundown. Six, as a rule . . ."

"Was he there tonight?" asked Bill.

"Yes, of course."

"Does he always phone to the house when somebody comes?"

"Yes."

"Who came tonight?"

"Why, I — nobody. Except Charlie Ingram. And you . . ."

"Is anybody else here? I mean besides you and Mrs. Wales and your father and — Marny, and me and Charlie Ingram and Durant?"

"Why, the servants, of course, but . . ." Winnie's eyes widened. She stared at Bill. Her breast moved quickly under the folds of blue chiffon. Slowly one large hand went up toward her throat. *"None of us killed her!"*

Bill dropped the lump of sugar into the cup.

"Here, Marny," he said, and put the cup in her hand. He turned to Winnie. "There are other ways to get on the island — boats — other ways. That doesn't mean that somebody on the island killed Cecily."

But it did mean it, thought Marny; and he knew it. His denial was really like an affirmation.

Unless the murderer came in a boat.

Winnie said, "There's the bell. It's the police. I'll go. . . ."

69

CHAPTER VIII

The police left at exactly twenty minutes after two after what seemed a very long time; however they did not question Marny beyond a few formal questions as to the position of the body, and her discovery of it, and she did not tell them of Cecily's visit to her room and Cecily's threats.

So far as she knew she made no decision about it. She accepted Bill Cameron's decision as instinctively as if it were a lifeline or a safe and unexpected path through a dark and treacherous swamp. His logic, however, was irrefutable and forceful. The police might suspect her if they knew the whole — indeed they would certainly suspect her. Cecily's words, the gun, Marny's discovery of the murder could all be, in the hands of the police, terribly damning evidence. Jury evidence, strong and tight and convincing. She knew that; yet there was a certain security in her own knowledge of her own innocence. It might be a deceiving sense of security, but it was there. She hadn't murdered Cecily and somehow, somewhere, there must be a way to prove it. But perhaps no such proof existed for Andre; and in any case her story would damn him even more certainly and inevitably than it would herself, for Andre was, as Bill Cameron had said he would be, the immediate suspect of the police.

It was instantly evident. They didn't even question anyone at length, except Andre. Andre and Laideau, who came at once in response to a telephone call from Andre and arrived soon after the police came.

Led by Tim and Charlie and Bill they tramped down across the lawn; policemen in uniform and detectives and, later, the medical examiner. Their flashlights shot long dancing rays of whiteness over grass and shrubbery and the black water which broke into a thousand small, glittering waves. And then disappeared behind the bamboos.

They made Andre identify the body, watching him probably, as he did so, for any betraying word or look or move. She must warn Andre, thought Marny rather desperately. She must tell him what had happened; she must put him on his guard. There was no possible way to do so, then.

Later, photographs were made. Marny and Winnie, standing on the porch, could see the explosions of light outlining the bamboos and lighting the water in flashes. Eventually someone brought an enormous electric torch which lighted up the area down by the pier. They searched the island, and Marny and Winnie watched that, too, and heard the voices of the men. All the lights on the grounds were turned on, and all the lights in the house. They stamped through the house, opening closet doors, asking questions. They found no one hiding, and Edward, brought from his post at the bridge, said that no one had come onto the island from the public causeway, except Commander Cameron and Mr. Ingram, whom he identified.

Shortly after that an ambulance came and men carried away a burden which seemed light, from the way they walked across the lawn and toward the drive, without entering the house. Judith came then, and watched them go, her lovely face a mask, her dark eyes lambent. Winnie shivered a little, and put her arm around Judith.

Marny turned away, unable to watch that small, somber procession, with the light from electric torches glimmering eerily around it. She went into the drawing room. She'd get a cigarette; she'd do anything, she'd simply sit down there by the calla lilies and stare at the beige and white rugs and wait.

And Andre was in the hall. She heard him come in. She heard the door close and his footsteps, slow and uneven, and she went to the door of the drawing room and Andre was standing in the middle of the hall. He looked shrunken, somehow, his shoulders drawn in. His face was pale and glistening. He was wiping it with his handkerchief and he looked over it quickly, jerkily at Marny.

"Andre," she cried, but low, remembering Judith and Winnie on the porch. She went to him. "Andre, I'm so terribly sorry."

He looked at her without speaking, wiping his face, his dark eyes black and bewildered and unfathomable. "Andre," she looked over her shoulder. No one was in the dining room and it was at some distance, anyway; no one was on the broad stairway; she had left Judith and Winnie on the porch. She said, whispering, "Cecily came to me, Andre. She had a gun. She said you had told her that you wanted to leave her. For — for me. Because of me."

Still Andre did not speak but only stared at her, as if not understanding, wiping his face. She shook his arm a little. "Andre, you must listen. You didn't tell Cecily that?"

He moved his lips twice before a sound came out. Then he said, "Tell Cecily what?"

"That you — that you were in love with me. That you wanted to — to marry me. That you didn't want her."

He shook his black head. "No. Certainly not. Never."

"She said — she thought . . . Andre, you're not listening. I know it's horrible, but don't you see, you've got to know. They'll suspect you. They'll . . . Andre, did you see Cecily tonight at all? I mean after we got here from the airport?"

Andre blinked slowly. "No. She . . ." His eyes quickened, as if at last the thing she was trying to tell him had got through his terrible, tragic preoccupation. "Marny, what are you saying?"

"Sh-sh. Listen . . ." Half whispering, quickly, she told him the story. His face was still unmoved and white like a wax mask, but his eyes, staring at the floor, were alive and comprehensive. He said, when she'd finished, only two words, "Poor Cecily."

"Andre, don't you see . . . ?"

He looked at her then. "Marny, you are so good. So — normal and generous and — and *right,* somehow. Not like Cecily. It was horrible, Marny. I tried to make things better. I didn't know when I married her. Poor child, it wasn't her fault. It was — it was in her blood, I suppose. And she was so young. I only thought she was young, you see, and changeable and . . ." He pressed both hands over his forehead with a kind of groan. "I thought things would be all right; I couldn't give up. Yet even when I began to realize that there wasn't any hope, I hoped. I couldn't tell you about her. How could I? How could I tell anyone? How could I bring the shadow of — of *that* into anyone's house? I didn't see her tonight, I didn't know she was on the island. If she said all that to you, it was another of her fancies. She had them. She hated women. She was crazily jealous. It was one of her — her delusions."

Footsteps were entering from the porch, across the drawing room. Marny whispered, "Someone is coming. . . ."

Andre gripped her hands. "Who did it, Marny? Do you know? Did you see anyone — anything . . . ?"

Winnie came to the door, saw them and stopped.

Andre let go Marny's hands. Winnie said, "Can I help you Andre? Has anything happened? I mean . . ."

Andre touched his face again with his handkerchief. "No, no, Winnie. It's only that the police have been questioning me and are going to again. As if I had killed her . . ."

Winnie waited a moment, her hands automatically smoothing down her blue dress, her eyes anxious. She said then, "But you didn't, Andre. You couldn't have. We have faith in you, all of us. Don't let them trap you into saying something that is wrong or suspicious. Be very careful. Things will blow over. I'm sure of it. Some tramp killed her, or somehow, she shot herself. I don't know how but she must have done that. She . . . Listen, Andre, I'm going to order some food. We'll all be the better for it. You haven't had anything to eat — none of us have had. Go in there and — and have a drink. Not too much, of course, and when they question you, just tell the truth and no more. I'll speak to Rilly."

She moved toward the dining room. Even her neat hair and her square brown shoulders rising above her blue dinner dress seemed, somehow, adequate and comforting. Andre said, "Winnie is so sensible. Yes, I'll do that. I'll . . ." His eyes met Marny's. "Thank you."

"I had to warn you. . . ."

"Oh, not for that. For something much greater. For having

73

faith in me," said Andre, and went into the drawing room.

Rilly came with sandwiches and coffee and Winnie made them all eat.

The photographers and the fingerprint men had gone; the police had apparently done everything they could do at the pier, and drifted to the house. The police by that time consisted of three policemen in uniform, and a chief of detectives in a neat gray seersucker suit with a blue tie, and tanned face and extraordinarily honest-looking, light-blue eyes. It was strangely matter-of-fact. Winnie had the plates of sandwiches and coffee brought out on the porch and put on a long table there, and had candles lighted and put in hurricane lamps. Everyone ate or pretended to; even Andre, sitting on one of the gaily cushioned chairs, made a pretence at it and gulped several cups full of coffee quickly as if he needed it. But he seemed, Marny thought, more like himself, less stunned and frozen.

Poor Andre. And poor, tragic little Cecily.

She must have killed herself — somehow, some way. Freakish, queer, seemingly inexplicable things could happen in cases of suicide. Couldn't they?

It gave the women something to do, moving about, seeing that cups and plates were supplied that is, it gave Winnie and Marny something to do. Judith sat back in a low chair, with her small, slender feet in their black sandals crossed on a hassock, and twisted her emerald on her finger and did nothing. There was very little talk while they ate. There was no way to know whether or not there had been any discoveries leading to the identification of the murderer or to any sort of reconstruction of what had taken place there, so silently (yet the girl had been shot), so swiftly (while Marny was dressing), so stealthily (for no one had known of it).

Tim said once, looking up from his coffee with his little bright eyes shrewd and his face sharply lined and guarded, that they hadn't known the girl. "I never saw her before," he said. "None of us knew her. She wasn't well. . . ."

"So you said, Mr. Wales," said the chief of detectives. His name was Jimmy Manson. He was a captain by rank. He was thinnish, with thinning brown hair, a sun-tanned, rather wrinkled face, just a man such as one would meet a hundred times in a day, on the streets, in the bank, at the post office, anywhere. He took the last bite of a sandwich and lifted his cup, eyeing Tim over the rim of it. "So you said. I'll get some statements from all of you as soon as we finish eating. This was a good idea, Miss Wales. Nothing like food where there's a hard job ahead. We don't have many murder cases here and" — he glanced at Andre — "there's no use saying they are easy on anybody. You did right to call the police right away. It beats all sometimes the way people get so upset they don't know what to do and it's a long time before actually they think about calling the police. You'd think that'd be the first thing anybody would think of. Reminds me, how about lawyers? Any of you folks feel you'd like to have your lawyer in on this? Sometimes a police investigation takes a long time, you know. Sometimes we get a break right away but sometimes not."

"Are you advising us to get lawyers?" asked Tim sharply, looking surprised.

Captain Manson shrugged. "Sure, if you want to. You're a pretty famous man, Mr. Wales. I want everything to be on the up and up."

"But I don't know anything about the girl's murder!" said Tim angrily.

"That's what I mean, Mr. Wales. But it did happen on your island, you see. All of you — your wife," said Captain Manson easily, looking rather hard at another sandwich, "everybody — is likely to get into the papers about it. We can't help that, you know. Reporters'll be here soon as they get onto what's happened. You know that's their job, of course. News. How about you, Mr. Durant?"

Andre lifted his head with a jerk. "I didn't murder her, either," he said.

"Now, now," said Captain Manson "It's only for your own good. If you don't want a lawyer, you don't have to have one."

Something inside Marny roused for an instant and said, the man is smart. He knows now that no one will call a lawyer. He'll question and inquire without interference. What did he

75

mean by that crack about Judith? Or was it a crack? Or did it mean anything?

Bill Cameron, his Navy whites no longer immaculate but wrinkled and stained with grass across the knees, slapped at a mosquito and Winnie said, "Perhaps we'd better go inside. There are so many bugs. . . ."

They were circling around the candles, beating against the glass shields. Tim said slowly, "Why, yes. Yes, that's a good idea, Winnie. Shall we . . . ?"

He led the way, host-like, holding the door open for Judith, who rose gracefully, still without speaking, and preceded him. In the long living room with its low tables, its calla lilies, its pleasant, gay and everyday atmosphere, Captain Manson made a little speech about murder. He stood beside the white piano, leaning on it as Andre had done, and said he had to tell them that a murder inquiry was very difficult and that they must not think, when he asked questions or when another detective or policeman asked questions, that they were going outside their line of duty.

"It's our job, you see," he said, and took a cigarette and lighted it. "So I wanted to say now that it'll make everything easier for everybody if you'll answer and not be worried about getting involved in anything. Nobody's going to be accused of murder falsely, if I can help it, and I'll do everything I can — and that's quite a lot — to keep anything out of the newspapers that you want kept out."

"I don't think we have anything to hide, Captain," said Tim Wales at once. Tim is smart, too, thought Marny, in another odd flash of something that was normal and sensible and everyday — which again was lost in nightmare. For that naturally was what it was; a nightmare with a nightmare's occasional flash of some small detail, some picture, some sensation that seemed clear and real, as if to disprove the nightmare.

One of the policemen took out a paper-bound notebook and a pencil and the slight motion caught Marny's eyes. It was one such detail — this was a nightmare, Cecily was murdered, things like that didn't happen. . . . And the notebook, and the policeman putting pencil to his lips and examining the point of it matter-of-factly, seemed to prove that it had happened.

"Now, as I understand it," said Captain Manson, smoking, "it happened like this. Miss Sanderson . . ." his blue eyes traveled around the room and reached Marny, who found herself nodding. (And thinking briefly that it had not taken him long to learn their names and to link those names with the right people.) "Miss Sanderson, walking down to the pier, found her just as Commander Cameron got there. They saw she was dead and then Mr. Ingram came and Mr. Ingram and Miss Sanderson came back to the house and you" — he looked at Bill Cameron, sitting solidly on a hassock, smoking also — "stayed with the body until Mr. Wales came. Then all three of you came to the house and you, Mr. Wales, called the police. Now then, you say you didn't touch the body, Commander, but you looked about the shrubbery and didn't see a gun anywhere."

"That's right," said Bill Cameron. "I told you. . . ."

"Got a record of that, Willie?" said Captain Manson, looking at the policeman with the notebook, who looked rather big and awkward and slow and who was making lightning like marks, shorthand probably, in his notebook. He nodded without looking up. The detective said, "Now let's try to get some of the main facts straight. Mr. Wales, you said you didn't hear the shot?"

"No, I didn't."

"Did anybody hear it?"

There was a silence. Judith, on the sofa, twisted her emerald ring. Winnie had picked up her knitting big and was holding it in her lap, gripping it tightly as if the touch of something homely and matter-of-fact was comforting. Andre sat huddled in a great armchair, his head leaning on a hand that shielded his face. Laideau stood behind him.

The light was on Laideau's face. Marny had not seen him when he arrived. He had been met by Andre and the had gone immediately across the lawn and not through the house, to the pier and the bamboo hedge where Cecily lay. Marny had been aware of him on the candle-lighted terrace — a man of medium height with great stooped shoulders and long arms; a man who looked large because his features were heavy and his head big; but he had said nothing, had kept close to Andre, had refused anything but coffee. He wore a white shirt, open at the throat, rather soiled white trousers and rubber-soled tennis shoes. He was the man she'd seen in the boat with Cecily. His thick, gleaming black hair, parted on one side, his powerful-looking shoulders, were unmistakable. Laideau had to know something of the story. He had brought Cecily and had taken her away, and then probably had brought her back. *Did he know why Cecily had come? Did he know why she had returned?*

His face was sallow, his eyes, half hidden under thick black eyebrows, his mouth unrevealing. He did not seem to look at her, he did not seem to look at anyone. He only listened and stood beside Andre. Bill Cameron shook ashes from his cigarette and said that probably nobody had heard the sound of the shot because there was so much noise about the place.

"Noise!" cried Winnie, looking surprised. "But it was so quiet . . ."

"I mean the radio was going," said Bill. "When I arrived. Nobody was down yet and I sat there on the porch. Several boats passed — motor boats — and once an outboard and you know what a hell of a racket they make. If the girl was shot here on the island, the noise of the boats might have covered the sound of the shot."

"If she . . ." Tim shot him a look of quick comprehension which had something like gratitude for the suggestion in it. He said coolly and promptly to the detective, "But then I don't see how she could have been shot here on the island, Captain. She must have been killed some other place and brought here. By boat . . ."

Laideau spoke. It was the first time Marny had heard his voice. It was metallic and rusty-sounding, as if he hadn't used it for a long time. His little dark eyes, too close together over the bridge of his large nose, sought the captain. "I told you," he said, "that I brought her here. I did. But she was alive."

"Let's have that again, if you please," said the Captain. "Only a brief statement for the record."

"Well." Laideau seemed to hesitate. He turned to the policeman who was writing. "She wanted to come to Shadow Island. She asked me to bring her in a rowboat. So I did. She came up to the house and I waited down there at the pier. She came back and got in the boat and we started away. Then she said that she wanted to come back. Said she'd forgotten something. So I rowed her back to the pier. She got out and said for me not to wait but go on back to Miami Beach. Said she'd get home all right. So I did. That's all."

"Okay," said the Captain. "Now let's see. Why did she want to come to Shadow Island?"

Laideau's opaque dark eyes shifted to the captain. "She didn't say."

"Why did she want to return?"

"She didn't say that either."

"I see." The detective had a disarming appearance of accepting every statement at its face value. He was smart, thought Marny again, her business sense (the sense that Tim Wales had trained and cultivated) rising to the surface again, touching this new Marny who didn't seem to know what she was doing, who was perplexed and horribly bewildered and frightened.

"Mr. Durant," said the detective, suddenly turning to Andre. "This has been a shock, of course. Can you . . . ? I've got to ask you some questions, you understand."

Andre gave a kind of shiver, like a dog coming out of water. "All right," he said in a muffled voice behind his hand. Judith made a sharp motion forward, opened a crystal cigarette box, took out a long cigarette, reached for a match and then accepted a light from Charlie Ingram, seated beside her, his monocle in place and glittering this way and that as he listened avidly. The detective said as the match sputtered, "What was your wife's maiden name?"

"Watts," said Andre, behind his hand.

"Cecily Watts?"

"Of course."

"Where was her home?"

There was a slight pause, then Andre said heavily, "In Jamaica. She was the daughter of an English planter. He owned

79

a sugar plantation." ("It was in her blood," Andre had said. "She was so young. . . .")

Marny held tight to the arm of her chair.

"Is he alive?"

"No."

"Relatives?"

"I don't know. I believe there was a cousin in England. Cecily didn't correspond much with her."

"When were you married?"

"About a year ago."

"Was her father alive then?"

"He died the week we were married. He'd been sick a long time. His name was Harrison Watts." Andre moved restively. "There's a record of everything there at Kingston, if you want it. I don't see what this has to do with Cecily. . . ."

"I was thinking of people to notify. Had your wife any enemies?"

"Not that I know of."

Laideau said raspingly, "She was her own worst enemy. She shot herself and threw the gun into the sea. She was not well."

"That would have been impossible," said the detective so completely without emphasis that it was flatly convincing. "She was murdered. . . . Had she any enemies?" he repeated, looking at Andre.

"No," said Andre after a pause. "Laideau is right, though. She wasn't well. It is why we were not living together."

"I see. Had you taken her to a doctor?"

"No. She wouldn't let me. She had fancies like that."

"Yes," said Laideau heavily, little eyes fixed on the detective, sallow heavy face impassive. "She had fancies like that. It is why I did not question her when she wished to come here, and when she wished to return to the island. It was always best to humor her."

"You mean that she was mentally unsteady? Erratic?"

"Yes," said Andre.

"But did you not consult a doctor?"

"No, I thought it best to — to wait. I hoped she would be better."

"Mr. Durant, I must ask you if you quarreled with your wife. I could ask the employees, the maids and the bellboys at the hotel where you tell me she lived, but I would prefer getting your statement about it."

He'll ask them anyway, thought Marny. He is saying that to warn Andre. Andre was aware of it too. He said, "I told you she was not well. There were times when she was hysterical. It was not easy."

Laideau said, "I was there. He did everything he could for her."

The detective put out his cigarette and took a fresh one and lighted it. He said, "Mr. Wales tells me that he had never seen Mrs. Durant. Did you know her, Mrs. Wales?"

Judith said, "I knew of her. I had never seen her."

She did not add to it; she did not explain. Her lovely face was cool and unmoved. She returned the detective's glance with every appearance of candor. He said, "I understand Mr. Durant is a guest here."

"Yes, he is," replied Judith. "He has been here almost a month. Except for a trip to New York."

"I didn't know about that," said the detective. "When did you return, Mr. Durant? Did you take your wife with you?"

Andre said, his hand still over his eyes, his mouth apparently steady, "I went to New York a week ago, a little over a week ago, on business. Cecily remained at the Villa Nova, the hotel. I got back this afternoon."

"We all arrived together," Tim Wales explained. They had come in by plane; they had reached the house before seven o'clock.

"Did you communicate with your wife, Mr. Durant? I mean during your visit north?"

"No."

There was a little silence. An insect buzzed loudly at the screen. The detective said, "Mrs. Durant must have had some purpose in coming here. Was it to see you, Mr. Durant?"

"No." Andre took his hand away and looked at the detective, his eyes bright and hard. "I did not see her. I did not see her or talk to her. I know nothing of this. Nothing."

"Miss Sanderson saw her," said Bill Cameron suddenly. "I told you about that. Mrs. Durant was on the balcony, so she did reach the house."

"I understand she told you her name." The detective was looking at Marny and Marny replied as if somebody else were speaking, not Marny; somebody over whom she had no control; somebody who'd been told what to say, and why, and how to say it. "Yes. Yes, she told me her name."

"About what time was that?"

"I'm not sure." She thought back. It had been a quarter after seven when she had returned to her room from the pool. She had talked to Judith, rinsed her hair, had a long bath. "I think it was after seven-thirty. I'm not sure."

"Had you ever seen her before? Did you know her?"

"No. She . . ."

"She was very nervous, Miss Sanderson said," intervened Bill Cameron, with every appearance of being helpful and informative. "Then she went down to the boat and I saw it leave." He jerked his head toward Laideau. "As you know, Laideau was with her, rowing."

"Did anyone else see her?" asked the detective. His blue eyes went slowly around the room. No one spoke. He said, "I'll have to ask for statements, by the way. I may as well do it now. So far as we know now the girl was killed between seven-thirty and a quarter after eight, when she was found. Is that right, Commander?"

Bill Cameron thought for an instant, frowning a little, his mouth tight. Then he gave a quick nod. "Yes, I think so. I arrived about seven-thirty, perhaps a little after that. No one was down yet; the butler showed me to this room and I went out on the porch. As I told you, I saw her leave. It was not later than eight-fifteen when we found her."

Judith stirred. She sat up straight. A long gray ash dropped from her cigarette onto her lap, and she said clearly, "If you want alibis, Captain Manson, then I can give you at least one."

Tim said, "*Judith* . . ."

"You seem to believe that Andre — Mr. Durant — may have murdered his wife. Simply because she was his wife and you must have a suspect. But I can tell you that he didn't." She lowered her eyes, slowly, so the white eyelids veiled them. She appeared to look at her cigarette burning down almost to the slender, white finger tips. She said, "He was with me."

But Andre, thought Marny suddenly, in the sudden silence, had not told her that.

CHAPTER IX

Tim Wales got up with a violent motion and stood with his shiny, fat hands doubled up, his face red. Winnie got up quickly, too, said repressively, "Now, Father," and went to sit beside her stepmother.

"I'm sorry, Tim," said Judith, without looking at her elderly husband. "But obviously the police suspect him, and he simply couldn't have done it. He . . ." She looked directly at the policeman with the notebook and made her statement. It was brief, concise and simple. She had gone to Marny's — Miss Sanderson's — room and talked for a few minutes. She had happened to note the time when she left and it was just past seven-thirty. She had returned to her own room, and Andre, already dressed for dinner, had come to her there. He had wanted to tell her the outcome of his business in New York. She was in the dressing room adjoining her bedroom and had heard him knock at the bedroom door and told him to come in.

"I told him I was dressing, to sit down and wait. He sat in a chair by the window and talked through the door. It was open a little. He had several cigarettes, I think. I had only to get into my dress and I did so, and came out into the bedroom where he was waiting. He sat there and talked until we came downstairs to dinner. That's all, except if Cecily was murdered during that time Andre couldn't have done it."

Winnie put her arm around Judith, with a defiant glance at her father. The detective said, "You corroborate this, Mr. Durant?"

Andre rubbed his hands through his hair, hesitated, glanced nervously at Tim Wales and said hesitantly, "I — well, yes. That is — yes."

"You may have to tell this in court, you know, Mrs. Wales," said the detective. "Have you thought of that?"

Judith's lovely chin, went up. She still would not look at Tim. "It is quite true, Captain."

Winnie's face flushed. She cried unevenly, "It doesn't matter. It isn't the way it sounds. That is, it's just Judith. Just . . . I mean . . . Oh, don't you sec, it is only her way. We . . . Why, we all go into Judith's room. We have breakfast coffee there or . . . It's just a custom. . . ."

Tim Wales said in a strange voice, "Winnie, don't try to explain." And Captain Manson said quietly, "Will you take the other statements, one at a time, Willie?" He put out his cigarette and said, "We have some routine to see to. It's late. You've all been very patient," made a quiet little bow and walked out of the room, through the hall, so his footsteps were clear and sharp on the tiled floor, and out the front door. It was so late and so still that they could hear even at that distance the murmur of voices outside, where apparently a squad car waited for him, and then the sound of an automobile starting up.

It gave them all perhaps a curious sense of shock and surprise. It was as if he had seen something they had not seen, had gathered some evidence that none of them had gathered, and had gone away to do something about it. Winnie half started up, sank back on the sofa, her face bewildered. "But he — he's gone. *Why* . . ."

Tim said to Judith, "It's late. You'd better go upstairs."

"My statement . . ." began Judith, and Tim said roughly, "He's got your statement. He'll have you sign it. You've said enough."

Bill Cameron crossed to Marny and sat down on the arm of her chair. His face was cold and hard-looking, his eyes enigmatic. He said, "This may take a little time. Cigarette?"

Judith got up from the sofa gracefully and went to Tim. She put her hand on Tim's shoulder and looked at him with a strange, still expression. This time, however, it was Tim who would not look at her. He said, "You'd better go."

All at once Judith became again the beautiful, self-possessed and charming woman they were familiar with but did not,

85

Marny thought suddenly, really know. She lifted her bare shoulders in a faint shrug and said, "Very well. I'm sorry, Tim, but I had to tell them the truth. They would have charged Andre with murder in another minute or two." She went calmly, with great self-possession, to the door, her black chiffon skirts trailing softly after her. There she turned and, incredibly, smiled and said good night.

Winnie started to wring her hands, seemed suddenly aware of it and stopped, with a queer look of amazement in her face. She went to her father and Tim said, roughly again, "Not now, Winnie . . ." and went abruptly out on the porch. And the business of making statements began. Statements which at once reduced themselves to the recital of a few simple facts.

Marny listened automatically, thinking of Judith and Andre and Andre's alibi. Winnie had been dressing and seeing that the table was properly laid and the flowers arranged. Bill Cameron had been sitting on the porch and had seen Cecily leave; then he had joined the others for cocktails. Charlie Ingram had arrived at eight, and had come immediately into the drawing room where everybody but Marny herself was already gathered drinking cocktails.

Bill Cameron knew when and in what order people had arrived in the drawing room and told the policeman succinctly. He had looked at his watch, he said. He wasn't sure just when Mrs. Durant had come down the stairway from the balcony and had crossed the lawn, but he did know that it was five minutes to eight when Andre and Judith came into the living room for he had heard their voices and had joined them. Winnie had come in a few minutes later and then Tim Wales and Charlie Ingram. Miss Sanderson, he said definitely, had come down the stairs from the balcony, had strolled across the lawn . . . "She went down toward the bay. It looked very pretty just then. I went after her to tell her dinner was ready. I reached her just as she found Mrs. Durant. . . ."

It was the truth as far as it went. The policeman made quick marks in his notebook and went out onto the porch to question Tim.

At twenty minutes after two exactly he, too, went away.

Charlie Ingram went home, looking shaken and red and worried. Bill Cameron stayed in the house and so did Laideau.

Winnie invited them. "You'll want to stay with Andre," she said to Laideau. "Please do. There is a vacant room next to his, a small one but . . . And you too, Commander Cameron. I'll get a razor and pajamas for you. You can't get a taxi at this hour, I'm afraid."

"Thank you," said Bill Cameron. "I'd like to stay."

Winnie led him upstairs. The servants had gone to bed long since. The light was on at the top of the stairs and along the corridors that branched irregularly from a central landing above. Andre and Laideau had disappeared together, and Tim was at the telephone, getting long distance. "The reporters will get at the New York office first thing in the morning," he told Marny. "Have to tell somebody what to say."

Marny went on up the stairs. She felt exactly like a mechanical doll, wound up but running down. She opened the door to her own room and entered it and sat down on the bed.

The bed was turned down. The carafe of water refilled and the stopper replaced. Otherwise the room was exactly as it had been when she'd left it to find Cecily.

Well, she'd found her.

Quite suddenly the thing that had sustained her, the wound-up spring, ran down completely. She flung herself over across the bed and put her head in her arms.

She couldn't cry and it wouldn't help anyway. She couldn't think and she must think.

For one thing, she had to decide for herself a course of conduct. She had followed Bill Cameron's lead, obeyed him blindly, failed to tell the police what she knew of Cecily's visit to Shadow Island.

Was it because it was easier? because she dreaded the ugly implications? because they would say she had murdered Cecily? or because of Andre?

But Judith had had courage. If Judith had not given Andre a firm and prompt alibi they would almost certainly have arrested him and charged him with murder. It was in the air; it was in the detective's eyes; it was in the way all of them looked at Andre. Andre was the obvious suspect; no one else except Judith even knew of Cecily. You had to know somebody very well, thought Marny; you have to have some very strong and very urgent and very personal motive to commit murder. But Andre was with Judith when Cecily was shot in the back.

How long did a police investigation last? Until they found the murderer, of course. Until they discovered who it was who met little Cecily Watts — Cecily Durant, married to Andre a year — there by the pier and behind the bamboos and shot her. So no one in the house knew that that shot had been fired.

Somebody was walking along the balcony.

One does not immediately accept a thing so bizarre, so awry, so vehemently outside the ordered scheme of things as murder. Marny thought merely, without much interest, someone is walking on the balcony, someone is approaching this room.

Murder had walked that night — somewhere on the island, somewhere near.

She sat up, her heart pounding in her throat, her eyes fastened upon the black screened door, open, with its little froth of insects gathered on it outside.

Then Tim Wales was there. Tim in a light bathrobe, Tim looking queer and pale in the half-light. He said, in a whisper, "Marny . . ." and opened the door.

Only Tim. She took a long breath and pushed her tumbled hair back. He came in and sat down on the foot of her bed. "Got a cigarette?"

Her heart was still beating hard in her throat. It was atavistic, this sense of danger. A man you knew as well as you knew anybody in the world walked along a balcony and stopped at the door, and that primitive sense of danger operated like that. Because of murder.

She said, "Yes," and went to the dressing table and came back with the small green cigarette box and matches. Tim was in pajamas and a pongee bathrobe, piped and handsomely initialed in red. His face was drawn and sunken-looking, not round and shiny as usual. His eyes very bright and nervous. He took the cigarette and lighted it jerkily. "Marny, you'll have to help me. The newspapers will be on us like vultures in the morning. I don't know how Manson kept them off tonight." He rubbed one hand over his head. "Judith won't talk to me. She's gone in her room and locked the door. If she'd kept still they'd have arrested Andre Durant, and a good job. He killed her."

After a moment Marny said, "He couldn't have killed her. He has an alibi."

"You mean Judith gave him an alibi. She saw it coming. We all saw it coming. He hadn't the chance of a snowball in hell. None of the rest of us even knew the girl. He wanted to get rid of her. He wouldn't have left her if he hadn't wanted to get rid of her. I don't believe all that stuff about her being crazy. She was crazy to marry him — but that's all. He saw a chance for better game and left her. Got himself wedged in here. Told Laideau to see that he kept Cecily out of the way. Didn't even tell anybody he was married."

"Judith knew it."

Tim hunched up his knees and wrapped the bathrobe around him, so he looked old and sagging and fat and helpless. But he wasn't helpless; he was as wily as a fox and as strong as a wolf. He said, "Yes, Judith knew it. Judith . . . That's why we came to Florida, Marny. I didn't tell you. It didn't seem fair to Judith. I imagine you guessed. She . . . I've always been afraid of it, ever since we married. She's young and she's beautiful and men like her and why shouldn't they? I've been afraid, but if or when she got mixed up with a man I wasn't going to let it hurt her. I wasn't going to let it be an Andre. He . . . I've investigated him a little."

"You what?"

His small shrewd eyes shot her a suspicious glance. "I said I investigated him. Not very thoroughly — yet. But enough."

"Enough . . ."

He made a vague gesture. "Oh, he's never been in jail, but his record . . ."

"Records can be wrong. What do you mean by record?"

"I've — well, I've inquired. Some. I . . . You see, Judith sent him to me with a letter asking me to consider giving him a job. I never knew Judith to take much interest in getting anybody a job, so I sized the fellow up, not that it needed much thought. I kept him around, as you know — let him talk, watched him. I didn't find out about Cecily. I'll know more about that by morning. So will the police. From here I'd say he got hold of her when her father was sick and couldn't do anything about it, married her as soon as he was sure her father was going to die, and got whatever money there was."

"Tim, you are . . ." She checked herself. She couldn't say jealous — suspicious — determined to get rid of Andre in the same inexorable, all but unscrupulous way in which from time to time he'd got rid of business rivals. She said, "You are not quite fair, Tim. You are letting yourself be influenced by . . ." There it was again — jealousy, and suspicion. Jealousy of Andre's youth and vitality, suspicion because Judith was young, too, and beautiful. She substituted ". . . emotions," but he didn't apparently hear her. He went on, "Not much money, I fancy, for he seems to be very thoroughly out of cash right now. Of course this fellow Laideau may have got his share. They're always together. They're an unsavory pair. Well, I came down here to get rid of Andre as quickly but as quietly and easily as I could. You see . . ." Tim took a long puff from his cigarette and looked hard at his slippered feet.

"You see, Marny, I have to go slow. I have to ride with an easy rein. I couldn't come down here and order him out of the house and tell Judith never to see him again. I couldn't fish up everything in his record, and I'm convinced I could find plenty to fish up — and then put it before her. If I were younger . . . If I were a — a" — he said with a wry twist of his lips — "if I were a more romantic lover, I could do that. As it is — no. I had to do it easily, skillfully. At least that's what I planned. That's why I came. I didn't think Judith would let herself get involved with a man of his type. God knows there are plenty of them floating around. But Judith seemed too smart, too sophisticated. I thought I could do it slowly, find out just how much she was involved. Get rid of him without fireworks. And mainly without antagonizing Judith. But I didn't figure that she really loved him."

The disarming thing about Tim Wales was that even at his

shrewd, suspicious, all but unscrupulous worst you liked him. She said quickly, "She doesn't love him, Tim. . . ."

"You're kind, Marny, and you're fond of me. You're trying to save my pride. Would a woman like Judith put herself out on a limb like that for a man she didn't love?"

"Tim, we all know Judith. She's always been casual, informal . . ."

"Informal," said Tim and gave an ugly short laugh. "The trouble is I can't, now, kick him out of the house. I can't . . ." He checked himself and smoked and said: "Everything's public now. I've got to stand by him to save Judith's face. Winnie says there was nothing to it. Judith and he were simply good friends. Judith likes anybody who amuses her. She always has . . ."

"Winnie is right, Tim."

He shook his head. "Winnie'd swear herself black in the face to stand by Judith. I talked to her just now for a while. I . . . God help me, I questioned her. Judith's in love with Durant, and God knows how far she's got herself involved. I'll bet anything I've got that he's made his livelihood by women — rich women, not rich, any kind of woman. I know his type. Why, he even made a play for you, Marny."

"Tim . . ."

"While he was trying to get me, Judith's husband, to give him a job that paid well and involved very little work, he went after you! Thank God, you had sense enough to know it."

"Tim, you're wrong. You're — you're jealous and unfair. It's blinding your judgment; you're being stupid and cruel. He wanted nothing from me . . ."

He swept on, staring at the floor, unheeding, "I'd like to kill him with my own hands. I was so damned happy, Marny. I love her so much."

Suddenly she couldn't bear the look in his face. All the life and bounding energy had gone out of him. It was a Tim Wales nobody had ever seen. She put her hand almost timidly on his arm. "Tim," she said, "give yourself and Judith a chance."

Again he did not listen. He went on, "We've got to plan things. We've got to fix up a story for the newspapers. I've got to save Judith from the headlines, from the things that could happen to her all the rest of her life. But he murdered that girl and he's going to hang for it. And," said Tim, hard and white and grim, "I'll be there to see it."

"*Tim* . . ." Again she checked herself. But he wanted to believe in Andre's guilt. He was determined to believe in it. He went on, "The police will be here tomorrow. They didn't even get unlimbered tonight. That fellow Manson is smart. He's going to look over the ground, investigate, check. He left loopholes — all kinds of loopholes — questions he could have asked and didn't. He was going to arrest Durant. I'm sure of that. And Judith put a spoke in his wheel. So now he'll go about it cagily, getting the dope quickly, sneaking around, and then spring it on us. I know his type." He got up and found an ash tray. His fat, shiny hands, usually so firm, so determined, so steady, were shaking. She said, trying to overcome a kind of sick horror, trying to speak calmly and sensibly, "You'd better go to bed now, Tim. It's horrible, all of it. It's stunned us. I can't think anything that's straight and logical and makes any sense. Neither can you. Go to bed and take something to sleep. You've got those pills the doctor give you last winter when you weren't sleeping, haven't you?"

"I don't know. Yes . . ."

"Take one. Talk to Judith in the morning. Don't be emotional about it. You're so smart, Tim. Use your head. You . . ." she forced herself to speak crisply, matter-of-factly, "You've got out of worse scrapes than this."

He looked at her then. It was a strange look, sad and bright and rather terrible. He said, "I'd kill him now if it were not for Judith. But I'll see him hang . . . all right, Marny. I'll go. We'll talk in the morning."

He went without another word by way of the door into the hall instead of as he had come, by the balcony.

It was three o'clock. She looked at the little gold hands of the clock for a long time. She knew Tim when he was like this. There was never anything anybody could do with him. And now, because it was Judith, because it was not business but something that went infinitely deeper into that stubborn, crafty, not too scrupulous heart, than any business feud could possibly go, he was even more obstinate. Tim Wales was an enemy who never gave up.

She'd better go to bed, she thought dully.

She got out of her dress and into pajamas, and tied her hair with a ribbon. She turned out the light and got into bed.

She thought suddenly of Bill Cameron. He was level-headed and cool. He might help. He had befriended her, at least.

Or had he?

Had he instead obligated her to him? So he could ask for whatever he wanted of Tim?

She sat up again and clasped her arms around her knees and stared at the faintly lighter space that was the door upon the balcony.

Was that his motive in seeming to protect her and Andre, in telling her story for her, so adequately, so convincingly that the police did not even question it? In imposing his apparently disinterested and wise advice upon her when she was bewildered and sick with horror and did not know what to do?

It was curious that there was a solid shape of blackness against the door. It almost took the shape of a man's head and shoulders and it moved and . . .

She reached out and snatched at the tiny chain on the lamp. It was a foolish and a dangerous thing to do but she was not yet used to the fact of murder. Light flooded the room and a man was standing, his face pressed against the screen, looking at her.

It was Laideau, fully dressed, his sallow face white against the night. He opened the door and slid into the room as lithely and swiftly as a snake and whispered sharply, "Don't scream."

She couldn't have screamed; she couldn't have moved. He said, "I was not sure that this was your room. Be quiet — I won't hurt you. I've come on business."

He too came to the bed and stood there, his powerful shoulders and long arms and crafty eyes looking, again, incredibly sinister and ugly. He said in a rasping whisper, "Don't scream. It'll be the worse for you if you do. I said I came on business."

"Business," she said, with her hands at her own throat.

"We've talked it over, Andre and I. He wants to know how much you will give us not to tell the police that you killed Cecily."

CHAPTER X

The house was silent. The night beyond that open door was still and black. There was no sound anywhere except the droning buzz of one of the night moths, fluttering against the screen, trying to get at the light beside her.

An unsavory pair, Tim had said. Laideau and Andre. *Andre!*

Laideau's great, big-knuckled hands clasped the railing at the foot of the bed. His small eyes flickered toward the door into the hall and then came back to her. "You're supposed to be a smart woman. Andre told me. You may be smart enough about business; you're going to learn something now, though, about people."

About people? About Andre. About herself.

She was cold. She pulled up the silk blanket cover and huddled it around her shoulders, staring at Laideau, not knowing what she did.

"Cecily threatened you with that gun. You told Andre all about it. Women always tell him things. Women are fools about him. But I'll say that Cecily told me. I'll say that Andre told her he was going to get rid of her, leave her and marry you. She threatened you and you got her to leave. I'll say that she told me all about it in the boat, then she made me turn around and come back. I'll say that I left her at the pier. I didn't want to be mixed up in anything, so I rowed down past the point where there are trees, and I waited there for a while. Then I decided she wasn't coming so I went home. You see my story is complete. Andre's clever; I'm not. But I'm useful to him."

There were rules in life. Things that had sounded trite and meaningless because she had never thought that she could conceivably be it a position to which those rules might apply. But nevertheless they existed. She whispered, her lips dry and

95

stiff, "I didn't kill her. I won't be blackmailed."

"Blackmail is not a pretty word, dear young lady. Blackmail and murder. You have money."

"I don't . . ."

"You are successful. Andre said so. Tim Wales has money. You are valuable to him. You must have money. If you don't have, you can get it. Don't forget what it means to you. She threatened you with a revolver; it was your life or hers. And you wanted Andre . . ."

"I don't — I didn't . . ." But she had, she thought sickeningly to herself. Hadn't she? She had at least come close enough to it to consider seriously whether or not she was in love with Andre. He laughed without making any sound, his pale mouth jerking upward. "Don't tell me that. They always want him. Well, think it over. We'll give you till tomorrow."

If you can't think and don't know what to do, stick to the rules. There was only one thing to do and say and someone outside herself seemed to tell her what that thing was. "I'm going to tell the police myself. I'll not pay you anything."

"Oh, yes you will. Think about the newspapers. Think about the police." He leaned over and put his great hand on the bed. It was like a gesture of comfort, a travesty, a mark of complacence. It was actually more convincing than the things he said. "You are young. Your future is before you. Or, if you choose, it is already behind you. You can get money; you must have money. Think it over."

He turned and slid out the door again as swiftly as he had entered. She could not hear his retreating footsteps on the balcony.

So Tim was right about Andre. Tim and Cecily. Laideau had said — secure in ugly knowledge — they always want him.

After a long time she got up, closed the balcony door and bolted it. Her room, she thought wryly, was too easy of access. The night had turned very dark. Clouds were thick and sullen and black. Not a ray of starlight showed through them.

"You're smart enough about business, now you're going to learn something about people."

So she had learned about Andre.

There was no doubt in her mind as to the truth of Laideau's statement. She wanted to disbelieve but she could not. Beyond reason, more convincing than logic was an irrefutable instinct. Small things, half-seen, wholly rejected, stubbornly denied, now linked themselves together. Laideau, Cecily, Tim, had been right.

And what could she do, now?

Perhaps no one in the house slept that night.

Marny saw it grow gradually lighter, the palms and Casuarinas take slow shape against the quiet, pearly sky and the water turn light gray and sleek. Every clearer shape of palms against the sleek water and sky, every heightening tinge of green along the fringe of Casuarinas brought her interview with the police nearer. Police, reporters, jury. She began to play a grim little game — when the water turned blue, when bougainvillaea around the balcony rail turned sharply green and purple, when the sun came out, she would go downstairs and telephone to Captain Manson.

But the sun did not come out, although the sky continued to lighten. It was, in fact, an ominously quiet day with hurricane warnings over the radio, along with the news of the murder. And before the Casuarina trees had emerged, green and fringy, from the gray mist, Winnie came.

She opened the door quietly, without knocking, and seeing that Marny was sitting up in bed, arms clasped around her knees, she entered the room. Everybody, thought Marny rather grimly, came to her room. It was like the Grand Central Station. Even Winnie came bursting in. "I knew you'd be awake," said Winnie. She wore a pale-blue silk dressing gown, immaculate and well-tailored. Her brown hair was in a neat short braid, tied with a blue ribbon. She carried a tray with coffee and orange juice and put it down on the table, and closed the door carefully behind her.

She looked at Marny. Her fresh color was gone, and her lips, without lipstick, looked pale and shapeless. Her thick, short brown eyebrows stood out. "I knew you'd be awake," she repeated. "Here's coffee. I'll pour it. You take sugar, don't you? I don't imagine anybody slept last night. Judith's light was still on when I passed her door a while ago to go to the kitchen. Marny," said Winnie, "you've got to help me." She put the coffee in Marny's hands and poured some for herself.

Marny felt as if her eyes were on strings, pulling from behind. She lifted the cup to her lips and eyed Winnie over it. There was something grimly humorous about helping Winnie. In all probability she herself would be in jail in a few hours' time. Winnie stirred her own coffee resolutely and said, blue eyes the exact color of her dressing gown, "It's Judith. And Andre."

Judith and Andre. Of course. Marny and Andre. *Anybody* and Andre!

Marny drank more coffee. It was funny, she thought wryly, how one did commonplace things in all the crises of life. Life was a process of getting through the moments, wasn't it? Winnie leaned forward. Her thick, shapeless eyebrows lowered across her short straight nose, with a puzzled, helpless look. "You're not listening to me, Marny. I'm nearly out of my mind. I understand Judith. Other people don't. They think she's lovely and charming and stunning and glamorous and all that, but they don't . . ." Winnie seemed to hunt for a word and finally said again, ". . . they don't understand her. She's never serious about men. Until now. And Father knows."

I can't listen to her, thought Marny rather desperately. Andre and Judith. Andre and Cecily. Andre and any woman. She said abruptly, "This is between your father and Judith."

"No, no, Marny. You must listen to me. Father is — he's not — himself. He's so terribly in love with her. I'm not good at talking. But you see, oh, I know how silly it sounds, Marny, but from the first minute I saw her she was like a fairy princess." Winnie stopped and looked at her rather defiantly for a moment as if she might laugh, and then went on quickly, "She was everything I wasn't. Oh, I'm all right. It's only that — I'm bread and butter and she's caviar and champagne. Father needs me and depends on me. But Judith is — is different. . . ."

"Winnie, what are you trying to say?"

"I'm trying to say — I don't know how — I'm trying to . . ." Winnie put down her coffee cup. She stood up, firm and attractive and neat. She put her hand in her pocket and came to the bed and put a small handkerchief on the blanket cover. It was lacy and delicate and crumpled and stained heavily, apparently with a brown liquid which had dried. It had a large J in one corner. Winnie said, "That's blood. It was soaked with it. I don't know what she tried to do after she killed her. She must have not intended to; she must have tried to stop the bleeding."

"*Winnie!*"

"Sh— she — Marny, you've got to help me. Father's going to find out."

Judith and Andre. Andre and Judith. Cecily, dead, in the shadow of the bamboos. Marny stared at the crumpled, dried, stained handkerchief.

"I covered for her last night, yet I didn't say anything that wasn't true, Marny. Judith is casual like that. I mean, her big bedroom is like a living room. Everybody strays in and out and sits around and gossips and . . . It was perfectly true, what I told the police, I mean. There wasn't anything unusual about Andre or anybody else going in there and smoking and shouting through the dressing-room door at her while she dressed. Only Father doesn't believe it. . . ."

"Winnie, what do you mean? What are you going to do with this?"

Winnie took a short, hard breath, stared at Marny and snatched up the handkerchief. "I'm going to burn it, of course."

"But that . . . Winnie, do you mean that Judith killed Cecily?"

Winnie's face took on a stubborn look. "No. At least she didn't mean to."

"Where did you get that handkerchief?"

The stubborn look deepened. There were hard, black pupils now in Winnie's blue eyes. She said obstinately, "I'm not going to tell you."

"Winnie . . ." Marny sat up straighter in bed and pushed her hair back from her forehead with a desperate wish that she could be able to brush away confusion and fog. Judith's handkerchief, stained with little Cecily's blood, in Winnie's hands.

Winnie said in a sudden rush, "If you think the police are going to get this, they're not, If you dare tell them, I'll say it isn't so, I'll tell them you made it up. I'll tell them you were jealous of Judith. . . ."

"Jealous of Judith!" Could Winnie have guessed about Andre? How could she have known? How could anyone . . . ? Winnie flashed with a kind of triumph, "Because of Father. You've worked so closely with him. They'll believe you are in love with him and jealous of Judith. That's what I'll tell them."

There was a silence. People were beginning to stir in the house. Someone went along the hall and down the stairs. A door was opened and closed sharply somewhere. It was as if Winnie had suddenly taken leave of her senses. Marny could not even feel anger and indignation. She said at last, feeling queerly baffled as if her words went out against a concrete wall, "There is not a word of truth in that. . . ."

Winnie shoved the bloody handkerchief into her pocket. She sat down on the bed and gave in as suddenly as if the concrete wall had collapsed. "Oh, Marny, I know it! I wouldn't really do anything like that. But I've been so worried and I couldn't sleep and I don't know what to do. Because Father won't stop. You know what he's like. He never gives up. He thinks Judith and Andre were having an affair and he's going to find out about Judith and Cecily just as sure as anything unless you stop him."

Marny took a long breath. "Listen, Winnie, I can't do anything with him when he gets an idea in his head. And if Judith really killed Cecily . . ."

"I tell you it was — it was an accident. Judith wouldn't hurt a fly. She'll be safe, if you'll only keep Father out of it till the thing blows over."

Suppose when Cecily came back she went to Judith's room. Suppose she said the things she had said to Marny; suppose Judith followed her down to the bamboo hedge. ("Then she must have tried to stop the bleeding," Winnie had said.) Marny took a desperate hold on herself. "Winnie, you've got to get things straight. If Judith killed Cecily . . ."

100

"It wouldn't bring the girl back to life, would it, to tell them Judith did it?"

Winnie got up. She reached swiftly for the little, gay ash tray on the bed table. There were matches in it, a folder with Shadow Island and palm trees outlined on the silver cover. Marny realized what Winnie was about to do just as she struck a match. She jumped up and Winnie caught her by the shoulder and forced her back against the bed and lighted the handkerchief.

"Winnie . . ."

"Stay there . . ."

"You've got to . . ."

"Wait . . ." The wispy handkerchief was in flames. Winnie's hand was hard and tight on Marny's shoulder. She wriggled away from it and Winnie ran to the bathroom door, snatching up the ash tray, holding it under the flaming handkerchief so the small, charred bits could fall into it.

"Winnie, you can't . . ."

"Oh, can't I," said Winnie, and reached the bathroom door, banged it against Marny and clicked the bolt.

An airplane droned overhead, came nearer, diminished in sound. The room seemed hot and humid. After a moment Marny went to the balcony door, unbolted and opened it. It was extraordinarily still, outside, the water as flat as a gray, shiny plate.

Suppose Judith *had* shot Cecily!

Judith had known that there was a Cecily; she had admitted that. She had said, "Andre, what are you going to do?" As if they had — well, talked of Cecily, speculated about her.

And suppose the lacy scrap that Winnie had burned could have saved her, Marny, from a murder charge! Police, reporters, jury. The words haunted her. Yet she still had a sense of unreality and security. She hadn't murdered Cecily, so how could anybody actually believe that she had!

But it was a deceiving sense of security; she knew that, too.

Winnie came out of the bathroom. She had washed the ash tray clean; even her hands smelled soapy. She put it down on the bed table.

Occasionally a spark of her father's determination showed in Winnie. AIlied with her mother's placidity it had a certain power. With weary dismay Marny recognized it now. She had to extract whatever it was that was in Winnie's mind and Winnie was not going to permit it to be extracted.

Winnie warned. "I'm sorry, Marny. I behaved rather badly. I know that you are loyal to Father and to Judith and you wouldn't give her away. But I was — well, frightened." She stopped again. Winnie was never adept with words. She bit her lips and said, "Please forgive me. I was upset. It's a horrible thing."

The thing to do was to reason with her quietly, slowly, without appearing to exert any pressure. "I understand, Winnie. None of us are quite sensible and reasonable this morning. But why do you feel that Judith murdered Cecily?"

It wasn't going to succeed. Winnie's mouth became straight and firm.

"I don't. She didn't. Or if she did it was sheer accident. But I won't admit, ever, even to myself, that she had anything to do with it. I burned the handkerchief and — and that's the end of it."

"Where did you find the handkerchief?"

"I won't tell you."

"Winnie, suppose I do tell the police."

"You won't. I didn't mean what I said, Marny. I know you too well. I know I can count on you."

She knew, too, that the evidence no longer existed. Winnie was not Tim Wales' daughter for nothing. Marny said slowly, "Suppose someone else is accused of murder? Suppose someone else is arrested and charged with it. What will you do then?"

There was a pause. Winnie's thick eyebrows drew together. Finally she said, although rather uncertainly, "Father and Judith come first."

"You mean you'd let someone else be tried and perhaps convicted . . ."

Winnie said, "Nobody else will be. They'll never find out who did it. If you can stop Father."

"I can't do anything with Tim. . . ."

"Yes, you can. He'll keep after Judith. She's so — so careless. She may have left other things to be found. She might do anything. Father'll never give up till he gets at the truth. Unless you stop him."

"But how can I stop him, Winnie!"

"By telling him that Andre was in love with you," said Winnie.

CHAPTER XI

The house was fully awake now. Perhaps it had been for some time. Now that the balcony door was open, small sounds drifted upward and through it. The clatter of china as if someone was having breakfast on the porch below; a distant voice; another airplane which, now, seemed very loud.

It didn't matter, of course, whatever Winnie had seen or guessed. Everybody would know soon enough. It would be in the newspapers, broadcast for anybody to read who cared to read it. Marny shut her eyes for an instant. When she opened them Winnie had taken a cigarette from the box on the table and was lighting it. Belatedly she held the box toward Marny, "Sorry. I *am* upset. Light?"

"No, thanks. *What do you mean, Winnie?*"

"You look very queer, Marny. Hadn't you better sit down?"

"No. I — yes." She sat down on the chaise longue and looked at Winnie who was lighting her cigarette.

Winnie put out the match and leaned against the edge of the table and said, "Are you in love with him, Marny?"

In love with Andre? Blackmail and murder and Laideau's horrible hands. Nothing was coherent. Everything was in words and phrases and flashing pictures. Marny pressed her hands into the arms of the chaise. "I am not in love with Andre."

It seemed to her that her voice alone was betraying. But Winnie said, "It was only that you really did look so very odd for a moment, Marny. Of course, I realize he was in New York only a week. But he's so Latin, somehow." Some sound in the hall outside or somewhere in the house seemed to have caught her attention. She turned and listened sharply and said, "I'll go now. Only please do it, Marny. No one else need know, only Father. And it will put him off Judith and — and things will have a chance to blow over."

If she says that again, I'll scream, thought Marny suddenly and rather horribly. The door closed firmly behind Winnie's blue dressing gown. The Winnies of the world always thought things would blow over. But they didn't.

There was a faint smell of burned cloth, floating like an ugly little ghost in the room, acid and disagreeable above the light fragrances of sachet and soap and perfume that inhabit a bedroom. She had to escape it. It was like a sudden, urgent claustrophobia.

So it was actually because of Winnie and her incredible request (that yet came ironically so near the truth) that Marny slid her feet into the small scarlet mules beside the bed, wrapped her white robe around her and went out onto the balcony. And Andre Durant was waiting.

She did not see him at first; he was sitting on the railing, down at the end of the balcony where it turned to follow the line of the house. The vines were thick and he was seated in their shadow, staring out at the bay. But waiting.

She knew that as soon as she saw him. It was in every line of his figure. She drew back, but he heard the creak of the door. His head jerked around and he sprang up and came toward her.

He looked no different. There was only a curious blankness about his face. As if he had not put on his usual mask of charm, of gaiety, of humanity. He drew nearer. His eyes were blank, too, and curiously opaque. It was the look of a creature from another and unknown world, something alien, something walled and untouchable by its own choice and being — and something evil.

This was the Andre Cecily must have seen the night before.

The humid, tropical air was heavy. The bougainvillaea was very bright. Palm trees at the edge of the narrow strip of lawn between the house and the water, stood out with broad, sharp outlines. He said, "I was waiting for you."

He touched the end of his cigarette against the balcony railing to shake off the ashes, and went on softly, with matter-of-fact precision that was indescribably practiced, as if he had

105

said the same words many times. "I don't like scenes. Don't make one. Laideau thought you did not believe him. He told you the truth."

He made no attempt to evade her eyes. His look was remote, impersonal. . . . Again it seemed to her blankly alien to any world she knew. She said slowly, "Why did you lie to Cecily? Why did you tell her we wanted to marry? Why did you send her to me?"

She was sure he heard her. He couldn't have helped hearing; yet there was no flicker of response in that blank, handsome face. "Laideau will come to you today. Tell him the amount you are prepared to pay."

He was going to turn away. She said, "Did you kill Cecily?"

Again it was exactly as if he hadn't heard her. "Laideau will see to the details. It may take a few days for you to make the necessary arrangements. We understand that. Any securities you will have to sell yourself. If you wish to include jewelry, I imagine Laideau can dispose of it more profitably than you."

"I will give you nothing."

But he had turned and was walking away, gracefully, lightly, a man whose face and walk she knew and who was and always had been a stranger to her.

He turned the corner of the balcony and disappeared. And she thought suddenly, poor Cecily. Knowing him for what he was, yet unable to free herself from his spell. Poor tragic Cecily.

And how many other women? And how near she had come to being one of them.

Yet in one way, of course, she had not escaped She turned back into her own room.

The faint small odor of burned lace and cloth still haunted it as she dressed.

It was later than she had thought. When she went downstairs Tim Wales was just outside the hall door talking to reporters, who were apparently leaving. (Murder on Shadow Island; Home of Tim Males: Prominent in Aviation Circles. It was all in the papers that day.)

She stopped at the foot of the stairway. Voices floated in through the open door. She had heard Tim deal with reporters many times. She knew his every manner; she could tell now that he was employing his very best and most disarming tricks.

". . . of course we'd all think it was suicide, if they had found the gun. They may find it yet; one never knows."

"Do you believe it was suicide, Mr. Wales? Can we quote you about that?"

"Well, it's hard to say. As I told you she was very young, not very well. She and her husband were separated temporarily. She may have had a fit of nerves, depression . . ."

"She was shot in the back, wasn't she, Mr. Wales? At the morgue . . ."

"Yes, yes, I know. You saw the body, did you? It's all a terrible shock to everybody. Yet — well, you know as well as I do what freakish things can happen with guns."

"According to the police statement the gun was not found at all." This voice was rather gentle but definitely skeptical. Tim, of course, knew it, too. He said in his most candid sounding manner, "That's just the trouble, boys. Shot in the back, and apparently the gun gone completely. Of course, the place where the body was found is only a few feet from the water."

There wasn't any question of suicide. The police had settled that instantly and with a decision which left no room for doubt. Not that any doubt could actually exist or be conjured up even by Tim Wales' artfully artless-sounding implications. Cecily was shot in the back and was dead and there was no gun and it was murder.

And blackmail. She held tight to the stair railing; the reporters were leaving. She could hear their footsteps on the gravel; one or two appeared to linger.

"We'd like a statement from Durant, you know, Mr. Wales."

"I know, I know. He'll give you one later, I'm sure. Just now he's not able to see anybody, believe me."

"Photographs . . ."

"All you want. Everything. Grounds — house, place where she was found."

"We'd like a shot of you and Mrs. Wales."

Marny could detect the icy edge in Tim's voice. His manner remained cordial and friendly and regretful. "Can't give you that. My wife's not up yet. It's been a shock to everybody — a suicide right here on the island."

"But it wasn't suicide, Mr. Wales," reminded the reporter gently.

"No, no, of course not. At least — well, poor child," said Tim. "Poor girl . . . I'll tell you what, as soon as we can pull ourselves together a bit, I'll let you come around and take all the pictures you want. How's that?"

"Oh, it doesn't matter," said the other voice rather airily. "We've got lots of pictures of you, Mr. Wales. Every paper in the country has them — and of course Mrs. Wales and your daughter, too."

There was a sharp, small silence. Then Tim laughed — very brightly, very shortly and very falsely.

"Yes. Yes, I suppose so. Well, I'm sorry I can't give you any more information. It's a bad business, any way you look at it. But Manson is a great fellow. I have every confidence in the police. Thank you, boys, thank you. . . ."

Footsteps crunched away down the drive and Tim came into the hall and saw her. "Good God," he said. He got out a handkerchief and wiped his face, and his whole fat body seemed to collapse. He sank down in a chair and looked at her. All the small lines showed sharply in his face and there were gray hollows around his eyes. The brightly tiled hall with its gay chairs and sofas looked strangely wrong and awry as a setting for Tim Wales at that moment. "Marny," he said, "what do you think of getting a good fellow to do a personal public relations job for me? This is going to be bad for — for business."

Judith appeared quietly in the doorway to the drawing room. Apparently she had been standing just inside it, listening as frankly as Marny had listened. She wore white-silk slacks and a white shirt, open deeply at the throat, and a green belt. Her dark hair was, this morning, parted and hanging long over her shoulders, held back with combs from her temples so the features of her lovely face seemed to stand out in more marked relief, and even greater beauty. Her dark, straight eyebrows, her dark eyes, her gardenia skin, her painted dark-red lips all seemed accentuated, somehow, and more beautiful. One hand was on the door casing. She looked at Tim steadily, long dark lashes shading her eyes. "Bad for business or bad for us?"

Tim shoved his handkerchief into his pocket. "Both."

"You said a personal public relations job."

"Did I?"

"What exactly do you mean, Tim? I heard you with the reporters. You weren't too good. Your efforts at hinting at suicide were a little obvious. She couldn't have shot herself. She was murdered. Everybody knows it."

Tim bounced up suddenly, his eyes little and sharp and bright. "Where were you? This morning, I mean. Why wouldn't you let me talk to you last night? Your light burned all night. You wouldn't answer when I knocked. Good God, Judith, we've got to talk about this. . . ."

"What do we have to talk about? You made your feelings about me altogether too clear last night."

"Judith . . ." he took her arm but she moved away.

"If you wanted to ask me whether or not I murdered Cecily Durant because I was jealous of her, I didn't."

"Judith, I didn't mean that. . . ."

"And I don't know who killed her. Except it wasn't Andre."

"How could you have been so stupid, Judith? If you had to give him an alibi did it have to be like that? Nobody can keep it out of the papers. . . ."

Judith glanced past him. "Good morning, Marny. Don't mind our little conjugal pleasantries. Tim suspects me of murder, you know."

It was bold, forthright — and daring. Exactly like Judith, whether or not she had actually killed Cecily. (Trying to stop the bleeding with the small, bloodstained handkerchief! But she hadn't. Not Judith. Not anybody Marny knew! Yet Cecily Durant was murdered.) Marny said, "Hello, Judith. Tim, I want to see the police officer, Captain Manson. Is he here?"

Judith's eyes became a little fixed and watchful under those lovely eyelashes. Tim whirled around. "What in the world do you want to see him about, Marny? You told your story last night. For God's sake, don't add to it. Keep your mouth shut. . . ."

Bill Cameron came briskly, as if at a cue, from the dining-room door. Had he too been quietly and yet frankly listening?

"Hello," he said as coolly as if it were any day, not the day after a murder. Somehow he had got hold of a change of clothing. He was dressed again in green uniform and looked fresh and alert. He came quickly to Marny and put his hand on her own, still clasped tightly upon the railing. "Have you had breakfast?"

His hand was warm and strong and safe. It was a singular word to use but it flashed across her mind. She said, "Yes, thanks."

"I heard you inquiring for Manson. He was here a while ago, wasn't he, Mr. Wales?"

Tim's eyes were hunted. "I don't know. Some police were here earlier, going over the grounds, questioning the servants. I haven't seen Manson."

"Do you want to look for him, Marny?" asked Bill Cameron pleasantly, and drew her — rather firmly — toward the front door. Judith and Tim watched them go in silence.

The screened door closed behind them. The sun was still hidden but everything somehow was very clear. It was an eerie, unnatural clearness of light that seemed to bring every leaf in the thick hedge into sharper focus.

There was something queer and rather oppressive in the air, something too quiet. The water around the island looked very flat and slick. The skyline of Miami was hazy. Miami Beach in the opposite direction was veiled too in kind of soft, dull haze. Yet the sky was in no sense stormy-looking or overcast. It was merely intensely still. The bamboos and the palms did not move. The hibiscus and bougainvillaea blazed in scarlet and purple, the grass looked queerly and brightly green. They walked around the corner of the house, toward the balcony stairway with its view of bay and green lawn. No one was about, although the bamboos hid the pier. She glanced at the porch. Someone had been having breakfast; no one, now, was there.

110

The thick bougainvillaea, heavy with purple, hung heavily from the balcony, not a leaf moving. A motorboat went past, curving near the island, slowing up as it passed within a few feet of the sea wall. Marny was suddenly aware of people in the boat staring — at the house, at herself in her plain white-linen dress with its red belt and the red ribbon around her hair. She drew back involuntarily, understanding the reason for their curiosity.

Bill Cameron knew it. He said shortly, "There's been a steady stream of boats passing the place. Why do you want to see Manson?"

"I want to tell him . . ."

He interrupted, "That's what I thought. What's happened? Or have you only come to your senses overnight?" He turned to look at her and suddenly and unexpectedly he grinned. His gray-blue eyes lighted up. His whole face seemed younger and for an instant friendly and warm. "I wondered when you would."

Had she come to her senses! She wondered if Andre were watching from behind one of the windows of the rambling white house — or Laideau, with his great shoulders and little ugly eyes. She said with something like a shiver, "Yes. But not the way you think."

The smile vanished. "Something *has* happened. You'd better tell me. No, wait . . ." His gaze went upward over her shoulder and became very slightly fixed, then moved on coolly and came back to her. He said without a change of expression but in a very low voice, "Somebody is on the balcony. Listening, I should imagine. I'm going to find out who it is. Stay here."

CHAPTER XII

The stairway was only a few feet away. He reached it in a swift step or two. His solid gray-clad figure was rounding the curve, between thick loops of bougainvillaea when she turned to look upward. She could see only the columns of the balcony, heavily hung with green foliage. The vines were thickest along the end opposite the stairway — where Andre had sat and waited for her an hour or so ago.

She moved a little away from the porch to get a wider view of the balcony and still could see no one. There was no flicker of a motion anywhere, no door opened and closed, no shadow moved stealthily out of sight. Bill Cameron had reached the balcony and was running with incredible lightness along it toward the corner which followed the corner of the house; it was further shielded by several thick, ferny pepper trees, spotted brilliantly with clusters of orange berries.

His black head and green uniform disappeared.

It was perfectly still.

Bill Cameron did not return. Nobody came. Nothing moved. The house was always confusing to her; its rambling, half-modern, half-Spanish architecture produced unexpected corners and changes of level, odd stairways and halls — any number of ways in and out of it, she thought suddenly and sharply. And anyone could have walked through her own room (whose door, in a cut-off mid-section, she could see), or through any room along the balcony and stayed there quietly behind the vines, listening.

Because Cecily Durant had been murdered on that island the night before. Because conceivably the murderer was in that house — alert to every voice and every footfall, and every whisper. Somewhere in that house — gay and modern and brilliant in its vines and shrubbery and red and purple blossoms and white walls.

She didn't like the stillness and the quiet. She didn't like the empty look of a house which was not empty.

All at once, strangely, she felt exposed, as if eyes were watching her, as if the lush walls of green shrubbery might conceal something that waited for her. As Andre and Laideau waited!

And again, as she had done the night before, a sense of the deadly patient waiting of the tropics to reclaim its own came back to her. Shadow Island was man-made — of spoilage, pushed into shape by huge shovels, flattened out and curved and planted, and neatly arranged in driveways and paths, and lawn and hedges, with a sharply modern house set down upon it — and yet the tropical land held it, permitted its existence, as if by caprice, as if for the moment.

Behind that thick hedge of silvery green bamboo, quiet now and still, Cecily had died.

She took a step or two toward the house and Bill Cameron came around the corner of the balcony again, walking along coolly, without looking down at her, his face expressionless. He came down the stairway, and she waited. He passed the curve where she had stood in her white robe the night before and talked to him — and listened for the oars of the boat which had disappeared behind the Casuarina trees.

He reached her and she could read nothing in his face or attitude. He spoke, however, very low. "I don't know who it was. But there was somebody. There are a lot of French doors on the other side of the balcony and a couple of stairways, one going up to another small balcony on a different level, and nobody there; the other going straight down to the back entrance and nothing there but a trash burner. No way to find out who it was, except I know I saw somebody move back of those vines and I think I heard footsteps — running. I'm not sure. There's no one way of finding out who was so interested. I suppose we'll never know, and it doesn't really matter. Except there was somebody, in the house, interested in our conversation, who didn't want to be seen." He opened his hand and showed her briefly the end of a cigarette.

"It was still burning. It was on the balcony, just at the corner. There's no lipstick on it. And I suppose the house is full of cigarettes of this brand. It could have been anybody from Tim Wales on down. It only proves somebody was there. And somebody who wanted very much to hear what we were saying. Yet, in a house where there's been a murder, that's not exactly incriminating either. I listened to Tim and the reporters, and Judith, and all of you from the dining room, this morning, with no compunction whatever and with the greatest interest. And I didn't shoot Cecily Durant."

He's trying to convince me — and himself — that no murderer stood on the balcony, hidden by vines, listening, and then hurried furtively away, thought Marny.

Murderer is a strange and terrible word — nothing one can associate with daylight, and physical small facts of everyday life, with footsteps on a balcony, with a lighted cigarette, flung down, still burning.

It was the brand Tim smoked habitually and constantly. Yet, as Bill Cameron said, it was a popular brand and there were quantities of them, all over the house.

It could have been anyone. Not necessarily the murderer of Cecily Durant.

Bill Cameron shoved the cigarette end in his pocket. He had pinched out the light probably when he picked it up. Why was he going to keep it? He said, "Well, we'll walk a bit away from the house. Don't talk now . . ."

But he talked himself, making conversation. "The early newspapers are here full of the police reports of the murder and Tim Wales' biography. The reporters have been here. . . ."

"Yes, I saw them leaving."

"The radio has it that a hurricane is winding up somewhere in the Caribbean. It will probably pass us by. They haven't told people to put up shutters yet. I understand that is standard procedure when the storm center reaches a certain point . . ."

"You see, I've got to tell Manson . . ."

"Of course we are right in the middle of the hurricane season. Have you seen the tennis court? Not that it is anything much to see, but come along this way. No, don't talk. Too many shrubs, too near . . . It's this way. . . ."

It was on the eastern end of the island, well away from the house with the fringe of Casuarinas between it and the distant view of Miami Beach. They reached the flat white surface of the tennis court. The high fence around it, high enough to catch tennis balls and laden with thick-growing vines, was like a wall. The sky above looked light and thick somehow and very still.

"Now then," said Bill Cameron. "You're going to tell the police about Cecily's visit to you."

"Yes . . ."

"Why? Have you decided that I took advantage of your shock and confusion to over-will your better instincts, and thus obligate you to me in a business way?"

"You . . . I didn't say that."

"But you thought it? I see. I was afraid that the brilliant, brainy young executive — suspicious and a little hard — would eventually arouse in you." He laughed shortly. "Frankly, I liked you better last night."

"Bill," she said, "Laideau is trying to blackmail me. Laideau and — and Andre."

"Andre!"

She suddenly could not answer, but could only look wretchedly, miserably into his eyes which were all at once as gray and cold as the sea. He took her hands, hard.

"Andre knew that Cecily came to you?"

"I told him. Last night. To — to warn him . . ."

"Good God, Marny . . . !" He checked himself, and glanced swiftly around them. "You'd better tell me all about it. Quick . . ."

"But I . . ."

"But you don't trust me? Is that it?" He paused for a moment and then said dryly, "You haven't given me a chance to talk to you. You've fought me every time you've seen me. Last night I got a glimpse of the girl you might have been if

115

you hadn't been so hell bent to be . . ."

"To be what?"

"To be somebody else," said Bill Cameron. "All right. That's your choice. I'm here on business. I really was sent by well, some very important people. It's not a long story. I was wounded, convalesced in England. Aviation is my job; always has been. I knew some fellows there; I know some in America. Everybody in aviation is planning for the years after the war. I'm not going on at length about it — not now. But everybody knows Tim Wales' reputation for going it alone. I think — we all think — we've got to work together. So far Wales has refused even to talk to anybody. Nobody can reach him through the regular channels. So I — partly on my own, partly not — decided to try the — well, the irregular channels. Get at him, get him to listen. But that's all about that. It doesn't matter now. I mean it can wait — it'll have to. I want to persuade Tim Wales to string along with everybody else. He's so important that he's needed. I want you to help persuade him. That's my business here. But I'm not trying to get you in my clutches. I think you're by way of being a fool about — well, about a lot of things. But that's not the point. Now then: what exactly did Laideau tell you? Hurry . . ."

She remembered every word; she would always remember it. "Laideau came in," she began. "Andre sent him. And I saw Andre this morning and it's true."

It took actually only a moment or two. Bill Cameron stared out over the water and listened. It was queer how his tall, solid body seemed to stiffen and harden as she talked, yet there was no change in his face.

A flight of Army airplanes, five of them in a V, droned above through the still sky and disappeared toward the ocean.

She finished and for a moment Bill Cameron said nothing. His face was unfathomable, impossible to read, his mouth hard and tight. He took out cigarettes and lighted one for her and for himself, and looked away from her out toward the bay, smoking. Finally he said, "You believed Laideau last night? Before Andre backed him up?"

"Yes."

"Didn't have any doubt about it?"

She took a long breath. "No."

He put his cigarette to his mouth, eyes narrow, still looking out toward the bay. "You didn't believe Cecily, you know. You still had faith, I suppose, in him. In spite of the evidence."

She said unexpectedly, "I ought to have helped Cecily."

He glanced at her then quickly. "Don't say that or think it. You couldn't have done anything for her. She was lost, poor child, from the instant he walked into her life. She knew he was a heel and a . . . She knew all about him. But she hadn't the strength or the will to get away from him. Whatever he was, she wanted him. It happens, sometimes. There've been other Andres in the world. Not many of them," he said rather grimly. "And men know what to do about them. But women, even women with what passes for intelligence and sensibility and . . . Let's get down to brass tacks." He took her hands so hard that it hurt. "Was Andre planning to get rid of Cecily in order to marry you?"

"No."

"Exactly how far had this affair with him gone?"

"It hadn't . . . What right have you . . . ?"

"Answer me."

"It was silly. There wasn't anything, really."

"You're not lying to me?"

"No. No. It was . . . I'm not proud of it."

"Kisses in the moonlight? That kind of thing?"

She could feel her face growing hot. "Once. Last night. When we came in from swimming. After you left — it didn't mean anything."

"Did anyone see you?"

"No. We were beside the hibiscus."

He searched her eyes deeply. Then quite suddenly he let her hands drop. "All right. Can you prove that to the police?"

"No . . ."

"You didn't write Andre any — well, letters?"

"No!"

"And you've decided to tell the police about Cecily coming to you with the gun . . ."

"Yes."

He said unexpectedly, "Good girl! Andre and Laideau are almost certain to have a police record somewhere. I think Andre did it, or Laideau. And I think the police think so. It'll take some time to dig up their past record and it'll take some time to get the evidence they have to have. But as long as they suspect Andre, I believe you are safe. And of course your best defense is police proof, jury proof that somebody else shot Cecily, and who it was." He lighted another cigarette. "There were not many people on the island. Judith — Wales himself. Winnie. Laideau and Andre. Somebody might have followed Cecily here, of course, and killed her. But I think her contacts with life were entirely through Andre. I don't think she had either friends or enemies, except Andre and Laideau. Suppose her existence threatened one or the other of them. Laideau appears to be the muscle man for Andre's pretty little schemes. Suppose he killed the girl because Andre wanted to get rid of her and Cecily wouldn't give him up?"

"Andre has an alibi."

"So has Judith," said Bill Cameron, looking out over the water.

And Judith had the wit, and the instantaneous daring and decision to claim it. *Or to invent it, in a way that was extraordinarily convincing!* Why, the police would say, would this woman tell such a story, unless it is true? If she were lying she'd tell a story less likely to be made capital of by gossip and newspapers. There were a dozen — a hundred other stories she could have invented. But the one she told was convincing. Cleverly convincing? Or honestly convincing?"

There was the handkerchief.

Again Marny was caught by a swift debate in her own mind. Could anyone she knew have done murder? And again it had the same conclusion. Certainly not Judith. There must be another explanation for the handkerchief. When she succeeded in getting the whole story from Winnie, she would see the loopholes as Winnie, frightened, had not. She told herself that.

Bill Cameron said abruptly, "You like Judith. And I don't

know her. But Andre is — Andre. I don't think Laideau and Andre would have taken such a dangerous method of getting rid of Cecily, unless, for some reason, it was urgent. Look here, Marny. Did Cecily call you by name?"

"Why, I . . . No, I don't think so. I can't remember. . . ."

"You'd remember. Did she know Judith? By sight, I mean, to recognize her?"

"I don't know."

"Has it occurred to you that when Cecily came to you, she might have thought you were Judith?"

"Judith!"

He looked at her queerly. "I guess you're bright in business. You're not very bright about yourself. . . ."

"But Cecily said Andre had talked to her. She said she'd seen him.

"Andre says he didn't see her at all. He told the police that last night. I don't imagine Andre's word amounts to anything, but Judith's story supports it. Judith says Andre was in her room at the time when you were talking to Cecily. It gave Andre an alibi and it gave Judith an alibi and she's a very attractive woman. Now don't get your back up like a mad kitten. I'm only reasoning. And somebody killed that girl."

"Not Judith!" cried Marny. And Bill Cameron said all at once, very quietly, "Here is Captain Manson."

She whirled around. The detective and two policemen were walking across the court toward them. They were already so near that Captain Manson's blue tie seemed to loom up like a flag. Nobody spoke. There was only the slap, slap of their feet across the hard court. And then Captain Manson had stopped and one of the policemen took off his cap and scratched his head and looked meditatively up at the opaque, quiet sky. Captain Manson said, "Good morning, Miss Sanderson — Commander."

Marny opened her lips and no sound came out. Bill Cameron was right, she thought despairingly. She had no sense at all about people and human relationships. She ought to have snatched that handkerchief from Winnie. She ought to have it now, as evidence to give the police. It didn't matter whether or not she believed Judith could have killed Cecily. Nothing ought to matter when it was murder except your own safety.

They'd never believe it without the handkerchief; and Winnie would deny it and telling it would only strengthen the case against her for it would sound as if she were lying, trying to cast suspicion on Judith, in order to avert it from herself.

Even Bill Cameron would not believe it. Police proof, jury proof, he had said, and she had only a tale of a handkerchief that no longer existed.

Captain Manson said, "Is it true, Miss Sanderson, that Cecily Durant came to see you last night, just before you claim to have found her murdered, and told you she would kill you rather than let you take her husband?"

Bill Cameron did not move, did not speak, offered in no way to shield or to help or to do anything.

"Yes," whispered Marny with stiff lips. And suddenly a very disheveled, long-legged and gasping rocket, Charlie Ingram, shot out from the entrance into the tennis court and rounded a group of chairs, loping along, his face red, his eyes popping, his monocle jumping and dancing on the end of its ribbon. "I say — I say — I say, Captain," he shouted. "Chap on the telephone says he saw it. Young ensign . . . Was in an airplane over the island . . . Saw the girl murdered . . . Come on. He wants to talk to you. Says a woman in a white dress did it."

CHAPTER XIII

The young ensign's story was perfectly simple and straightforward, too simple as a matter of fact, and too straightforward. As Tim Wales said, later, he saw too much and too little.

But it sounded true.

He came at once, summoned peremptorily by Captain Manson, and escorted by two policemen in a squad car. He arrived within fifteen minutes. Captain Manson made no bones about letting them listen to the whole story; but then Charlie Ingram already knew it. He had arrived at the house, he said, as the telephone rang. No one seemed to be about and he had yielded, as one does, to the compulsion of a telephone bell, anywhere, and answered it. And hurried to call the police.

"Says he saw it," cried Charlie. "My God! Says he saw it."

"Maybe he did," said Tim, drily. "Maybe he didn't." But he was nervous, smoking rapidly, listening for the police car. Judith was there too, and Winnie — who had changed to a pink, tailored, cotton dress and combed her hair into a roll on her neck, and whose eyes sought Marny's with a look that was pleading, questioning and demanding all at once.

"Says it was a woman in a white dress," said Charlie, and then gave a rather panic-stricken look at Marny and began to polish his monocle nervously.

Probably everyone was thinking what was all too obviously in Charlie's mind. Judith had worn black the night before; Winnie had worn blue; Marny alone of the three women had worn white.

And who had told Manson the true story of Marny's meeting with Cecily?

They did not question her then. There was no chance to talk to Captain Manson alone. And with a spattering of gravel the police car arrived and the young ensign appeared, bright-eyed and rather white-faced, saluted snappily when he saw Bill Cameron, gave Judith a rather long and definitely admiring look and told his story.

Told it briefly, succinctly and apparently with frankness. His name was Burke Harcourt. He had been on a practice flight over the island the night before, just at dusk. It was, however, still light enough to see the layout of the grounds very clearly. He had flown rather low; idly noting the tennis court and the pool. Nobody had been in the pool or, in fact, anywhere about the house, but down by the pier, just on the east side of the bamboo hedge, there had been two women and they were struggling.

"Struggling?" said Captain Manson.

"Well," Ensign Harcourt hesitated uncomfortably, "it looked like that, sir. I mean, well, I just thought it was a joke or something. You know. Maybe they were — well, a little tight, you know. And one of them fell down."

"Fell down! What do you mean exactly?"

But Ensign Harcourt didn't know. "You go awfully fast in a plane, you know, sir. I just saw that and wouldn't have seen it at all if I hadn't been flying pretty low. I took my ship on in and didn't think anything more about it till I saw the papers this morning. Then I realized that this must be Shadow Island and I asked my superior officer and he said I'd better let you know." He turned his cap in his hands, shot a glance at Bill Cameron and looked embarrassed.

"You say you *saw* one of the women fall?"

The boy turned rather whiter and looked steadily at Captain Manson. "Yes, sir. But I didn't see the flash of a gun. I didn't see anything. Except one of the women was smaller than the other, I thought. The — the one that fell down," said the boy, and this time dropped his glance to his black oxfords.

Cecily, of course, was smaller than any of the three women. Judith was markedly tall, Winnie as tall as her father, Marny a good four inches taller than Cecily. Tim Wales said, "But look here — but look here . . ." and stopped.

Captain Manson said, "Was there anything else that caught

your attention? Anything at all?"

"No. That is, somebody was out in a rowboat, fishing, I guess."

"Where exactly?"

"Off toward Miami Beach. Around that green point that looks as if there were Australian pines on it."

Australian pines or Casuarina trees. Captain Manson said, "Who was rowing the boat? A man or a woman?"

"A man. Looked rather big. He was alone." The boy twisted his cap again. "I don't think he could have seen the women at the pier. The trees were between them. He was quite a distance off the island, really."

"What time was this?"

"Well, that — well, you see, sir, usually we check in right away and I could tell you almost to the minute. But last night, as I landed, I noticed a wobble in the tail. I stopped and talked about it awhile with a mechanic and we looked at the thing. By the time I checked in it was ten after eight."

"What is your impression of the time when you must have flown over Shadow Island then?"

"Well, it must have been between seven-thirty and eight. It was still light enough to see what I — what I told you about. Only I don't think she was shot then. I think I'd have seen that and I think I'd have seen the gun flash. I'm not sure, of course. Is that all, sir? I have a class . . ."

"You say the taller woman was wearing white?"

"Oh, yes, sir. I'm sure of that. Showed up clearly. A long skirt like a dinner dress. It's what caught my eye."

"Very well. Will you stand up, please, Mrs. Wales, Miss Sanderson, Miss Wales. . . . Thank you. Now then, Mr. Harcourt," he cleared his throat, "was either of the women you saw, one of these ladies? I'm sorry to have to do this but remember that your testimony may clear innocent people."

That was, of course, to disarm the young ensign — and to secure his honest opinion.

It was rather horrible standing there, like prisoners, waiting, while the boy's embarrassed, yet very keen eyes went from Marny to Judith (black head up, graceful body erect and, somehow, defiant, luminous dark eyes meeting the young ensign's boldly) and then to Winnie who looked frightened as Judith did not. Her square, rather stolid jaws were set. There were two spots of color high on her cheekbones. She stood with rigid stillness and looked indeed rather as she looked just before a golf or tennis match. She glanced at Judith and at her father and would not meet the ensign's eyes at all.

The young ensign shook his head. "I'm sorry, sir, but I didn't see either woman clearly enough to identify her."

Judith sat down and lighted a cigarette and crossed her knees. Winnie remained standing, her face still rigid and expressionless. Tim got out his handkerchief and wiped his face and dropped one cigarette and lighted another. Charlie Ingram said audibly, "Dear me, dear me. No other women on the island."

"Somebody could have come. Somebody could have come by boat. There are a hundred ways. Some woman interested in Andre . . ." began Tim. Captain Manson said to the boy, "Thank you. We can reach you later, if necessary. I'll have to ask you to let the police car take you to the morgue in order to see if you can identify Mrs. Durant as one of the women."

The boy turned still whiter and seemed about to expostulate and then made a short little bow in the direction of Judith, saluted Bill Cameron again and went away with the policemen who had brought him. Manson said, "Did any of you have an interview of any kind with Cecily Durant near the pier at about that time last night?"

Judith said, "No," clearly and as if it did not concern her in the slightest degree. Winnie said "No," too. Marny opened her lips to speak and Captain Manson said, "I want to talk to you alone presently, Miss Sanderson. Now then — I saw the dresses you ladies were wearing last night. I'd like to know if any of you changed between, say, seven-thirty and eight?"

Again Judith spoke clearly and promptly, her lashes lowered over her dark eyes.

"I've told you. I took off a short white dress and put on a long black chiffon for the evening. You saw it. . . ."

"Thank you, Mrs. Wales."

Winnie said, "I changed too. We all changed. I put on a blue dress, the one I was wearing when the murder — when you came."

"Miss Sanderson, I believe, was wearing white," said Captain Manson. "Now then, if you don't mind, I'd like to look in your wardrobes — dressing rooms, wherever you keep your dresses. Will you show me, Miss Wales?"

They disappeared up the stairway together, Winnie going ahead.

Bill Cameron said, "This doesn't really count as evidence. It is too vague. Harcourt doesn't know the exact time, he didn't see a gun flash or even get the idea that there was a gun." Judith said coolly, linking her hands around one knee, "It may not count as evidence, but I think he saw something."

"Too much and too little," snapped Tim, then, and got up nervously, and tramped through the drawing room and out onto the porch.

And Charlie Ingram said rather plaintively, "I say, Judith, where's this fellow Durant? Did they arrest him? I really think he did it, you know. Who else?"

"I told you, Charlie, he couldn't have. He was with me — at least he was in my room and talking to me through the door."

"But couldn't he have stopped talking long enough to sneak down the balcony stairs and catch up with the girl and kill her? Wouldn't take long, you know. I thought of that during the night. Seems to me very possible." He stuck his monocle in his eye and looked at Judith with a rather self-congratulatory air.

Judith said coldly, "Listen, Charlie, he couldn't have murdered her. I tell you he sat there and smoked and talked — maybe not constantly, but there was never a long enough pause for him to have done all that — the whole time. I was dressing. I couldn't see him, but I could hear him."

"Now, now, Judith, don't get worked up about it. I . . . See here, you know, my dear, no matter what you think of the fellow, he's not worth your going to such lengths to protect him. Andre Durant," said Charlie so earnestly that his monocle fell out and he snatched it up and replaced it, "Andre Durant is a rat. Only have to look at him to know that. Knew it the first minute I saw him. Couldn't see why you kept him around. And that fellow Laideau is a thug and a cut-throat if ever I saw one!"

Unexpectedly a little smile touched Judith's heavily painted mouth. She said as unexpectedly, "Dear Charlie, he may be a rat, darling, but he couldn't have murdered Cecily."

Charlie Ingram sighed. And Judith added, smoking, "Andre always sleeps late. Perhaps I'd better call him."

She got up with the utmost composure and went upstairs, moving gracefully in her white silk slacks, the beautiful line of her hips melting into her small waist, her black head held high. Bill Cameron watched her go, an odd expression on his face. Charlie sighed again and polished his monocle. "She'll bring him down, just as if nothing had happened," he said gloomily. "Want to bet on it?"

Nobody apparently did; but before Charlie could prove his small prophecy Captain Manson and Winnie returned.

Captain Manson spoke to Winnie for a moment, as if asking directions, and then asked Marny to accompany him to the small study, done all in white and coral and rarely if ever used, which lay back of the coatroom and on the other side of the stairs.

He closed the door. The study was rather dark in spite of its white and coral decoration; there was only one window and it was overhung with vines. He told her to sit down and sat down himself opposite her. What light there was fell on his face rather than her own, which seemed to Marny wrong, somehow, and not like the third degrees she had read about.

Neither were his questions. She had thought it would be much harder to talk to him than actually it was. Although of course that was part of his job, to win your confidence, to lead you on to talk. And talk and talk and talk. To tell him everything; tell him about Cecily and the gun and everything she'd said.

"Had you talked of marriage?"

"No. He . . ." A queer memory returned to her; she flushed

126

a little, she could feel it in her cheeks for now she saw the meaning of something that, at the time Andre had spoken, had meant nothing. "He said he asked nothing of me."

The detective looked at the vine outside the window for a long moment. Then he said, "That is a good line. One of his stock in trade, I imagine. Convincing to women, yet holding him to nothing. If what I think is true, Miss Sanderson, you are to be congratulated. Cecily Durant was not so fortunate."

He got up with an abrupt motion, and began to walk up and down the little room. "I'm going to be honest with you, Miss Sanderson. I think you've told me the truth. I think Andre Durant killed his wife. Durant or Laideau between them. I'm going to prove it, if I can. It's hard even now to get in touch with people who can give you complete records of anybody living outside this country. But he has apparently floated around, wherever the picking was good. He and Laideau. I telephoned to the police in Jamaica; he seems to have married this girl after only a short acquaintance. The pity is that she was held by him as by a spell. With time and luck I can get a complete record of his activities. I imagine, however, he's managed either to stay within the law or prey on some woman who couldn't fight back. Now, then, tell me again, Miss Sanderson, everything.

She went through the whole story again. This time when she'd finished he asked questions. What time had it been when Cecily came? What time had it been when she left? Was she sure that the boat had returned or had she only thought she'd heard the oars? What kind of gun was it? Oh, she didn't know. Couldn't anyone else have taken it from her room while she was talking to Commander Cameron? Oh, someone could. Did she think Cecily really meant murder, or did she think she was merely hysterical?

"Hysterical," said Marny. "She'd been talking to him, she said. He was everything to her, life and" — she stopped, but Captain Manson finished it grimly —" and death. Yes, death. So far as I can discover up to now she had no friends, no other contacts whatever, except through him. Well, you did right to tell me about their efforts to blackmail you, Miss Sanderson.

127

I'd like you to go into court with a charge against them. Well, we don't consider that, just now. Who knew of Cecily's visit to you?"

"Andre, as I told you. Laideau. Commander Cameron."

"Anyone else?"

"No" She added suddenly, "How did you know? Who told you? "

He replied promptly, almost as if she had a right to ask it. "Charlie Ingram. He came down to the pier where I was watching them hunt for the gun. He told me."

"Charlie Ingram! How did he know?"

All at once something changed in the little room. It was almost tangible, almost something she could touch with her fingers, yet could not identify. It had something to do with Captain Manson. She knew that, but there was no perceptible change in him. He said, "That's all now, Miss Sanderson. I told you I'd be honest with you. I'm a fair man. I do not intend to give your story to the newspapers. Murder sticks to people. But I have to say, too, that if I can satisfactorily prove that Durant and Laideau did not murder Cecily Durant, then — well, you did wear white last night. And neither Miss Wales nor Mrs. Wales has a white dinner dress. And with this story you could plead self-defense. If the gun, when we find it, was one we can trace to Cecily Durant. And . . ." Someone knocked at the door and he went to open it. A policeman stood there; he looked excited and came in quickly. He did not appear to notice Marny. He cried, "Look, it was in the water. Not far from the pier. We found it while we were trying to find the gun. . . ."

He held it in his hand and Marny could see it and it was Andre's gold cigarette case with the sardonyx showing only dimly through clots of mud and sand.

128

CHAPTER XIV

They called Andre.

He came downstairs, his handsome face a mask, his curly black head high, looking coolly with those blank eyes at everyone and no one.

Marny saw him come and turned quickly away, into the drawing room.

He remained in the white and coral study with Manson and another detective for two hours. Some time during that time they sent for Laideau. He appeared from somewhere on the island in the company of a policeman, and disappeared also into the small study.

It was a strange and an ominous day.

A day that actually existed in two layers — one the outward, visible layer, the surface of facts as Marny knew them, and the other a hidden, secret layer, composed, really, of many layers. As many layers as there were people on the island, active and intent upon their secret and, in at least one case, rather desperate activities.

The outward facts were few, and while specific enough, did not reveal much of the progress of the police inquiry — if progress there was.

Their fingerprints were recorded, separately. It was a rather gruesome little ceremony, taking place in the washroom off the hall with an obliging policeman standing by with towel dipped in cleaning fluid which removed the ink from their finger tips. Andre and Laideau emerged eventually from the study and disappeared but were not placed under arrest. They did not, however, appear to make any move to leave the island and Tim did not, so far as Marny knew, ask them to do so. Policemen came and went. Judith sat on the porch and did nothing.

Winnie sat on the porch and knitted a sweater. Tim fretted, and pounced, disappeared on mysterious errands and returned, smoked incessantly, and talked several times over the telephone to the New York office. Charlie Ingram stayed on, prowling restlessly about the grounds, watching the men at the pier, coming back again to report that they had found nothing.

For all that day men searched the island and the house and particularly the shallow water near the pier, rowing about in short circles, holding a kind of box with a glass bottom out over the edge of the boat and staring down through it. But no gun was found.

It began to seem a very important piece of evidence; no secret was made of that.

Captain Manson, returning to the island after rather a long absence, talked to them with apparent frankness about it. "They've extracted the bullet that killed her," he said. "We've got to find the gun."

"I'm afraid of them," said Tim Wales with a shrug. "Too many accidents happen with guns. I don't like them."

"And never had one?" asked Captain Manson.

"And never had one," said Tim definitely. "Neither had Judith or Winnie. They know how I feel about them. Anyway a gun's no good. If you're going to be robbed, go ahead and be robbed, and let the insurance company pay your losses. Don't invite trouble by waving a gun around."

Charlie Ingram said rather nervously that he had had several guns for years and still had them. "They are in my study, over on Silver Point. You can see them. They were still there this morning. I checked it. Just to be — well, just to be sure. Because the girl was shot, you know," he added, as if it were news.

"What about Andre Durant?" said Tim, an ugly gleam an his eyes. "What about Laideau?"

Captain Manson looked over Marny's head. "Durant says he had no gun. So far we've found no proof to the contrary. Laideau says he had a gun, but he believes that Cecily may have" — he hesitated and said — "may have taken it. Certainly it was not in his room at the Villa Nova. And it was not in

Cecily Durant's room, in the same hotel."

"See," said Tim. "She must have thought of suicide! That proves it."

Again Captain Manson rather ostentatiously did not look at Marny. "I don't think that was why she took his gun," he said quietly.

Tim was still excited and rather triumphant. "If the girl had a gun, and you can prove it, it puts the whole thing in a different light," he cried.

"I'm not so sure," said Captain Manson, and went away. But at least, thought Marny, he had not told them about Cecily's visit to her; for that she could be grateful.

And rather oddly Charlie Ingram had not told them. How had he known? There was no chance to ask him. Even if she had chosen to do so, point-blank, and risk Charlie's bland, blank evasion. She had never known Charlie Ingram well. He had been merely a figure of the Shadow Island scene, pleasant, rather neutral, interested in tennis and fishing, a squire for Judith and Winnie.

There was no chance, either, to talk alone to Bill Cameron.

Late in the afternoon men were still rowing about the pier, slowly and somehow inexorably, as if they were to be a permanent part of the landscape. If the police considered Andre's cigarette case evidence against him then it was by no means conclusive evidence, for Captain Manson went away again, still without making an arrest.

Laideau made no effort to seek her out and demand a decision.

But, after Manson had gone, Winnie did. It was Winnie who, all that queer, hot day with its sense of waiting, and brooding quiet, and stillness, somehow managed to keep the routine of the house running almost as usual. Meals were served; telephone calls were answered; messages were received and sent. She came out on the porch, looking hot and tired. "Rilly's been difficult," she said. "They want to quit, both Rilly and his wife. I told them the police would make them stay, so they may as well work and draw wages. I don't suppose it's true, though." She sighed and pushed back her hair and said to Marny, "I want to get out of the house. Let's walk around a bit. . . . Will you, Marny?"

Winnie was never subtle. Any of them might have guessed that she wanted to talk to Marny alone. Only Bill Cameron looked up, however, and made a half motion as if he thought of going with them; he sat back, though, deliberately. Marny rose and went along, strolling with Winnie across the narrow strip of lawn, around the house, down toward the swimming pool. Andre and Laideau were there.

Andre, in swimming trunks, sat on the edge of the pool with his legs in the water and his handsome black head sunk in his hands. Laideau lay at full length on the grass, staring up at the sky. He still wore the white sports shirt and rather soiled white slacks he had worn the previous night. Neither of them were speaking yet there was about them a curious air of communication, of shared speech and thought.

Winnie drew back. "Not here," she said, and pulled Marny back through the opening in the brilliant red and green hibiscus hedge. And, once they were well away from the pool, apologized.

"I was wrong this morning, Marny. I'm sorry I talked as I did. Trying to get you to tell Father that Andre was in love with you, I mean. You didn't do it, did you?"

"No."

"It was a silly idea. But you see I'd found — *that* — and I couldn't sleep all night for worrying about it. You didn't tell the police about it, did you?"

"What good would it have done to tell them! You said you'd deny it."

"Yes," said Winnie. "I would. But if somebody is arrested and charged with murder, I'll tell about it. I promise you that. I hadn't thought of it, that way, somehow."

"Where did you find the handkerchief, Winnie?"

But she was still stubborn. It was in her eyes before she spoke. "No, I won't tell," she said. "I can't. Not even you."

Nor Manson. Marny knew that. There was never any use in trying to influence Tim when he looked as Winnie looked just then. And the story of a non-existent, bloody handkerchief was not going to help her own case, but the contrary.

They walked slowly back to the house. The sky was as quiet as it had been in the morning. The bay was glassy and sleek. There was no breath of air and it was still in no sense overcast and threatening. It was merely terribly quiet.

And still Laideau did not come to Marny.

It was one of the strangest things in that strange and nightmarish day. Every time anyone spoke to her, every shift in any group, at every moment and every instant she expected Laideau to make an attempt to see her and he did not. Yet perhaps Manson had told Andre that there was to be no blackmail; that she had already told him the story of Cecily's visit and the gun.

When Marny and Winnie reached the porch again everybody was having cocktails and listening to the radio from the drawing room, turned on very loud, just as if it were any day.

That, of course, was Judith's doing.

Judith who wouldn't admit a toothache if she could help it, Judith who liked the pleasant things of life and simply wouldn't accept anything else.

The storm center, said the voice over the radio, was between Bermuda and Nassau, moving due west at an estimated rate of twenty-five miles an hour.

"Better get the shutters up," said Tim, smoking with nervous, rapid puffs. "Better move to a hotel."

"It'll turn north," said Judith. "It almost always does."

Charlie Ingram turned his glass meditatively in his hands. "I'll have my boat tied up, just the same."

"A good dance band comes on after the news," said Judith.

The news, however, was not finished. The murder on Shadow Island, luxurious home of Tim Wales, president of the Wales Airlines, came next. Mrs. Wales, prominent in society. Miss Wales, well known, too, and winner of last week's tennis tournament. Cecily Durant, wife of one of the Wales' guests, Andre Durant — shot in the back. No gun found. Brutal and revolting murder. Police dragnet thrown out. According to rumor, a startling arrest was to be made within the next twenty-four hours.

Judith got up at that, went into the house and snapped off the radio.

Charlie Ingram said thoughtfully, "It's queer. I always thought the people directly concerned in a murder case knew all about it. I don't know a damned thing. Who do you suppose they're going to arrest?"

"Andre, I hope," said Tim Wales. "He did it. He and Laideau."

Judith returned.

The men in rowboats off the pier, having apparently added themselves inexorably and permanently to the spot, suddenly rowed in, tied their two boats and departed by way of a police car. No one spoke until the sound of the car died away. Then Judith said restively that there was a dance at the Bath Club that night and she'd like to go, and Tim said angrily that it might be nice, too, if she made the rounds of the night clubs. "Nice for the papers! Swell! Go right ahead!"

Bill Cameron got up. "Can I borrow a car, Mr. Wales? I'd like to get my duffle from the hotel. That is, if I'm still invited to stay . . ."

Tim shifted his omnipresent cigarette from his mouth to his fingers. "It's like an invitation to a pest house," he said. "But if you can put up with us, stay."

Bill said, "Thanks, then I will. How about coming along with me, anybody? Do you good."

He looked at Judith and Winnie. Judith shook her head. "But get all the newspapers you can, will you?" she said. "New York papers, too." Winnie looked uncertain. "I'd like to. It's so horrid. Waiting around like this. Not knowing what the police are doing or — or anything except what we hear over the radio."

Tim said, "Don't be a fool. Some idiot reporter'd spot you the minute you got off the causeway. You're both too well known around here. Seclusion is the thing. Stay put. Marny might go with you, Bill. Nobody'll know her."

Bill Cameron said briskly, "Fine. Let's go right along."

Charlie Ingram rose. "I'll be getting along, too. Walked over. You can give me a ride, Commander." He took Judith's hand. "Didn't get much sleep last night. None of us did. I'll turn in early tonight. Just thought I'd come around. Rally, and all that, you know. Not that I'm doing any good."

"You're a darling, Charlie," said Judith.

"There's gasoline in my car," said Winnie. "Charlie will show you."

"Will the police let you go?" Tim asked Bill Cameron.

"We'll soon find out," he said, and Charlie led them to the white, vine-hung garage. They took Winnie's small gray coupe, and all three sat in the front seat together. At the gate Edward, the chauffeur, sitting morosely on a bench, merely glanced up as they passed. Three policemen were there. They did not stop the car but one of them followed in a moment, on a motorcycle. Charlie observed it cheerfully. "Fellow seems to be taking a sporting interest," he said. "He'll chase you all over the beach. I'd go along for the fun but I'm tired." He yawned and his monocle dropped out. "Let me off at the entrance to the next island, old chap. I'll walk to the house. It's only a small place, Silver Point. Nothing like Tim's place. Here we are . . ."

They stopped at a narrow road leading from the causeway to another island, very small and masked with Casuarinas so the house was not visible from the entrance. Charlie Ingram waved and nodded and started down the narrow road.

Bill Cameron let in the gear, peered into the mirror and started on. "The Wales family are now having a heart-to-heart conversation. And our policeman is sticking right with us. Now then — I thought I'd never get you alone. Tell me all about what Manson said."

She told him. They crossed Indian Creek and turned on Collins Avenue. Houses, walled, and laden with vines; brilliant hibiscus, bougainvillaea and pepper trees lined the wide street. The water on Indian Creek was as still and gray and even flatter than the bay. Occasionally, between houses, there were glimpses of the ocean, flat and gray too, with the surf remarkably even and breaking very slowly and heavily. As they neared the section of hotels Bill slowed down and the policeman behind them slowed down, too.

"Manson's okay," he said thoughtfully, but frowned a little

135

too. "Well, tomorrow's another day. Let's have dinner somewhere. It's early, but I can't take another meal today at the Wales place. I don't like the island. I don't like the house. And I think we're going to get the hurricane, sure as hell." He leaned out and waved his hand at the following policeman, as they turned on Lincoln Road. "This way, buddy," he called.

But over the small table, a few minutes later, they talked. Rather guardedly, as there were tables near them, but the dance band muffled their words somewhat in music. The place was crowded. It was attractive, large, cool and gay, with murals which were large aerial photographs of various cities, and a long bar at one end from which the policeman surveyed them, and where eventually he enjoyed a meal himself.

"The cigarette case is news to me," said Bill. "I'd like to know what they made of it, finally. Well, there's one thing certain. They won't arrest you until they have satisfactorily proved that Andre didn't kill her. The cigarette case was a break in a way, but it doesn't really prove anything as long as Judith sticks to her story."

"You feel sure that Andre did it?"

He shrugged. "Andre or Laideau. But the police are not going to do anything too quickly — anything that might make monkeys of them later. It all takes time. There are some funny angles, though."

He frowned, tracing circles on the tablecloth with his fork. "How did Charlie Ingram know Cecily had seen you? I was sitting on the porch when she left. Charlie Ingram definitely was not there, then. He might have come quietly into the room off the porch while you and I were talking and overheard us. I didn't see him, but I stayed on the porch for a while after you went back to your room. It was at least twenty minutes before I went into the drawing room. Judith and Andre came in and then Ingram and Tim Wales and Winnie. I was introduced to Tim, so I wasn't paying much attention to anything else. But Ingram wasn't in the drawing room when I entered it. So if he didn't see Cecily leave, and see you follow her down the steps somebody must have told him. And if, say, Judith told him, how did she know? Did Cecily, for instance, tell her?

136

And if so, when? I don't like this business of a woman in a white dress, either. Our young ensign saw a lot, considering the short time it took him to pass the island; but I'm sure he was sincere about it. However, when I got to figuring the time it takes to approach and pass any given point, I decided he could have seen just what he says he saw. But it was still fairly light. And if he saw all that, I think he'd have seen the gun. If, that is, it was then that Cecily was shot. So maybe Cecily was then talking to somebody else, in a white dinner dress."

"A dress can be destroyed quickly and thoroughly." He thought for a moment. "Judith wore black later, but she could have changed after meeting Cecily. The time is obscure and a few minutes one way or the other would make a great difference. Winnie wore blue, but she could have changed too. And of course" — he signaled to the waiter to bring the next course — "it may not have been a woman at all. It's an easy disguise. At night and at a distance."

Andre! Laideau! Andre had the run of the house and knew the place. He could have taken a white dress from Judith's or Winnie's wardrobe and later destroyed or hidden it.

Bill said, watching her, "Of course, whoever owned the dress, knows it's gone and is protecting Andre by not telling it. Don't look at me as if I'd discovered a gold mine. It doesn't get us anywhere. It's merely an idea. Now then — oh, hell." He got up abruptly. "Let's dance."

They did, quite as if murder did not exist and had not touched them with chill, inexorable fingers.

Bill Cameron danced well. He was light on his feet, extraordinarily light for so big a man. He knew just where he was going and when. For a moment the rhythm, the music, the pressure of his arm made a tight, invulnerable world. While they were dancing a rather odd thing occurred. The master of ceremonies said something Marny did not hear and suddenly the lights went out except for spotlights, roving in graceful arcs of light over the restaurant and over the dancers, and someone bumped against them. It was only one of the small collisions that happen on a crowded dance floor, but she lost her balance momentarily and Bill Cameron caught her. Caught her and then held her for a moment, rather tight and hard against him, so, somehow, her cheek was pressed against his own.

It was the way he had held her when he kissed her. *Only it wasn't Bill who had held her and kissed her!*

That, incredibly, had been Andre — yet it did not seem as if it had been Andre at all.

Bill Cameron had scarcely so much as touched her hand. It was contradictory; it was all wrong. Yet the warm, hard pressure of his cheek seemed extraordinarily familiar. As if she had known it, some time, somewhere, before. And as if she had liked it!

He moved his head away. "On your feet?" he asked rather brusquely, and they began to dance again, but this time, it seemed to her, with a certain self-conscious formality. They went around the dance floor once and then back to their table as the lights went up.

Through the rest of the dinner, through coffee and cigarettes, he talked of impersonal things and looked at her with friendly but impersonal eyes, and when they'd finished, did not linger but asked promptly for the check. They picked up the policeman at the car.

But they did not immediately go back to Shadow Island.

Instead, with the policeman coming along behind them, they drove back along Collins Avenue and eventually parked the car, before a hotel. "I'll get my stuff. Then let's have a drink and watch the sea for a while," said Bill.

That, too, was normal, everyday, as if they had escaped a world where everything was awry and out of focus and terribly, horribly wrong. The people about the lobby looked gay and normal and pleasantly matter-of-fact.

They sat in deep chairs above a strip of sand and watched the black ocean roll in and break in long creamy lines of white surf.

A radio was going somewhere in the lounge behind them; they could hear occasional words.

"Hurricane's still heading this way," said Bill. "Cigarette?" He lighted it for her. "It's queer how the surf is breaking. Looks, somehow, so slow. As if it knew it could afford to take its time. If the big blow comes, you know, we'd better get to a hotel quick. Manson won't stop us. He's a good guy." He paused and watched a long, white ridge roll in and break, and added, rather somberly, "Except maybe he's too good."

"Too good?"

"He'll do what he thinks is right, come hell or high water," said Bill Cameron. "I wish to God you were out of this thing." He got up. "Forget I said that. You didn't murder her and there must be ways of proving it. Tomorrow, if you want me to, I'll talk to Mr. Wales about a lawyer for you. Not that I think you'll need one. But it's sensible. Unless you'd rather talk to Wales yourself."

She remembered suddenly that Tim had called him "Bill." She said, "You talked to Tim today, didn't you?"

"Some," said Bill Cameron. "But not about you." He put down his hand for her. "We'd better be getting back. I don't know how much good a lawyer would do just now. Merely getting one is an admission of fear, so in that way it's not a good move. The fact is," said Bill soberly, staring out toward black ocean and black sky, invisibly blending somewhere, impenetrable and somehow ominous, "the fact is unless they definitely remove Andre from the suspects, you are safe. Andre's their pick. So . . ." he gave her hand a quick but very impersonal pat, and they went back to the car and a yawning policeman.

Even now, however, they did not go directly to Shadow Island. They went instead to Charlie Ingram's house.

"I'm going to ask him point-blank who told him that Cecily had come to you," said Bill and stopped the little coupe, with a spattering of gravel, in front of a low white house which loomed up in the car lights beyond thick, shadowy foliage.

But Charlie was not at home. At least he didn't answer the bell and there were no lights anywhere in the house. Eventually they gave up, backed cautiously around and, still followed by the policeman whose motorcycle engine woke the still and black night, continued along the causeway back to Shadow Island.

At the gate, which was lighted, Edward gave them a sleepy nod, and the two policemen stopped them, peered into the rumble seat and then let them go on. The third policeman left them there, leaving his motorcycle against the gatepost. The sweeping lights of the car glanced this way and that upon the green banks that lined the driveway. Bill let her out at the front door. "I'll put the car away. Go on in; don't wait for me."

She crossed the gravel as he turned the car toward the garage. The engine sounded loud in the stillness. The car lights shot ahead and disappeared around the corner of the house as she put her hand on the latch.

The door, however, was locked.

She tried it and tried it again, and started to ring the bell and stopped. The house was perfectly still. Off somewhere, seeming very far away now, the car engine was turned off, so Bill had reached the garage.

Everybody must have gone to bed early, and comprehensibly, considering the wakeful hours of the previous night. Obviously Rilly or someone, forgetting or not knowing that she and Bill were out, had locked the door.

She'd wait for Bill.

But Bill did not come.

Minutes passed. There was not a sound anywhere. The gate and its lights were far down the driveway and hidden by foliage. There was not a star in the sky. She listened for Bill's footsteps; suddenly it seemed to her that she had waited a long time. She left the step and walked slowly in the direction of the garage, expecting Bill's figure or the crunching sound of his footsteps at any instant.

But she reached the garage and it showed vaguely light in the darkness, and the doors were closed and Bill was not there.

Had she missed him somehow, in the thick, hot darkness? But surely she'd have heard his footsteps on the gravel. She went back along the driveway, her own footsteps making small sounds which seemed somehow furtive and yet too loud. She reached the front entrance and the steps which showed dimly white and still. Bill was not there.

There was nothing to do but ring. She put her thumb on the bell and, as she touched it, before she actually rang it, she remembered the porch and the door into the drawing room.

140

That would be, if it were open, the simplest way into the house.

The grass around the house in that direction muffled her footsteps; objects were dimly perceptible — the faintly light bulk of the house, the thicker shadow of the vines, the black line of the curving stairway, the shadow under the balcony, deeper even than surrounding shadows. There was no light on the porch and no light from the drawing-room door.

And no one anywhere.

Well, she'd cross the porch and try that door.

She was confused by the darkness; her sense of direction was awry; she brought up against the lower step of the vine-laden stairway, and flung both hands out to discover a stable thing, a guiding point, the railing . . .

Her hands encountered something that moved — heavily, sluggishly, only a little.

It was soft and sagging; her fingers touched cloth. Like a coat. Like a man's coat, hanging there in the thick, hot blackness. Hanging as if it were on a man. She flung back her hands and her body; a scream in her throat could not utter itself.

A man was hanging there, suspended somehow, anyhow — from the balcony, from the stairway, from any nameless thing she could not see or know, but which was only black and hidden.

The senses have a language of their own, intangible, swift, certain. Recognition derives from anything and everything even a dim, pale outline, only and mercifully half-seen, the outline of a man.

Andre Durant.

"I'd like to see him hanged," Tim had said.

It was as if the words repeated themselves, disembodied, terribly clear in the black silence. And then she heard a light, soft patter of footsteps on the balcony above her head. Footsteps that did not diminish or dwindle but simply, abruptly stopped.

CHAPTER XV

Nothing moved on the balcony. The light, stealthy footsteps did not resume. Nothing moved anywhere except suddenly Marny had a fantastic notion that the horrible thing, sagging there in the darkness within reach of her hand might sway nearer. There was a sound though, hard and heavy and fast, pulsing in her ears and her throat; the frantic thudding of her heart. She must run, escape, put distance between her and the balcony. Before the footsteps turned and came down that winding stairway. Before the thing so near her swayed and moved again!

The darkness was bewildering. Her pulses beat hard and heavy in her ears, in her throat, all over her body. She was running, pushing herself through the hot blackness, her out-flung hands grazing shrubbery at the corner of the house; she avoided the front steps, gravel spattering sharply in the still night; the hedges were enormous and tall and black; the tropics claimed the night and claimed the island and all the man-made things upon it. It reached out with primitive tenaculum to take back everything it had relinquished.

An area of light suddenly turned the driveway white and outlined the hibiscus sharply black against it. She whirled around a curve and saw the gatehouse ahead. A policeman was sitting on a bench, directly under the light, smoking. He heard her and jerked upward to listen and then came pounding along the driveway.

She must have told him the thing she had found. His bulky figure was running back toward the house. He had shouted toward the gate. Other figures, two policemen, and Edward came too, thumping heavily through the night and then becoming part of it as they passed her. But there were flashlights,

142

cutting fine, sharp fingers through the blackness. She reached the front steps and the pounding, heavy figures of policemen and the glancing rays of flashlights disappeared around the corner of the house. She'd better follow, better not to stay there, alone again, with all the enclosing shadows of the inexorable tropic night. She did, and they were standing together, in a queer disjointed group, lighted erratically by flashlights, in a pendant, heavy shadow below the balcony.

She reached them and Bill was there, too. A ray of light fell on his face. He was staring at that heavy, hanging shadow. His face looked strangely white. Everyone was talking, she thought, and yet she could really distinguish no words. But light streamed out all at once from the balcony, and Tim Wales shouted down, "What's going on down there?"

Bill was saying, "But there was somebody. When I was going toward the garage to put the car up. He was in the shrubs there by the garage. He ducked out of sight just as my lights swung around. I started after him but he got away and I came around the other side of the house and . . . Good God, it's Andre Durant!"

A flat, yellow ray of light was full upon the face of the thing that hung so heavily from the balcony railing, just beside the iron stairway. The dark hair had fallen forward. She had to get away. The night was too full of chaos and of something that surged too loud now and heavily in her ears.

There were more lights from the balcony. One of the policemen swung around toward her. "Was he like this when you found him, Miss?"

"*You found him* . . ." began Bill. Then he was at Marny's side. His arm was tight and warm around her. "*I* found him," he said to the policeman. "I came around that corner of the house. I found him just as you . . ." The policeman said, "She found him. At least she said she did. *She* came running down the drive to the gate. That's how we got here."

Edward mumbled something incoherent and disappeared. The two policemen stared at the thing, brightly, eerily illuminated. Bill turned Marny so she couldn't see. He pressed her face down against his shoulder. He said, "See here, we had just left the car. It hasn't been five minutes. You know that, you saw us come in. . . ."

The drawing room and then the porch sprang into such bright light that the flashlights paled; red and orange cushions stood out; homely details, ash trays and the newspapers, and a glass and a half-empty soda-water bottle on a tray as if someone had had a solitary night cap. Tim Wales, in a dressing gown, came charging across the porch and out the door and stopped. He stared, as the others stared, as if mesmerized horribly by that forever silent thing. Then all at once everybody, again, was talking. Bill Cameron held Marny tighter and said in her ear, "You've got to get away from this. Come on . . ."

Tim and the policeman were talking and Edward, very wan and sick-looking, added himself again to the scene. Bill's arm seemed to move her, without any volition on her part. He took her into the drawing room. He slid her down onto the sofa and stuffed a pillow not under her head but under her feet so they stuck up absurdly in their white pumps. There was a sharp black mark across one toe; she'd got that dancing. Before they had come back to the silent, fearful island, with Andre hanging . . .

"Bill . . ." she cried and turned so she was wholly in his arms, clinging to him, hiding her face as if to shut out everything the night had held.

He held her warmly for a moment, his face against her own as he had done, not meaning to, dancing. This time it was deliberate and strong and indescribably comforting. She felt safe again, as if within an invulnerable wall; as if his arms could shut out horror, everything. "Marny, Marny. Don't tremble like that. Don't, Marny. I promise you I'll fix things. I don't know how, God knows, but I . . . Well, I promise you. Somehow I'll make them come right. Understand?"

She clung more tightly. Her arms were around his neck and she decided quite simply that she wouldn't let go. She'd just hold on, like that, to something that was real and sane and strong. If she did so nothing could happen. He said, "*Marny, listen.* You've got to pull yourself together. Quick. This is going

144

to be a damn sight messier. For God's sake, listen. You're not paying attention to me."

He took her arms from around him and gave her a queer, hard shake and made her look at him. "Now answer me. I left you on the steps when I put the car in the garage. Did you see anybody?"

"No — no . . ."

"What did you do?"

What had she done? She thought back past an infinite, terrible gulf. "I got tired of waiting. The door was locked. I went to the garage. You weren't there. I came back and thought of that door . . ." She pointed toward it. "So I came around the house. And — it was there."

She thought he was going to take her in his arms again and she wanted him to, but he held her tighter and said, "What did you do?"

"I ran back to find the police. There was somebody on the balcony. . . ."

"What did you say?"

"There was somebody on the balcony. Just — just light footsteps. It — whoever it was — stopped. Just like that. Stopped. And I ran down to the police and it was dark and they came and . . ."

"Who was on the balcony?"

"I don't know. I couldn't see. I only heard somebody and then it stopped. Bill — Bill . . ."

"All right. That is safe to tell. That much. But no matter what you think or remember or anything don't add a word to it. Understand? Tell them only that . . ."

Judith said from the doorway, "What has happened?"

And when Bill got up, as if he wanted to think, Judith saw the lights and the men outside and she swept across the drawing room in her trailing scarlet dressing gown. Bill ran after her. At the door of the porch they saw her stop, the long scarlet silks swirling around her. They saw her hands flung upward to her eyes. They saw her whirl around, stumbling, running back toward them. Bill caught her. "Here — where are you going — wait . . ."

Her face was chalk white. She dropped her hands and stared at him. He said, "The police are there. Tim is there. They'll question us."

"What have I done?" said Judith. "Oh, what have I done?"

Bill said, "What do you mean? Sit down. Here." He shoved a chair toward her and she sat down mechanically, her great dark eyes staring up at him, her hands locked between her knees, the scarlet silk flowing around her, her black hair streaming over her shoulders. "What do you mean?" said Bill again, but she shook her head, numbly, staring at him.

Bill looked at her for an instant. "Marny, remember what I told you," he said. "Hold everything . . ."

He was, incredibly, gone, through the brightly lighted porch, back to that muttering, gesticulating group with the flashlights and the eerie white faces and Tim Wales shouting above them, "Where's Laideau? He did it! Where's Laideau? For God's sake, search the place. Don't let him get away."

Winnie came running into the room, blue dressing gown clutched around her. Judith lifted her head and cried, "Winnie, don't look. Don't go. Your father . . ." She put both hands over her mouth. Winnie stopped dead. "Judith, why are those men out there?"

Judith knew exactly what was happening. She said, "Andre . . ." and stopped and seemed to select words and then in a sudden rush, "Andre has killed himself."

Winnie looked at her and then at Marny and went to the porch, blue dressing gown held tight around her, brown braid over her shoulders. She stopped in the porch doorway and after a long moment came back. Her face was so white that the thick eyebrows stood out; then suddenly she sat down in a straight chair and stared at Judith.

And the men searched the house.

They searched the island. They sent for Manson and for the medical examiner and automobiles began to make a swift, speeding line along the causeway. It was like and yet horribly unlike the night before when Cecily had been found; that had been bad enough; this was different. Worse, owing to a few salient and very important differences.

Winnie hinted at those differences first. For, as they sat there, listening to the voices over the telephone in the hall, watching and trying not to watch, aware and trying not to be aware of everything that happened, Winnie said suddenly, staring at the beige and white floor, "They had the island under guard. Policemen were at the gate."

Judith, gave her a sharp look. "Someone could have come by boat."

"Then he didn't kill himself. You don't really think so, either."

"He was hanged," said Judith. "I saw that. I don't know what happened."

Winnie seemed to make a motion to go out on the porch again. Judith said, "You'd better not. It's — horrible." She shivered and looked out toward the porch. "I wish Tim would come in."

But it was Manson who crossed the porch, the screened door banging behind him, and called back to someone in that clustered, lighted group outside. "Tell Doctor Meade to come in here when he's finished." He crossed the drawing room without apparently looking at any of the three women. His face was white, his eyes looked black and brilliant as obsidian. His seersucker suit was wrinkled and his thin, brownish-gray hair disheveled. He looked into the hall and snapped, apparently to another policeman, "Bring them all in here. Everybody. Servants too. Keep the reporters out; tell them I'll give them the story in half an hour; tell them to wait. They can have all the pictures they want as soon as Doctor Meade has finished." He turned around, looked at Marny, Judith and Winnie as if they were not there at all and, as Tim Wales and Bill came in from the porch, he said, "Now then. That man didn't hang himself. Who did it?"

"What do you mean by that?" demanded Tim Wales. He pulled his bathrobe around his paunchy middle. His fat, shiny hands were shaking. He didn't look at Judith. Captain Manson said, "Answer my question. Do you know who did it?"

"If anybody killed him it was Laideau," said Tim Wales and selected and lighted a cigarette.

147

"When did you see Durant last?"

"Me, personally?" said Tim, his little eyes hard and brilliant and obstinate. "I'll be glad to tell you. Dinner was sent to his room on a tray. He and Laideau had it together. I wouldn't have them at my table, and I couldn't get rid of them just yet on account of the newspapers. They'd say — well, I couldn't. But I wouldn't eat with them. I haven't seen Durant since about seven o'clock, when I saw him come in from the swimming pool and go up the stairs to the balcony. From there, as you know, he could walk around to his room. I never saw him again. I don't know anything about this. Except if ever a man deserved hanging, he did."

"Tim . . ." began Judith in a stifled way and stopped.

CHAPTER XVI

The detective's face jerked toward Judith. "How about you, Mrs. Wales?"

"You mean — you mean . . ." Judith's face had no beauty then. It was strained and white with terror, above the scarlet silk.

"I mean when did you last talk to Andre Durant?"

Judith's hands were locked so tight that they looked bony and hard. "After dinner. I went to his room; it adjoins the room Laideau is using. I talked a minute . . ."

"What about?"

"I said" — Judith swallowed — "I said that I thought if there was anything he knew of Cecily's past that might possibly explain her murder, I thought he ought to tell it. That it would help us all and couldn't hurt Cecily now. Or — or anyone."

The detective looked at her. Tim put his cigarette to his lips, jerkily, not looking at Judith.

"And what did he say?" asked the detective.

Judith touched her lips with her tongue. "He said he didn't know anything. I went away. It was then, I suppose, about eight o'clock."

"What did you do then?"

"I went to my room. I was tired. My husband and Winnie were down here on the porch. I went to bed. I read and then I took a sleeping pill; about ten, that was."

"And that's the last time you saw Andre Durant?"

"Yes."

There was no way of knowing what or how much the detective accepted as true. He turned to Winnie. "And you?"

"I saw him at the pool," said Winnie. "Marny was with me. It was, I think, between five and six o'clock. Then Marny and

149

Commander Cameron went to the Beach and they took Charlie home. Judith told me that it would be better to have dinner sent up to Andre and to his friend, so I did."

Rilly and his wife and the smart, little colored maid who had unpacked for Marny, were in the doorway. Something was going on in the hall behind them. Some sort of commotion, voices, but the only thing that seemed to matter just then was the frightened nod Rilly gave as Winnie looked at him for confirmation. His wife, slender, frightened too, but intelligent-looking and neat in her red-and-white cotton house coat, put her hand to her hair and nodded too, her large dark eyes fastened on the detective. The smart little maid in a smart black dressing gown, turned to stare curiously over her shoulder, into the hall. Captain Manson said to Winnie, "Then what?"

"Then what happened, you mean? Why, nothing exactly. We had dinner, Father and Judith and I. Judith went upstairs; she said she was tired. Father and I talked awhile on the porch. I went to bed about ten-thirty, I think. I didn't see Andre again."

"How about you, Mr. Wales?"

"I've told you," snapped Tim. "I sat out there after Winnie'd gone to bed and smoked, and had a night cap. I was dead tired. We all were. I don't know just when I went to bed, but it was shortly after Winnie'd gone. I didn't see Andre again. I didn't hear anything. I took a couple of pills and slept until all the hullabaloo outside the balcony waked me. Then I came down and . . ."

"What about you, Miss Sanderson?"

Bill Cameron said quietly, "I told you about that, Captain Manson."

"Go on, Miss Sanderson."

Marny's voice was uneven and suddenly it seemed to her horribly unconvincing. She heard herself talking as if it were Judith or Winnie or anybody except herself, Marny.

She had waited on the steps; she had gone to the garage; she had returned; she had remembered the door from the porch; she had found . . . At that point the other woman, the woman who had got into her body and obligingly was talking for her, stopped there and could not go on. Captain Manson said, "Go on, please. You found Durant?"

"Yes." It wasn't that other woman any more. It was Marny herself, whispering with a throat that felt tight and stiff.

"How did you know it was Durant? Could you see?"

"Not — exactly."

"How did you know then?"

"There was something — a sort of — outline — I knew who it was."

"What did you do then?"

"I remembered the police at the gate. I ran to tell them."

"How long a time elapsed between your being left at the step by Commander Cameron and your notifying the police of your discovery?"

"I don't know. A few minutes."

Captain Manson turned to a policeman. It was the man who had followed her and Bill Cameron on a motorcycle, who had watched them from the bar while they danced. The policeman said, "It was about twelve minutes, sir. I was listening to the chauffeur's radio and the commercial had just come on at the end of a fifteen-minute program. It's one of my favorite programs and I was hoping we'd get back in time to hear it. Twelve minutes is my guess."

Laideau appeared in the doorway and Rilly and his wife and the maid moved aside, glancing sideways at Laideau and the two policemen holding his arms. Manson did not even look at him, although Laideau's tiny, ugly dark eyes fastened themselves on the detective as if drawn by a magnet. In the same moment the medical examiner and another policeman came across the porch, and into the drawing room.

The doctor was short, fat, round and hot. He wiped his hands with a handkerchief. "You were right, Captain," he said. "Fellow was killed before he was hung. Skull fracture just behind the ear. Some heavy, hard instrument. Don't know what."

"You mean," said Captain Manson, "that it's possible that somebody hit him, fracturing his skull, and then tied that rope around his neck and pulled him up over the balcony railing?"

Doctor Meade nodded. "Looks like it."

"Could a woman have done it?" asked Captain Manson.

"I don't see why not," he said and walked briskly across the room and into the hall.

Manson said, "Let him go. I'll see to him."

He meant Laideau. The two policemen dropped their hands. Laideau gave a kind of shiver and rubbed one arm as if it had been bruised and did not shift his hard, black gaze by so much as a fraction from the detective. Manson said to the policemen, like a postscript, "And take Miss Sanderson to her room. She'll show you. Keep her there. Don't let anybody see her or talk to her."

"*You can't* . . ." began Bill Cameron and started toward her and Captain Manson shot out a thin, arresting arm. "I can," he said.

The policemen were at Marny's side. It was easier to walk out of that room with everyone looking at her, with Bill Cameron standing there, watching too, not moving — than to let them make her walk. She went out through the hall. She went up the stairs. The policemen were directly behind her. If anyone in the drawing room spoke or moved she did not hear it.

She ought to have known; Bill had told her; Manson had told her; she had reasoned it out for herself. Andre had been their principal suspect. And, in a queer way, he had protected her.

But now Andre was murdered. So they would charge her with murder. Cecily had come to her with a gun, and the police knew the whole story.

She went into her room with her head high, which was queer, because she had no knowledge of walking, of moving, of even touching the switch; she only knew that the room leaped into light.

One of the policemen tramped across and went outside and stood on the balcony, just outside the balcony door which he closed. The other said, rather uncomfortably, "I'll — well, I'll stay in the hall, just outside the door, Miss. Captain didn't say

— well, anyway, I'll stay right here. Only don't try anything, Miss. You won't get by with it," and he closed the door.

She stood for a long moment in the brilliantly lighted room. She had changed places with Andre!

A macabre and horrible corollary seemed to reach out and catch at her. She recognized it and fought it back. Andre was dead, so he was no longer the main suspect of the police. Now she had taken that place.

She wouldn't think; but what did one do? What could one do?

Well, one thing was not to lose one's head. She hadn't murdered Cecily; she hadn't murdered Andre.

The bed was turned down. Her night things were neatly laid out. It was sharply normal, like the little black mark on her slipper, extraordinary simply because it was so unextraordinary, so out of pace with a world that had become fantastic. She looked down.

It was then that she realized that quite recently someone had been in her room.

As she had already discovered that night, recognition operates in a hundred intangible yet perfectly certain ways. She knew that someone had been in her room rather in the way one knows it if someone else has used one's pen, from a faint subtle difference in its balance. It was like a nursery rhyme: Goldilocks? "Someone has been sitting in my chair. . . . Someone has been eating my porridge. . . . Someone has been sleeping on my bed. . . ."

That was nonsense. Why exactly did she know someone had been there? Then the tangible small things that give rise to subconscious knowledge began to emerge and make themselves clear. Someone had sat on the bed. There were a few wrinkles and a shallow but definite indentation on the otherwise smooth linen and silk. Someone had dropped a cigarette in the ash tray and she had happened not to smoke in her room that evening. It was a cigarette like those Tim Wales smoked, but they were everywhere in the house, probably in every ash tray, along with other brands. It was the same brand that someone listening from behind the vines on the balcony had dropped, still burning. She looked around and then saw it. Between the door and the bed was an odd, long smear. It was a kind of reddish brown, showing not deeply but on the surface of the deep-piled rug. As if someone had dragged something along, over the rug, so it touched for a few brief inches.

Something that was newly painted. Something that made a short, small, red smear. It drew her like a dreadful magnet, as if she knew exactly what that smear was, so she moved across the room and knelt down on the carpet.

And after a long time, thought: cold water takes it out. Not cleaning fluid, not hot water. Only cold water.

Andre had been murdered. His skull had been fractured and the doctor had said he believed it had happened before Andre was — somehow — hanged there from the balcony. She had heard footsteps on the balcony and they had stopped. Because whoever was there had entered her room? And had stopped there to wait and listen in the darkness, and had even smoked a cigarette? And had dragged something over the rug, not knowing, because it was dark, that that smear had been made?

It was police evidence, jury evidence, but it also was evidence against her. There was no question about that.

She got up and went into the bathroom. Someone had been there too, had washed his hands and used two towels and thrust them wet and crumpled back upon the rack.

There were the towels. There was water splashed around the basin and a little puddle under the soap. There was a look though as if whoever had washed there had also washed the basin quickly. Suddenly and with a kind of cold horror, she looked for red smears there, too, reddish brown, diluted with water. There was nothing. Self-preservation operates, too, instinctively and strongly.

She must hurry. Get the smear off the rug first. Before the police see it. One of them had walked across it, toward the door — and only by luck had not been looking at the rug and had not seen that smear. Next time he would see it. She took a fresh towel, held it under the cold-water faucet and went back to the rug.

She knelt again, trying to force herself to the ugly but grimly necessary task and someone knocked and called to her. "Marny, Marny, can I come in?"

It was Bill Cameron. She got up. He opened the door, saw her, came quickly into the room and across to her, taking her wrist in his hand, staring at the dripping towel: *"What are you doing?"*

"There . . ." she said.

He looked and knelt, too. Finally he got up. "I'll get Manson."

"No, no . . ."

His eyes blazed down into her own. "Don't be a fool! It's a plant. Deliberate. Like fixing it so you would find Andre. It wasn't any coincidence, your finding Andre as you found Cecily. It was part of a plan; it had to be."

"Someone was here. Someone sat on the bed and smoked and washed his hands in the bathroom . . ."

He said. "Listen, Marny. It's a safe bet that whoever killed Cecily killed Andre. And I think I know why, too. And whoever did is trying to implicate you. Stupidly — yet so openly that the only thing for us to do is show Manson this." He went to the door and spoke to the policeman outside. "Get Manson. Quick." He came back to her. "Now then. I got Manson to let me see you about a lawyer. But he — I think if we can get him alone he'll give us the low-down. I think that he's got to consider you a suspect because of Cecily — because of the evidence, but I think he doesn't — well, want to. I think his instinct is against it. Therefore let's give him every chance to get at the truth, put everything on the table." He paused, frowning, looking at her as if he did not see her. He said, "I may not be right. My opinion may be governed by my own feeling about you. There is a certain . . ." He paused and, rather curiously, used the words that had entered her own thoughts, "There is a certain deceiving security in the knowledge of innocence. That's the way I feel about you. You didn't murder Cecily or Andre, so I keep thinking that they can't seriously accuse you of it. Yet — oh, maybe I'm wrong. But are you willing to put yourself in my hands and do as I tell

155

you? Knowing," said Bill Cameron, looking straight into her eyes, "knowing that I may be wrong. That I may make mistakes. And that it is, your life, quite literally, I'm asking you to put in my keeping."

Bill Cameron's face, clear and intent, his green shoulders solid and broad. Suddenly everything about him seemed right.

It was the only word that came clearly into her mind. Right — sane and solid and clear-seeing and *right*.

She made no decision because there was no decision to make. She looked back up into his face and said, "All right, Bill."

Manson himself knocked at the door and entered.

"Well?" he said and looked at Marny. "If it is a confession I'd better have the stenographer take it down."

CHAPTER XVII

Bill Cameron seemed to square his shoulders. "It is not a confession. Look here, Captain, I want to make a bargain with you."

Manson's intensely concentrated look seemed to grow more marked. "I don't think you are talking about bribes, Commander. I've had such offers in my time, but not for a long time."

"No, I'm not talking about bribes." She noticed that Bill had moved, so he stood squarely between Manson and the smear on the rug. He said, facing Manson directly, "I mean this. Apparently Miss Sanderson is on the spot. There is evidence against her. Cecily came to see her and had a gun, you know all that — and Miss Sanderson found her later when she'd been murdered. Now, tonight, she found Andre Durant. You had to go through a form of arresting her . . ."

"I didn't arrest her."

"You sent her up here, with a guard. It also seemed to me that if you were convinced in your own mind that she had killed either of them you'd have actually arrested her."

Manson said, "What is your bargain?"

"I have to say all this first," said Bill Cameron. "I don't think you believe she murdered either Cecily or Durant. But I do think that you cannot discount the evidence as it stands. Right?"

"Go on."

"Her discovery of Cecily's body was an accident. But her discovery of Durant's body was a deliberate plant, and I think whoever murdered Durant has planted another piece of evidence. Intended to cast suspicion upon her. So — well, it actually proves she didn't do it."

There was no way to tell what Manson was thinking. His face conveyed nothing but hard concentration. "What?" he said.

Bill Cameron paused. He gave Marny a glance, and then with something like a shrug, moved aside. "There . . ." he said, and pointed.

It was blood.

Men from police headquarters, expert technicians with apparently sufficient equipment to identify a bloodstain as such, were in the house then. There was not even a wait while they went to the laboratory. Marny watched, Bill Cameron watched, Captain Manson watched. And then he told them to take a specimen away with them and label it.

They went away. Captain Manson, standing in the open door, spoke rapidly to another policeman. "Search this room," he said. "Quickly."

"Yes, sir. What for, Captain?"

"Something heavy and hard. A — hammer would do it. An ax. Even, I suppose, a baseball bat."

Marny hadn't thought of that. Suppose whoever killed Andre had hidden the weapon that had been used somewhere in her room. She glanced at Bill Cameron and he was afraid of it, too. She could tell by the stiff, hard look in his face.

They found nothing. They opened the wardrobe and looked among Marny's clothes — things that seemed so familiar and everyday. The Captain lingered for a long time in the bathroom. The man looked in drawers and under the mattress of the bed, and along the draperies at the windows. They found nothing and Captain Manson sent them away.

And Bill Cameron said, his mouth very tight and Scotch-looking, "You see, Captain Manson? Miss Sanderson wouldn't have done that deliberately. She wouldn't have told you . . ."

"I'm not saying what anybody would do," said Manson. He sat down. His clothes looked damp and limp, his face withered, somehow, and tired. And Marny said suddenly, leaning forward, "I heard footsteps. While I was outside. Just after I'd found him. Somebody walked along the balcony. I heard it clearly and then the footsteps just stopped."

It sounded too pat, too circumstantial. Manson just looked at her. Bill Cameron said, "That's right. You told me. Did it sound as if whoever it was came into this room?"

"I couldn't tell. I couldn't have known, it was so dark and I had just found him, you see. . . ."

Bill said, "You couldn't possibly have seen anyone from where you must have stood. Besides, it was dark. But probably whoever it was came into your room, waited and smoked — listening, I imagine, to know just what would happen and what you would do. And then purposely, I think, left that smear on the rug."

Manson said, "Will you tell me your story again, Miss Sanderson? It detail. Exactly as it happened."

She did, rapidly and slowly, by jerks. When she'd finished he turned to Bill. "How about you, Commander?"

So Bill told his story again. It coincided with her own naturally up to the time when he had left her on the step. And, putting the car away, he had seen someone move quickly out of the beam of lights from the car, and had tried to find him.

"Who was this person you say you saw and tried to find?"

"I don't know. I just saw a motion and a black figure. He ducked out of sight behind the hedge. I had a quick impression, but it was clear enough. But I didn't see enough to know who it was."

"Man or woman?"

"I don't know. Except — well, I think I'd have known if it had been a woman."

"But you can't be sure? You couldn't identify anybody?"

"Well," said Bill and paused as if he longed to say yes, and finally said, "No."

"Why did you try to find out who it was?"

"Why? Because of the murder, of course. Because — well, because the fellow didn't want to be seen."

"Then what did you do?"

"As I told you. I put the car in and gave the door a shove as I went out. I ran down toward the hedge. I thought whoever it was had gone in the direction of the swimming pool. On the opposite side of the house from the porch . . ."

"I know," said Captain Manson rather tersely. "I'm fairly well acquainted with the layout by now."

Bill flushed a little. "Well, at any rate, I went down there, and hunted around and listened and whoever it was had got completely away. At least I couldn't hear anything. I thought Marny had come on into the house. I never thought of the front door being locked. At any rate, I came on back finally but since it was nearer, came around the other end, the back entrance of the house. I couldn't find my way, it was so dark, and I had my cigarette lighter so I got it out. I saw something there near the railing, and had got to Durant's body just as the police came from the other side of the house. But look here, Captain Manson. This is not my job, and I don't mean to be impertinent. But — there *was* somebody in the shrubbery, and he got the hell out of there as fast as he could."

"If you saw somebody, what about the footsteps Miss Sanderson claims to have heard? What about the blood on the rug? Your mysterious intruder couldn't have been in two places at once."

"I think there'd have been time for him to run round the house, instead of toward the swimming pool as I'd thought, and up the balcony stairs. Where I suppose he could have stopped and listened to be sure whether or not I was following him. Then he could have heard Marny, and tiptoed into her room and waited a minute to see — at least to listen — to what was going to happen. And deliberately place these false clues. Just as I think the door was locked on purpose, so Marny and I *would* come back from the Beach and find the door locked — think about the side door, come around that way and find Durant's body. Coincidences may happen but not that conveniently for the murderer. I simply don't believe that the fact that it was Marny who found Cecily and then again Marny who found Durant, could be coincidence. It was planned."

"Then to carry it further, you think somebody in this house locked the front door after murdering Andre, went down to the hedge and was seen by you, levitated himself somehow through the darkness and in what must have been a very short

160

space of time to the balcony, and waited for Miss Sanderson to find Durant; then left ashes and a bloodstain deliberately in her room; washed his hands and cleaned off whatever instrument of murder was used in that bathroom, walked out into the hall and to his own room and pretended later on to be awakened."

The smear of blood on the rug, the look of the washbasin having been used and then thoroughly rinsed! Marny hadn't gone that far. She'd only thought, vaguely and horribly, of hands stained with blood. What had Manson told them to look for? A hammer, an ax, anything heavy and hard. But now it would be washed clean. It would show no signs of the thing it had done. Bill said, looking very white, "I didn't say that. There's only Mr. and Mrs. Wales and Winnie in the house. Except, of course, Laideau."

"Why would Laideau kill his best friend?"

"Laideau would slit his own grandmother's throat for a dime."

"That's not the point. They worked together, Laideau and Durant. Laideau profited by Durant's brains. He wouldn't have killed the goose that laid the golden egg. No. Miss Sanderson, by your own testimony, they were trying to blackmail you. Laideau could not have done so without Durant's support. You see for yourself it provides a motive for your murdering him."

"But I told you about Cecily," said Marny. "They couldn't have blackmailed me . . ."

"They could still have made it bad for you if Durant had come to trial." Captain Manson paused, his eyes bright and hard. "I'm not the court or the newspapers or the jury. I'm only a police officer. They could still have used the threat of publicity and jury evidence."

Bill said suddenly, "Captain, we got a general idea from what the doctor said, but will you tell us exactly how Durant was killed?"

"He was hit on the head, behind the ear, twice. Hard. One of the blows apparently killed him. Then a slip knot was neatly put around his neck. The other end was looped around the

161

balcony railing, or rather, the pointed iron post that projects just at the top of the stairs. He was hauled up to a sufficient height to get his feet off the ground. Then the knot was fastened. It was not a herculean feat by any means. The leverage was such that" — he gave a slight shrug — "even I could do it. I tried. It was not too hard a pull for a woman. And it need have taken very little time. It only required three things — a weapon, Durant's presence at near enough that spot at near enough the right time, and a rope."

"You haven't had time to trace the rope?"

"Not yet. It may mean nothing when we do. It might have been merely a rope from the garage, pier, anywhere. Something anybody on the island could have got."

"Are you limiting your suspects to people on the island?"

"I'm not limiting the suspects," said Captain Manson rather wearily, "to anybody. But there are certain probabilities. One is that Cecily Durant and Andre Durant were killed by the same person. This is because murder is an unusual and desperate act. The law of averages and probabilities suggests one murderer rather than two. But if there was one murderer — as I believe — there is an extraordinary conflict of motives. For instance, who wished to do away with Cecily Durant if it was not her husband? The answer to that could be a woman who wanted to marry Andre Durant, and whom Cecily opposed — even to the point of threatening her with a gun. But would that woman murder Cecily to get Durant and then murder Durant? You see?"

"If Cecily had not been murdered . . ."

"If Cecily had not been murdered I'd have believed that the motive in the case of Andre Durant's murder was almost certainly fear or revenge."

Both words seemed strange and melodramatic and yet convincing, uttered in that quiet, businesslike voice.

"Fear?" said Bill.

"Fear of blackmail."

"Revenge?"

"The revenge of some — husband, father, brother . . ." Captain Manson shrugged slightly. "Any man who had a right

162

to resent Andre Durant's treatment of a woman, and did so."

Bill Cameron said suddenly and violently, "I'd have liked to do it myself."

"Frankly," said Captain Manson, "so would I. But the law requires me to discover his murderer and deliver that murderer into the hands of justice. And in this case that murderer is almost certain to have murdered Cecily Durant first. But I don't know why."

"Captain Manson, who told Charlie Ingram that Cecily had seen Marny?"

The detective replied to that too, simply and directly. "He said he had heard it, and had seen Cecily leave with Miss Sanderson following her."

"That's a lie," said Bill. "I was on the porch. I'd have seen him. Where was Charlie Ingram tonight when we went to his house? He wasn't at home."

"Are you suggesting that actually he did not overhear anything, but that Cecily told him of her meeting with Miss Sanderson? Are you suggesting he was the person you claim to have followed tonight and who got away from you?"

"Somebody was there near the garage," said Bill stubbornly. "Ingram could have rowed over, quietly, from Silver Point. So the police at the gate wouldn't have seen him."

There was a long pause. Finally Captain Manson said, "I've questioned Ingram and Ingram's record — for another reason. So far as I can discover he had no previous knowledge of either Cecily Durant or Andre. Why do you think he murdered Durant?"

Bill shrugged. "Fear," he quoted. "Or — revenge."

Unexpectedly Captain Manson went to the door. "Get hold of Charlie Ingram and tell him to meet us at the police station. In Miami Beach. In half an hour."

Bill had been sitting on the arm of a chair. He got up slowly.

Captain Manson said, "Come just as you are, Miss Sanderson. You can have someone pack a bag for you later, if you need it."

Bill Cameron looked white and rigid. He said quickly, "I'm coming too."

CHAPTER XVIII

The stairway, hall and drawing room were empty. There was no sign of Tim or Winnie or Judith except ashes from Tim's cigarettes in the many trays in the wide hall. The police car was drawn up at the door.

Laideau went with them. He was already sitting in the police car, huddled in a corner of the back seat, his thick, black hair and ugly pale face dimly visible, his great hands clasped together. He did not look at them as they got in and did not speak.

The night was still and quiet with no faint suggestion of a storm. As they went along the causeway and turned on Collins Avenue, the policeman driving the car turned the radio to a news broadcast and got the latest hurricane warning. The storm was still headed that way. They listened, estimated wind velocity, estimated the time which it would take for the storm center to reach the Beach. People were warned all precautions should be taken — windows boarded up, children kept at home. The Red Cross and the Coast Guard would stand by.

"It'll hit tomorrow night," said the policeman and turned the radio dial. "I'm going to take my wife to a hotel. We're too near the ocean." He paused, his shoulders a black, bulky shadow ahead and added thoughtfully, "May hit before then. It's hard to tell. They can't always get it right on the nose. But it'll hit."

Charlie Ingram arrived in another police car, shortly after Marny and Bill Cameron were ushered into Captain Manson's office, leaving Laideau, smoking uneasily, in another room. Charlie looked sleepy and annoyed, with puffs under his eyes, his thin hair ruffled and his monocle agitated. He admitted almost at once that he had not seen Cecily leave the Wales house on the night she was murdered.

It was hot in the high-ceilinged, clean office. The windows were open but no breath of air stirred. Charlie, sitting with his legs crossed, glanced rather nervously at Marny and at Bill Cameron and looked back at Manson who sat at the desk, leaning back, waiting.

"Thought you ought to know the girl was there," said Charlie. "But I didn't want to tell you who told me. Matter of fact, she asked me not to tell you at all. But I . . ." He shrugged. "I thought you ought to know it. So I just said that *I* had seen the girl leave."

Manson leaned forward and put his elbows on the desk. "You do realize that this is a murder inquiry, don't you, Mr. Ingram?"

Charlie blinked. "Why, certainly, old chap. It's why I thought I'd better not bring Judith into it."

"Judith . . ." said Marny and stopped.

Captain Manson said, "You mean that Mrs. Wales told you that Cecily Durant had seen Miss Sanderson?"

Charlie hesitated, swung his monocle on its ribbon, cleared his throat and said finally, "Well, yes. Said she had seen the girl, or overheard her talking to Marny or something. Said — well, I don't think she really meant to tell me. Asked me not to tell anyone. But it seemed to me you ought to know that the girl — Durant's wife, I mean — actually had a gun. Thought it my duty to tell you." He turned to Marny. "Hope I've not got you into trouble, Marny. I didn't mean to. I just thought the police ought to know the girl was running around with a gun. Shows she had some thought of suicide." He swung his monocle with a righteous and indignant air.

Manson said slowly, "A little thing like perjury wouldn't bother you?"

Charlie's eyes popped open. "Perjury! My dear fellow, really! I was only doing my duty."

"Didn't it occur to you that your story was likely to make the police suspect Marny?" demanded Bill Cameron hotly. "Do you think you were doing your duty when in order to protect Mrs. Wales you deliberately turn suspicion toward

Marny?" He was standing, big and solid and so obviously angry that Charlie Ingram gave an uneasy wriggle in his chair.

"Now, now, old chap," he said protestingly. "Now, now, no need to get upset. I didn't intend to do anything of the kind. I only thought they ought to know Cecily Durant had been there and had had a gun. I didn't think Marny had shot her. Not for a minute. But I couldn't tell about the girl without telling that it was Marny she had come to see, could I? And still there was no need to drag Judith into it." He lifted his scant eyebrows and stooped shoulders and turned appealingly to Captain Manson. "Seems perfectly clear to me."

Probably, thought Marny rather wearily, nothing had ever been quite clear in Charlie's mind except how to shoot and how to play tennis and how to tell a pleasant and innocuous story at a dinner table. He was devoted to Judith. The muddled reasoning arising from that devotion was perfectly comprehensible. Even Captain Manson seemed to see that. He fingered a blotter on the desk and said, "False witness is not a pleasant thing, Mr. Ingram, no matter how much you disguise it. Is there anything else you've told me that was not true?"

"Now, now, see here!" Charlie was ruffled and worried. He leaned forward in his chair, staring earnestly at the detective. "I'm no liar. It's not sporting, you know. I only — well, one must protect one's friends, you know. It didn't seem to me to matter whether *I* had seen the Durant girl or *Judith* had seen her! Merely a gesture on my part . . ."

Bill Cameron said, "A damned unpleasant gesture!"

Charlie Ingram jumped up. "I don't like your tone, Commander . . ."

Captain Manson interrupted crisply, "Will you sit down, please, Commander? You, too, Mr. Ingram. If you want to fight you can do it outside, but I'm too busy just now to bother with you. Now then, when did Mrs. Wales tell you that she had seen Cecily Durant with Miss Sanderson? How much exactly of their conversation had she overheard?"

Bill Cameron stood exactly where he was. Charlie settled

166

back into his chair and looked at Captain Manson. "I told you all that," he said sulkily.

"Tell me again."

"Well, it seems silly. It's already a part of your record, isn't it?"

"Go on."

"All right. All right. Give me a chance to get my breath." He frowned. "I think it was early the morning after the murder. After Cecily Durant's murder. Judith said . . . Oh, I told you everything. She said that she thought the Durant girl had killed herself because she knew that she had a gun. I said, I suppose — one can't remember exactly — but I think I said, 'How do you know?' Or words to that effect."

Bill thrust his hands into his pockets with a gesture of strongly withheld violence, seemed to remember he was in uniform and jerked them out again, as violently. Charlie glanced nervously toward him. The detective said, "Go on."

"Yes. Well, I'm doing the best I can, you know. One can't always remember these things exactly. However" — he went on rather hurriedly as Bill Cameron seemed again to control incipient violence — "however, I do remember that Judith said, 'Never mind how I know,' or something like that. And added that I'd better not tell the police because it might sound as if Marny had been having an affair with Durant. I said why? And she told me then that the girl had threatened Marny with the revolver and had said that Marny couldn't take Andre away from her, that she — I mean the Durant girl — wouldn't let her. It was something like that. I can't remember the exact words. I told you, Captain," said Charlie with suddenly assumed dignity, putting his monocle carefully in his eye, "I told you that I myself had heard the Durant girl and Marny talking. I told you then, when it was much fresher in my mind, what Judith had heard them say. The only difference was that I told you that I had been on the porch and they had been on the balcony and I had heard it all. The actual fact is, of course, that Judith must have been there."

"She was not on the porch," said Bill Cameron, biting out the words.

167

"Was she on the balcony?" asked Captain Manson, turning to Marny.

"Not when Cecily ran out of my room and I followed her. I saw no one. Except Commander Cameron, on the porch below."

"Was the door open? The door from your room to the balcony?"

"Yes."

"Then could Mrs. Wales have overheard without your knowing it? If, say, she happened onto the balcony?"

"Yes. Yes, I suppose so. But I didn't think . . ." A fleeting, odd memory checked her. Some time after her swim with Andre someone had passed along the balcony. She had not heard anyone. She had caught only a glimpse of a shadow passing briefly across the bed and vanishing. As if someone had been there. But it hadn't been Judith. She remembered the exact time. Judith had just gone into the hall. And it was before she had emerged from the bathroom to find Cecily Durant, pale and thin and young, standing there with her wide, frightened eyes and her badly painted mouth, and the gun hidden in her hands.

"What is it, Miss Sanderson? What have you remembered? Tell me . . ."

She told him slowly, trying to recapture what was at best an elusive and swift impression. The detective said, "But then it couldn't have been Judith Wales."

"Couldn't it have been Cecily?" asked Bill Cameron.

Captain Manson looked at him slowly and said pointedly, "Will you please sit down, Commander, and permit me to question in my own way?"

"Sorry." Bill Cameron was plainly not sorry and he was plainly still angry and resentful of Charlie's explanation. He went over to a chair and sat down, looking remarkably solid, as if he'd be very hard to move. Captain Manson rubbed his wrinkled brown hands through his hair and across his eyes. He said, "All these things take time. Now then, I'd like you to go back, please, to the time of your arrival in Miami, Miss Sanderson. Tell me exactly what happened. As if you were making a timetable. Up to the time you found Mrs. Durant murdered." He pressed a bell on his desk and a policeman came in. "Will you take this?" said Captain Manson and the policeman went to another small desk and came back with a pad and a pencil. He looked at Manson as he adjusted the tablet on his knee. "Fellow called Laideau says he wants to see you," he said.

"He'll see me all right," said the detective, looking grim and tired. "Now then, Miss Sanderson. You arrived at the airport at about six. Who met you? Start from there."

She did. Their ride home to Shadow Island, her swim, Bill Cameron's arrival.

Captain Manson interrupted there and said to Bill, "About what time was that?"

"I don't know exactly. I should say around six-thirty. At any rate, there was time for me to go to the house, present my letter to Miss Wales, and drive back to my hotel, after she asked me to dinner, change into whites and return to Shadow Island. In all it must have taken me a little less than an hour. I got a taxi both ways. Happened to get one without waiting, at the entrance to the causeway, and there was one at the door of the hotel when I came out. It was about, I think, seven-thirty, when I saw Cecily run down the stairs from the balcony."

"Will you go on, Miss Sanderson?"

Andre Durant had come while she was still talking to Commander Cameron. Commander Cameron had left the swimming pool. She had not known that he'd gone to the house. She and Andre Durant had remained in the pool for perhaps ten to fifteen minutes, or even longer. While they were swimming, Charlie Ingram had come past and stopped to speak to them. Again the detective verified it.

Charlie Ingram said, yes, that was right. "I'd been down at the tennis court. Winnie had had a racket restrung for me and I walked over from Silver Point to pick it up. Thought I'd just stroll around past the pool to see if anybody was there and there was. Marny and this Durant chap. Stopped to speak to them, although I never liked him. Thought he was a rat. Well, anyway, I was polite and then went on back home."

"Did you go to the Wales house at all?"

169

"No. Never went near. Knew my own racket, and Winnie'd been trying it; said she'd leave it there for me. Matter of fact, I'd nearly forgotten it. Wouldn't have done to leave it out overnight, you know. No, I didn't go to the house."

"Did you see anyone besides Miss Sanderson and Durant? Commander Cameron, for instance?"

Charlie shook his head. "Didn't see anyone. No, wait a minute." He paused, swinging his monocle, frowning absently, pale-blue eyes looking popped and anxious. "I didn't *see* anybody," he said carefully, "but I got a sort of impression that somebody was walking along the driveway as I came through the hedge from the pool and — well, as if whoever it was ducked into the shrubbery. Now understand, I didn't see anybody. I just had a — a notion that somebody was there." His manner was one of exaggerated caution and care as if henceforth, following the detective's reprimand, he intended to stick to the very letter of the truth. It was meant probably to be also exasperating for he still looked sulky. The detective said, "What gave you that notion? A sound, footsteps on the gravel? Someone talking? Or, say, the shrubbery moving as if someone had just passed through the hedge?"

Charlie, still sulky, gave himself a little more time to think than was absolutely necessary. He said then, however, with an effect of honesty, "I really don't know, Captain. I only remember that the thought crossed my mind that — well, it's just as I tell you. I thought someone was around somewhere, but I didn't see anybody." He considered for a moment and reaffirmed it with an energetic nod.

And Marny said suddenly, "I thought that, too. I thought someone was at the opening of the hedge, there near the driveway. I looked twice. But no one was there."

There was, she thought, something a little too sharp and shrewd in the detective's eyes. He said, "So you didn't actually see this mysterious presence either?"

Bill Cameron's hands clinched angrily again around the arms of his chair. She said, feeling her face grow hot, "No. I only remember it because I looked twice. I don't know why. I thought, as a matter of fact, that it was Commander Cameron."

170

"Did you linger at the hedge or did you go straight to the house, Commander?"

"I told you," said Bill Cameron. "I went straight to the house. The houseman answered the bell and let me into the hall. I waited for a minute while he gave my card to Miss Wales, who was, I think, in the dining room. At any rate she came from there. If you mean did I see anyone along the drive, I didn't. But I couldn't have seen anyone, the way the driveway curves and through all that heavy shrubbery. That doesn't mean that nobody was there."

Captain Manson said rather dryly, "I don't like a mysterious intruder whom nobody really sees. Can you swear that somebody was there, Miss Sanderson? Did you actually hear or see anyone after Mr. Ingram went away?"

"No. Except as I told you, I thought someone went along the balcony . . ."

"But that was just as Mrs. Wales was leaving your room and before Cecily Durant came to you," reminded the detective. Bill Cameron stirred restively and said, "Captain, if you don't mind, suppose that was Cecily Durant on her way to Durant, or someone else . . ."

"Who?" said the detective again.

Bill Cameron shrugged. "Anybody." Charlie Ingram appeared to catch some hidden meaning in his voice and turned to look at him sharply and antagonistically. "Do you mean that Cecily herself went to see Judith?" he demanded. "She didn't. For one thing, Judith's room is at the front of the house."

"If Cecily had never visited the Wales house, she couldn't know that."

"Well, it doesn't matter," said Charlie. "Judith would have told me if Cecily had come to her. Judith never keeps anything a secret."

"Except from the police," said Captain Manson again rather dryly. He turned to Marny. "After Mr. Ingram left, you and Durant swam for a while?"

"Yes."

"It was as you left the pool and were approaching the house that you had your — that is — interview with him?"

"Yes," said Marny. Interview! How unreal that moment with Andre seemed and how unimportant. As if it had never touched her life at all. She said, yes, conscious of Charlie's quick and interested regard. And went on. They had come to the house and had gone up the winding stairway to the balcony. She had gone into her room and there had talked for a few moments to Mrs. Wales. Later Cecily had come.

Bill had heard it all before and so had Captain Manson. Charlie listened so hard that his monocle fell out twice. She did not, because Charlie was there, mention Laideau's and Andre's attempt to blackmail her, and neither did Captain Manson. He made, indeed, no comment at all, but turned to Charlie. "Will you give me your story again?" he said.

"Mine! But I told you. I don't know a thing about . . ."

"Begin when you left the swimming pool."

"But you know . . . Oh, all right, all right. I've no objections, I'm sure. Question me all night you like," said Charlie with wounded sarcasm and began. It was very short. He walked along the causeway to Silver Point, went to his house, changed and returned. He saw no one along the way either time, except Edward, the chauffeur, who was reading the paper on the bench in front of the small gate house. He reached the house after Judith, Andre and Commander Cameron were already in the drawing room. Winnie met him in the hall so they entered the room together and Tim Wales came from somewhere . . .

"Somewhere?" queried Captain Manson.

Charlie shrugged. "I don't know where," he said testily. "I wasn't thinking of murder, for God's sake, or suspecting my best friends! Maybe the study. Maybe the dining room. I don't know. Anyway, there he was and I was shaking hands and Judith was introducing Commander Cameron, and Winnie said something about dinner and all at once, *he*" — he shot a sulky glance at Bill Cameron — "hared off through the porch. Disappeared. Marny wasn't down. Judith told me to go after Cameron and tell him dinner was about to be served. So I did. There they were by the bamboos. Girl was dead. That's all."

"How about tonight?"

172

"Tonight? Good God, I don't know a thing about it! If you think I killed Durant . . ."

"Where were you tonight? About eleven?"

Charlie turned bright purple and exploded. "It's none of your business! I didn't murder Durant and I didn't know a thing about it till one of your men phoned me and rousted me out to come down here. Durant deserved murder, but I didn't do it. And I'll raise hell with you for false arrest if you don't let me out of here."

Captain Manson looked singularly unimpressed and a policeman opened the door and stuck his head in. "Captain, this guy Laideau out here wants you to arrest him. Says he had nothing to do with the murder, but if he goes back to Shadow Island he'll be murdered himself!"

CHAPTER XIX

"Bring him in here," said Captain Manson.

Laideau came in, sallow, his great shoulders hunched, looking at no one. And he was either genuinely afraid or he achieved a remarkably convincing pretence of fear. After the first few moments, Marny unwillingly acknowledged that to herself and she thought Bill Cameron did the same. Charlie Ingram, obviously having decided that Laideau and only Laideau could have murdered Cecily Durant and Andre, swung his monocle and listened with an air of haughty disbelief. There was no way of telling what the detective believed, but he questioned Laideau at length, as the minutes of the hot night ticked away.

It was clearly, in many ways, a repetition of former bouts of inquiry. But Marny had not heard Laideau's story in detail; neither, probably, had Bill and Charlie Ingram. She wondered why the detective went over it again so lengthily and concluded it was for the same reason that he had asked her to repeat her own story — in the hope of finding some previously overlooked loophole for inquiry, and because the murder of Andre Durant had given a different slant to the course of that inquiry. Before his murder, the detective had admittedly suspected Andre. His inquiry had been, naturally, directed by that suspicion. Now he must backtrack, repeat, seek again through a maze of facts for someone who could have murdered Cecily and Andre.

But Laideau's story, she thought from something in Captain Manson's attitude, did not vary from his previous story. He had taken Cecily in a rowboat to the island because she had insisted upon going.

"She knew her husband had returned from New York?"

"I told you that. He told me he was coming and I made the mistake of telling her. She insisted on going to see him.

She'd been nervous and hysterical all week. I couldn't do a thing with her. She threatened to come by taxi and make a scene, so I thought it better to take her myself."

"Why did you row across."

Laideau's little eyes shot a quick, ugly look at the detective and lowered swiftly again. He thrust his great hands into the pockets of his soiled white slacks. "No reason. I thought it was a good idea, that's all."

"You didn't do it because you didn't want anyone to know you and she were on the island?"

"I didn't want a public scene. Maybe I thought the row would calm her down. Anyway, that's what I did and I can't change it. I let her off at the pier and I stayed in the boat."

"You didn't come on the island at all?"

"No. I've told you . . ."

"Go on."

It was brief. He had waited for Cecily, but he didn't know how long. He had no watch. It seemed a long time but probably wasn't. She came at last, running down to the pier. She wouldn't answer any of his questions. She got into the boat and they started off away from the island and all at once she said she had to go back. Again she was hysterical and determined, so he took her back. She got out on the pier, and this time instead of waiting near the pier, he rowed out into the bay, toward Miami Beach. "Why?" said Captain Manson and Laideau shrugged. "I didn't want to be in on anything. I was ready to wash my hands of her. I didn't know what she was going to do and I didn't care. I thought I'd done enough for Durant to keep her quiet for the last month or so."

Captain Manson leaned forward. "Why should you keep her quiet for the last month or so?"

But Laideau's eyes were stubborn and impenetrable. "No special reason, except she'd been hard to manage ever since they separated. I stayed at the Villa Nova to be near her. Andre went to another hotel and then was invited to the Wales' island. It seemed a good idea for him to go, we — he was short of money."

"You say you rowed out into the bay?"

"Yes. I told you that at least twenty times. I didn't hear any sound of a shot. I didn't know she had a gun. I suppose it was my gun, for it's gone, as I told you. I did hear an airplane go overhead and it seemed very low and may have been the Navy plane, but I didn't look up. There were several motor boats — I remember that. After a while — it's exactly as I told you — after a while it was getting dark and I thought she'd gone to the house to see Andre and he could see to her. I rowed back to the Beach and had a bite to eat and had just got back to the Villa Nova when you phoned."

Captain Manson said suddenly, "I understand you wish to be arrested? On what charge? Why?"

Laideau got up with the sinuous, slow ease of a feral animal. His little eyes shone in the light. "Because whoever got him is going to get me next. That's why! I don't care what the hell charge you arrest me on. But if you've got any decency you'll put me where I'm safe. I'm afraid of Shadow Island."

Charlie sat forward. Captain Manson said, "Why?"

"I told you."

"Why was Durant killed?"

"I don't know. I don't know anything about it. I was asleep."

"Did he know who murdered his wife?"

There was a slight pause, then Laideau said, "No."

And stuck to it. He knew of no motive for either murder, but he was afraid. He reiterated it, he turned ugly and mean, he refused to return to Shadow Island and said that his refusal alone ought to make them place him under arrest. Eventually Captain Manson sent him away with a policeman.

"But he did it," cried Charlie. "He did it. He's lying! He thinks if he pretends to be afraid it'll go to clear him. He murdered both of them."

"Why?" said Captain Manson. "There's no motive for Laideau to have murdered either of them."

"He's a thug and a cutthroat. . . ."

"That's your opinion, Mr. Ingram," said Captain Manson and got up. "Can you prove it? Now will you all come with me, please?"

They followed him into another room. The policeman with

the notebook went with them, another policeman in the hall unlocked the door of the room into which they were led, and turned on the lights. It was a small bare room with extraordinarily bright lights. Marny was suddenly aware that both policemen had placed their hands in a businesslike way upon the revolvers at their belts. And then she saw why.

Charlie Ingram gave a kind of squeal. Bill Cameron stopped dead still and stared. On the table, brightly lighted, lay a curious small assortment of objects.

One was a revolver. Another was Andre Durant's cigarette case. On a plate was a little horde of half-smoked cigarettes. On another plate lay three brown and withered flowers, hibiscus, broken off short. There was a small, plain gold earring; there was a narrow black ribbon which looked as if it had been twisted and broken.

Charlie recognized the ribbon. He clutched at his monocle and cried, "That's mine! That's like . . . *How did it get there?*"

It matched the ribbon on his monocle. Captain Manson said, "Exhibits. The revolver was found tonight, not in the bay but hidden under some sand along the sandy strip there by the pier. We found it by pouring water over the sandy strip; bubbles came up just there and we dug. The revolver belongs to Laideau; we've checked it."

"*My ribbon . . .*"

"Wait, please. The cigarettes are the brand smoked constantly by Mr. Wales. They are in every room in the house at Shadow Island. But we managed to get one (rather smudged but identifiable) fingerprint which checks with the middle finger of Mr. Wales' right hand. These cigarette ends, three of them, you will note, were found down by the pier, not far from the bamboo hedge. Mr. Wales had already told me that he had not gone to the pier until after Cecily Durant was murdered. The gold earring is one of a pair belonging to Winnie Wales. The other was in her jewel case in her dressing room; it was unlocked, in a drawer. But that earring was found only a few inches from the body of Cecily Durant, under the bamboos. Miss Wales has admitted owning it, but says she had not worn the earrings in several days and does not know how it got there

177

and that she, too, was not at the pier or near it during the time when Cecily Durant must have been murdered. Those withered flowers are hibiscus blossoms and Miss Sanderson is the only one in the household who has admitted to being at the pool and near the hibiscus hedge that night."

"I didn't break off a flower. I never thought of it. . . ."

Bill Cameron interrupted. He said, "I'm the only person not represented here. I — and unless I'm wrong, Judith Wales."

Captain Manson did not reply.

And they were wrong. There was Judith's bloodstained handkerchief, thought Marny. Only Winnie had found that instead of the police, and had destroyed it. Bill said, "False clues? All of them? Planted?"

"I don't know," said the detective.

"But I tell you my ribbon . . ." began Charlie, sweating. The detective said, "It too was found not far from the place where the body lay."

"But I wasn't there till after she was murdered! I swear it! I don't know . . . I can't imagine . . . I often break ribbons . . . I keep a supply of them. They seem to break so easily."

He was twirling his monocle madly. Bill said, "You work them too hard."

"Did you break one anywhere near the pier recently?" asked Captain Manson quickly.

Charlie was again a deep, angry purple. "No! I've not been near . . . Well, anyway, I can't remember. I don't know. But I didn't murder the girl!"

Bill Cameron said quietly, "Which is the true clue, Captain?"

The detective looked at him quickly. It was a brief, oddly communicative glance. Bill added, "Or perhaps there is no true clue. Perhaps it's the absence of a clue. There is nothing there which leads to Mrs. Wales."

Charlie, slower on the uptake, stared, spluttered and cried, "You can't mean that you suspect that Judith did this on purpose! Planted clues to everybody except herself on purpose! To make you suspect everybody — Tim and Laideau and Andre and Winnie and Marny and me and — everybody but

Cameron! Why, it's impossible! It's mad! It's . . ." he stuttered and searched for a word and cried, "It's fiendish!"

"But there was a clue to Judith," said Marny. "A handkerchief with her initial on it. . . ." She told them, quickly, the bright lights beating down upon her face and in her eyes. And told it again, slowly, while the policeman with the notebook and pencil took it down word for word. Captain Manson questioned her. "Where did Miss Wales find it?"

"She wouldn't say."

"You are sure it was a handkerchief belonging to Mrs. Wales?"

"No. But it was initialed with a 'J'."

"Are you sure the stains were blood?"

"Yes. Well, no. I thought it was blood. It could have been anything reddish-brown. It looked like bloodstains."

"Why didn't you tell me this before?"

She explained swiftly. "I didn't think you'd believe me. I had no proof. And it would have sounded as if I had invented it to try to clear myself by implicating Judith. Besides I — I don't think she did it."

"It's hard to believe that anybody could murder," said the detective quietly. "Murder itself is almost incomprehensible. But it happened."

Charlie blustered, "It's all nonsense! Judith didn't kill her or Durant. Somebody's trying to implicate everybody but himself." He glared at Bill Cameron, who grinned a little, unexpectedly and said, "Do you think that makes me the prime suspect, Ingram?"

Captain Manson coughed. "But there *is* a clue. Will you come over here, please?"

Another table stood against the wall. The policeman snapped on a bright drop light above it, disclosing an array of gray, white, irregular shapes.

"Casts," said the detective. "We made a moulage of footprints and marks around Cecily Durant's body as it lay on the grass, just beyond the strip of sand. We did not get anything satisfactory. However, we did get this, Commander." He touched a cast lightly — an irregular, rough-looking surface,

179

with marks made upon it. "If you look closely," said Captain Manson, "you'll find that these marks make a 'C' and an 'A' in capitals and this wavering line following them could be a broken attempt to draw an 'M'. They were obviously made with someone's finger, hurriedly. We measured the distance from Cecily's hand to the strip of sand and she could have reached it. Trying to tell us, before she died, who killed her."

"C — A — M," said Charlie, staring. *"Cameron!"*

"Fortunately," said the detective dryly, "the marks on the sand were not disturbed by the various footprints made around the body before the police arrived. You'll find marks that fit your shoes, there, Mr. Ingram. And yours, Miss Sanderson. And your own, Commander," he added conversationally.

"And part of my name," said Bill, studying the moulage showing the traced letters with a queerly absorbed look in his face. "I've already told you I only saw Cecily when she came down the balcony stairway."

"You did, Commander."

Charlie was beginning to look pleased. "Seems very odd to me that two strangers — Cecily Durant and Commander Cameron — turn up at exactly the same time. Are you sure you didn't know her, somewhere, Commander? In Jamaica, for instance?"

"Very sure," said Bill imperturbably. "For one reason, I've never been in Jamaica and can prove it by the State Department passport record and by my Navy record. I didn't follow that girl to the pier and murder her, Captain."

"Neither did I," snapped Charlie. And Captain Manson sighed. "Durant's name was Charles Andre . . ." he said, and left the sentence unfinished and snapped out the light.

Twenty minutes later they were taken back to Shadow Island. Charlie took Laideau's place in the back seat of the car. Laideau, however, was not arrested. Captain Manson told them. "He had no motive. He had everything to lose and nothing to gain. Good night," said Captain Manson politely, and a policeman escorted them to the car.

So she was not to be arrested either, thought Marny wearily. Not then, at least, and in spite of Captain Manson's statement, when they left Shadow Island, about sending for her things later. But if anything had occurred during those two hours which tended to exonerate her, she did not know what it was.

It was by then nearly three o'clock. There were a few lights along the way home. The air was hot and still. The car lights cut a bright path through the shadows and across the causeway. Bill looked very thoughtful and said nothing. They stopped to let Charlie out at the entrance to Silver Point. Charlie mumbled something which could be taken as a good night and started along the driveway toward his house — as he had done, ages ago, it seemed to Marny, when she and Bill had left him there before dinner.

They passed the lights at the entrance to Shadow Island and policemen again, and this time the front door was open and lighted. They got out. The police car turned and backed and disappeared along the driveway back toward the gate house. The hall was lighted and the drawing room, and two policemen appeared in the drawing-room doorway as Bill and Marny came into the hall. Bill glanced at them. "Any news?"

One shook his head. The other, eyeing them, said, "Captain Manson just telephoned. He said to tell Miss Sanderson to . . ." he glanced up the stairs and came closer, his voice lowered to a hoarse whisper ". . . to be sure to bolt the doors to her bedroom. Both of them. The one leading onto the balcony and the one from the hall."

Bill Cameron's face tightened. "Why?"

The policeman shrugged, but eyed Marny with curiosity. "He didn't say. Told us to stay here tonight. Or what's left of it." He yawned. Bill put his arm around Marny suddenly and turned toward the stairway. They reached the upper hallway, and it was empty, although lights were shining brilliantly there, too. He opened the door to her room, glanced around, and then drew her inside the room. He glanced into the glittering, gay-colored bathroom. He crossed to the balcony, looked out along it, closed the door and bolted it, testing it to be sure it held. He came back to her. "Nobody here," he said.

She was so tired that everything seemed to whirl in a kind of impressionistic chaos around her. Only then did she realize

181

the meaning of his search. "But nobody . . . There's no reason . . . I'm not in danger," she said jerkily. And looked up at Bill Cameron. "Am I?" she whispered.

His eyes held her own for a moment. Then he put both arms around her and held her close against him. Perhaps she turned her head, perhaps he turned it. His mouth met her own and held it and everything else in the world fell away and there was nothing that mattered outside the circle of his arms and the warm, hard pressure of his mouth.

He kissed her and lifted his head and looked down at her. It was a strangely clear and uncomplicated look, as if the problems of earth and the path she had yet to journey upon it were solved and settled forever. Then, his eyes very bright, he bent and kissed her again. It was queer how warm and sweet and tender that tight, Scottish mouth could be. She was bewildered, swept as if by a tide of an emotion that was new and strange yet deeply familiar, as if she had known it for a long time. And as if she wanted only to remain where she was forever.

Bill Cameron lifted his head, looked down into her eyes again and grinned. It changed his whole face. There was nothing guarded and cold about it. He said nothing, however. He put her down in the chair and went to the gaily paneled doors of the wardrobe and opened them, whistling very softly. He came back to her with a nightdress in one hand and her white robe in the other.

"Take these," he said. "Go in the bathroom and get into them. This may shock the whole household but I can't help it. Go on. Hurry. It's practically morning and you look as if you hadn't had any sleep for six months."

"What are you going to do?"

He was pulling the chaise longue so it stood between the bed and the door, whistling again very softly and somehow rather happily. He said, "Stay here, of course."

"But I . . ."

He lifted her out of the chair. "Hurry up. I'm dead tired."

When she came out he was established on the chaise longue and was already (or pretended to be) asleep. She sat on the edge of the bed for a moment. His eyes were firmly closed and he looked very comfortable leaning back against the beige cushions. There was still a suggestion of a grin lurking at the corners of his mouth and she regarded it suspiciously, but he did not move.

She reached up and turned off the bed light. She closed her eyes, thought suddenly and clearly, "Forever? But I've only known known him since yesterday," and sleep caught at her as if it had comforting arms.

When she awoke he was gone and light was streaming into the room. The chaise longue had been pushed back into its original position and the pillows plumped up into round surfaces.

She yawned and shut her eyes and after a while opened them again with a start. This time, fully awake, she looked at the clock. It was noon and the light outside was full and strong and from somewhere came the sound of pounding.

It came, in fact, from everywhere, multiplied and repetitious, as if a number of people were pounding very constantly and very hard.

She sat up and looked around. A white folded paper lay on the rug by the hall door and it was a note from Bill. She'd have known it from something very definite and vigorous about his handwriting, she thought, sitting on the bed and reading the note.

It was very short. "At four-thirty exactly, will you put on a dress of Judith's or Winnie's — long skirt but *not* one of your dresses — and go down to the pier. Be sure nobody sees you. This sounds silly. I don't want to scare you to death, but I don't want you to take any chances either. If you are seen give it up and get back to the house as fast as you can. Bill."

Below was a hasty triple postscript. "Judith says she did not tell Charlie about Cecily and you. Don't go wandering off alone with *anybody*. I don't think I was seen coming from your room this morning. But if so, I might consider making an honest woman of you."

A shadow fell across the rug and pounding began sharply on the balcony immediately outside her room. She realized then what was happening. The windows and all the French doors were being boarded up. Yet the sky remained light and extraordinarily still. There was nothing anywhere to suggest that a hurricane was headed that way.

Where had Bill gone? What was his plan? And if Judith hadn't told Charlie about Cecily coming to her with a revolver in her hand, how did Charlie know it?

She read the note again and lingered over the last sentence. So he might consider making an honest woman of her! And who was it said the Scotch had no sense of humor.

Someone knocked very softly on the door and it was again Winnie. This time, however, she brought no coffee. Her face was flushed and angry. She said, "Are you awake at last? It's almost time for lunch. They're getting the windows boarded up. Marny . . ." She sat down heavily. She wore a neat blue chambray dress and every line of her stocky figure suggested the first Mrs. Wales, but her eyes were exactly like Tim's when he was in a seething rage. "Why did you tell the police about that handkerchief? You promised not to."

"I didn't promise. Besides . . ."

Winnie wouldn't listen. "They've been at me about it this morning. And now they've got Judith in the study questioning her."

"What did you tell them?"

"Tell them!" flashed Winnie. "I told them there was no handkerchief, of course. I told you I'd say that." She got up abruptly. "You'd better get up. What went on at the police station last night? Laideau has disappeared. Did they arrest him? There wasn't anything in the paper."

"I think they let him go. Winnie, that handkerchief . . ."

"I don't think that was very nice of you!" snapped Winnie and went away, closing the door behind her with a bang.

Eventually Marny went down to lunch. She slipped Bill's note under the blotter on the small white writing table before she left her room. Four-thirty and any dress which had a long skirt and did not belong to her.

She was tired and wished she could forget Andre. And the small queer assortment of objects that the police had, without any of them knowing it, gathered up and identified.

And Tim's words. "I'd like to see him hanged," Tim had said. The next night Andre had been hanged. And they had talked of revenge as a motive.

It would have been, in any case, a nightmarish day. The effect was heightened by the boarded-up windows and doors which left the interior of the house so dark that it was more comfortable — but eerie and uncomfortable in its way — to turn on lights. Yet outside it was bright and quiet with not a leaf moving and not a cloud in the sky. The door onto the porch was left open and it was queer to go out on the porch and hear everywhere the sound of pounding. It was so still otherwise that there were faint constant echoes of hammers from across the bay as everyone in Miami and along the Beach prepared for a possible big blow.

It made, however, a topic of conversation if, that is, there was conversation. By the time Marny got downstairs the police had gone and reporters had gone. Tim, again, had dealt with them.

They had lunch in the dining room in an air of unnatural gloom from the candles and the boarded-up windows. And nothing happened. Laideau did not turn up at all and no one seemed to know what had become of him. Bill Cameron did not return. Tim glowered and smoked and read the newspapers or pretended to, sitting on the porch that hot, queerly bright and still afternoon with the water of the bay like molten brass and the sky a pearly roof that seemed to press down rather closely upon them. Judith disappeared for a nap, she said. About three o'clock Charlie Ingram came and borrowed a hammer saying his own had disappeared and he was tired of trying to nail up shutters with a pair of pliers and a brick and went away again. There was some discussion about the advisability of going to a hotel, but Tim vetoed it again. "House has withstood any blow we've had yet," he said. "I don't care what the rest of you do, I'm going to stay here."

"Well," said Winnie, "the storm may turn yet. But I'll have to let the servants go. They all live on the mainland. . . ."

"Let 'em go," snapped Tim behind a paper he had already

read twice. Winnie went away and Tim waited until her footsteps had crossed the dusky drawing room and then looked at Marny. "Where's Bill Cameron?"

"I don't know."

"What happened last night? They took you to the police station."

"Nothing."

He eyed her sharply. "Okay, don't talk if you don't want to. But . . . Look here, Marny, who do they think did it?"

"I don't know." She looked away from Tim's bright, granite-like eyes, boring into her own. There were no boats on the bay that day and the singular brightness of green grass and purple bougainvillaea was even more marked. It must be nearly four-thirty. "I want to telephone," she said. And, passing, put her hand for a moment on Tim's shoulder.

"Thanks, Marny," he said, and cleared his throat. "Thanks . . ."

Where was Bill? And what was he doing? Well, she'd follow the letter of his instructions.

No one was in the hall. She went upstairs and hesitated. How did one go about abstracting another woman's dress? In any case it would have to be a dress of Winnie's as Judith was presumably still in her own room resting. She went to Winnie's door and knocked.

There was no answer so she entered it, very quietly, feeling both guilty and frightened, because of the darkness. Yet others were within call, she told herself. It was silly to let her heart pound like that, hard in her throat.

Others had been within call last night when Andre was killed.

She wouldn't think of that. She glanced around the shadowy room. Furniture loomed up dimly — the bed, light thick shapes that were chairs. For a moment she thought of retreat and rejected it. She went instead to the closet, selected the first long-skirted dress that she discovered, put it over her arm and opened the hall door cautiously again and again finding no one about hurried to her own room.

If anybody saw her going down to the pier at half past four

in a long dinner dress that didn't belong to her, with a hurricane in the all-too immediate offing, they'd arrest her on suspicion alone!

It wasn't going to be as easy as Bill's directions had made it sound, and she'd feel much better if he had told her his reason for asking her to do it.

She got into the dress. It was the dress Winnie had worn the night Cecily was murdered, all soft chiffon ruffles and much too big for Marny. And something was going on outside!

It was something very queer. A kind of stir and movement, a vibration like the approach of a distant army. She started toward the door to look, and it was boarded up. She glanced at the clock and it was nearly four-thirty. She'd better go.

She did not see that the blotter on the writing table was a little askew. She threw a raincoat around her shoulders and hitched up the long blue skirt below it, holding it up with one hand so it would not show below the coat. She went into the hall, and very quietly, pausing to listen and hearing only that great, distant motion and stir on the outside of the house, down the stairs.

The front door was not boarded up. She let herself out cautiously and did not think that anyone saw her, although, as she closed the door, it seemed to her she could hear a telephone ringing sharply inside.

It was still fairly bright but there was no more quiet. Instead, everything about her seemed to have taken on an independent, restless life. A strong, hot wind pressed against her like a hand and then was gone. The green banks along the driveway were murmuring and moving. She hesitated, on the verge of returning. But there was, actually, nothing very portentous about that momentary puff of wind. There was actually nothing very threatening about the way the heavy tropical growth was moving.

She skirted the house closely, got behind the row of bamboos and passed the spot where Cecily had been found and stopped. No one was there. The Casuarinas were waving. There was another strong hot puff of wind which rattled the bamboos. The sky and bay seemed suddenly darker. The two small boats tied at the pier moved up and down and outward and then back, banging against the pier.

She could not see Miami Beach. The waving, tossing Casuarina trees blocked her view. She could not see the house, either. She could hear, though; suddenly and very distinctly from somewhere near came the sound of oarlocks.

She whirled around and stared at the thick moving greens of the Casuarina trees and could see nothing beyond them. She went almost to the edge of the curling, moving gray water, and still could not see through the waving, green trees.

Was Bill in a boat behind the Casuarinas, approaching the island?

Or had someone else written that note?

A hot wind came from nowhere, came from everywhere, caught her and swirled her coat around her, and her hair in her eyes and was like a giant hand, buffeting her, blinding her, confusing her. The bamboos rattled sharply, too sharply, so she twisted around.

Something that looked like a black cloak, like the garments on a scarecrow, was standing there, as if it had body, flapping in the wind. There was no face; there was nothing recognizable and it was moving toward her.

Wind flung itself upon her, blinding her sight, making the flapping invisible. It snatched her breath out of her mouth and stung her face and she tripped in the long chiffon ruffles and fell, clutching at the sand, pushing herself back desperately from the gray, surging water.

CHAPTER XX

A boat bumped loudly against the pier. Wind hurled upon the Casuarina trees. The bamboos rattled like a thousand castanets. She must get away; she must escape the sightless, faceless thing that flapped like a black scarecrow among the bamboos. She got to her knees and was flung down again, and somebody shouted, "Hi, there! Hi, there!"

It was torn and carried off by the wind, but it was a man's voice. Again she struggled to get to her feet and somebody, nearer now, shouted, "Marny . . . !" and hands came under her arms, dragging her upward. It was Charlie Ingram. The wind swept them toward the bamboos. He shouted: "Who was that? Looked like somebody ran! What are you doing out in the storm?"

She caught the words in gusts. Charlie was half-dragging her along, his raincoat flapping madly. She stumbled and caught up the chiffon flounces and stumbled again. She had never dreamed that wind alone could be so strong, could have physical body, could tear at you like that. The bamboos clattered and clashed. The sky was darker. Rain was suddenly slanting straight into their faces. Charlie was panting, pulling her along with him. They reached the porch and the bougainvillaea was rending and tearing at the balcony railing as if it had a destructive, malevolent life of its own. A great wave rose from the bay and crashed against the low sea wall, spilling over it and rushing up across the strip of flat, wet grass almost at their feet. Charlie got the door open and thrust her inside the porch and someone must have seen them coming, for the door into the drawing room was opened. Tim shouted, "Come on, you fools, come on . . ."

They were inside the drawing room. Tim and Charlie both

flung themselves against the door and bolted it. Charlie collapsed into a chair, long legs out, panting, his face wet, glaring at Marny. He tried to speak and couldn't get his breath. Tim shouted, "What were you doing out in the storm? Good God, Marny, you might have been killed!"

The house had come alive as frantically, as madly as the Casuarinas and the bamboos. It wall creaking and banging and trembling. Charlie got his breath. "We're only getting the rim of the hurricane! I can tell by the wind! Rain straight in our faces! It'll blow itself out. . . ." He stopped and stared at Marny. "What were you doing down there by the pier?"

She had to change quickly, before someone saw her in Winnie's dress. Whatever plan Bill had had must have failed. He had not come to the pier at all. Instead that flapping scarecrow figure, half seen in the storm, wholly unrecognizable had come.

Tim's eyes were two bright, granite points; his voice was loud above the crash of the storm. He said roughly, "You'd better get some dry clothes on."

Charlie turned to Tim, mopping his thin hair with a handkerchief, and beginning to shed his long black mackintosh with its shiny, wet cape. "There she was down by the pier. Wind had knocked her over on the sand right at the edge of the water. Another minute and she'd have been in the bay. I was cutting it pretty fine myself. Doesn't usually come so fast. Usually we have some straight, steady wind for a while before the full force of the storm. I got my own boat tied securely and suddenly thought about yours. Knew Edward wouldn't think of it. He's only been around a week or so. So I rowed over. Faster to row than to come by the causeway. And I found her! Had barely time to lash my own boat, and I'm afraid . . ." He tossed his dripping raincoat on the floor and looked less like a gigantic black bird of prey. . . . "I'm afraid yours will get away, Tim. I simply had no choice. Gathered Marny up and dragged her to the house. Got a drink anywhere?"

"Some in the dining room," said Tim.

Either the light or the storm or something made him look different, a much older Tim Wales. Almost a beaten Tim

Wales. Charlie went off toward the dining room, hands thrust in the pockets of his tweed jacket, muttering about winds and hurricanes, and being on the rim of it this time unless it turned around on its tail. ". . . as it's been known to do," said Charlie over his shoulder and vanished. Tim said, eyeing Marny, "What are you doing in that dress?"

She looked down. Blue chiffon ruffles, draggled with rain and sand, hung to the floor, trailing below the raincoat. She snatched it up under the raincoat, mumbled something incoherent and hurried past him and up the stairs. He did not attempt to stop her. She ran up the stairs. The storm had fallen upon the island like a demon bent upon tearing it apart. The tumult drowned the sound of her feet. It drowned the sound of other feet too, for as she opened the door of her room someone cried, "Marny — Marny, stop!"

It was Judith. She came from the gloom of the hall, somewhere, and followed Marny into her room and closed the door and stood with her back against it, looking at Marny, her great dark eyes luminous as a cat's.

A changed Judith, thought Marny suddenly; changed as swiftly and as strangely as Tim had changed. Or was it merely the storm, the horror of the past two days, the eerie effect of artificial lights upon Judith's white face? So it looked ten years older.

A shutter loosened and began to bang savagely against the house.

"Marny, where have you been?"

"At the pier."

"Why?"

Why? Marny thought despairingly that whatever plan Bill had had must have failed. She said, "I wanted to go down to watch the storm." And huddled the raincoat around her. Judith waited a moment, looking at Marny. Looking at her hard and close and long. Did the dress show below the raincoat? Marny didn't dare look to be sure. But that didn't matter, really. Who had been there by the bamboo hedge?

Judith said, "That was rather dangerous, Marny. A storm like this! You could have been swept into the water. Did you see anyone else there?" Judith's eyes were filed and intense like a cat's, too, watching some infinitesimal moving object to see if it was worth snatching. Was Judith's bloodstained handkerchief the one real clue of them all — and ironically the one clue that was not laid out on a table and examined and classified by the police? Had Judith been at the pier, disguised by that flapping cloak, face hidden by hood or cape or whatever it was? And now wanted to make sure whether or not Marny had recognized her? There had been a definite sense of danger, of menace, about that fantastic figure seen so obscurely through the fury of wind and sudden rain.

Bill had said be careful. Go back to the house if anyone sees you.

The detective, Captain Manson, had telephoned and sent a message of warning to her.

Judith said suddenly, "What's wrong, Marny? Why don't you answer me? What has happened? Marny, do you know who murdered Cecily?"

"No — no . . ." She clutched the dress and the raincoat tight around her.

Judith said slowly, "There's something about you — something in your eyes, just now, Marny. Tim didn't do it. He hated Andre. He had no reason to, really. But he wouldn't have murdered him. He wouldn't have murdered Cecily. He didn't even know of Cecily's existence. I asked him and he said no. *I* knew Andre had a wife. He told me. He intended to divorce her. He told me that, too. But nobody else here knew of it. Tim or Winnie or anybody. So you see Tim wouldn't have murdered a woman he never saw before. He hated Andre because he thinks I was in love with him. Tim's got a violent temper. And when he once gets his mind made up you can't change it, no matter how . . ." Judith bit her painted, lovely mouth, and said, ". . . no matter how wrong he is. I . . . Andre was Andre. But Tim — well, never mind about that. The point is Tim didn't even know of Cecily's existence — unless he had investigated Andre."

But he had investigated Andre. Not fully, not thoroughly; there hadn't been time. Yet even if he had discovered the fact of Andre's marriage to Cecily, why would Tim have shot Cecily? Perhaps they were all wrong in assuming that the same person (the person who had been there among the bamboos, watching Marny, waiting for her at the pier?) had murdered both Cecily and Andre. Suppose Andre had murdered Cecily to get rid of her? Suppose Tim, believing that Andre had killed Cecily and that Andre menaced his own life with Judith, had murdered Andre?

He would have considered it justifiable. He would have called it, to himself, a necessary execution. Tim was not the kind of man to hesitate, once his mind was made up. He was not the kind of man to be troubled by conscience. He would have put Andre's murder on the same level as the killing of a rattlesnake.

Judith's watchful eyes seemed to follow Marny's thoughts. She said in a voice that was husky and low and yet violent, as if she had stamped her foot and shouted, "He had the idea that I was in love with Andre. I wasn't. He hated Andre, but he was wrong. And he . . . Oh, Marny, you know him so well. Surely you know that Tim has too much good sense to murder anybody. It's such a — stupid and terrible thing," whispered Judith suddenly, her face blank and white and cold, her eyes bright and observant. ". . . and it doesn't settle anything. Marny, if you do know anything — anything at all — *don't tell the police*."

Marny found the voice that had been lost somewhere, out in the storm, taken away from her by that fantastic, scarecrow figure that started from the bamboos and vanished. And yet had to have a human body and a human will. She said, "Judith, I don't know who murdered Andre — or Cecily. I tell you I don't know."

Judith waited for a moment. That new, strange, older Judith with her hard, strained, white face. The two women stared at each other in silence across the beige-and-white room with the storm lashing and tearing at the balcony outside — along which Cecily's light footsteps had fled and below which Andre had been killed. There was something, though, that Marny must ask Judith. She pushed back her wet hair. "Judith, did you know that Cecily came to see me? The night she was killed? Did you tell Charlie Ingram about it?"

"No," said Judith at once. "Commander Cameron asked me that, too. And the detective — Captain Manson. I didn't know Cecily was on the island. I didn't know she came to see you. Marny, were you in love with Andre, too?"

"Too?" said Marny.

"I mean — women liked him. I wondered about you. You seemed such good friends, somehow. He had a way . . ."

"I was not in love with him."

"But Cecily thought so?"

"I . . . Yes, she thought so."

"He must have told her," said Judith slowly. "He must have told her something. The detective said that she had a revolver and threatened you with it. She told you she wouldn't let you take him from her. The detective asked me if I knew it. But I didn't."

"Charlie Ingram said that you told him."

"Charlie!" An odd look of speculation, mingled with something else less definable came over Judith's face. "Oh," she said. "Oh. Neither of them told me that. I asked the detective but he froze up and wouldn't say. I suppose he thought I was lying. Why did Charlie say that? What did Charlie see? Did he meet Cecily? Did she tell him? Marny . . ."

Judith's voice became rich and coaxing. "Marny, tell me. You were at the police station last night. Everybody knows it. Marny, you *must* know something. Tell me. Do they think I did it?" She tried to smile. It was a travesty of her famous charm.

"I don't know," said Marny. "I don't know what they think." Suddenly the crashing of the hurricane outside, and the sense of cross purposes within the house held there inexorably by the storm was as frightening as the nightmarish, half-seen figure by the bamboos. (Who? Marny thought again, desperately, who? Judith? In a raincoat, face hidden?)

Had Bill really meant her to come to the pier, or was it, she thought again, a trap? But why should she, Marny Sanderson, be in danger?

194

Judith said suddenly, "Marny, Marny, if you've ever been our friend, remember it now." And flung out her hands in a very passion of entreaty and was gone.

Marny stared for a long time at the blank panels of the door, as she had done actually once before. She thought again how long ago that seemed. Judith had come to her and asked about Andre, anxiously, as if she had to know, and then had gone and a small brief shadow had flitted across the door, blocking off the light from the French window for an instant. Now of course there was no light from the boarded-up window.

She'd better remove Winnie's dress. There was no point in replacing it. She'd have to tell Winnie the truth, try to order another dress to take its place. She slipped out of the draggled, pale blue ruffles and hung the dress in her own wardrobe. It was torn and wet where she'd fallen. Why hadn't Bill come? Perhaps he hadn't meant to come? There was no way to guess what his plan had been or how she could have been a part of it.

Unless it wasn't a plan; unless it was a trap; unless Bill himself had not written that note. It was then that she went to the table to reread the note and reconvince herself, and found that it was gone.

She stood again for a long time looking down at the bare space the lifting of the blotter disclosed.

So someone had taken it. Someone had known where she was to be, and when. That person had come, disguised in the flapping cloak and found her there.

Charlie Ingram had saved her life. Unintentionally, arriving just as she'd tripped in the long skirt and fallen, close to the surging, crashing gray water, at the mercy of whoever it was in the bamboos. Unless it had been Charlie himself. He was wearing a shiny, black mackintosh with a flapping cape. He could have entered the house and taken the note — he had actually been there, that afternoon, borrowing a hammer. Saying his own hammer was lost. She hadn't counted the boats at the pier as Charlie all but dragged her to the house. Suppose the bump of a boat against the pier which she had heard had been merely the bump of one of the boats already tied there, surging in and out with the rapidly rising waves.

Yet there was the sound of oarlocks in that hushed, queer lull just before the wind came. And Charlie could have murdered her, easily, so it would look like an accident, sliding her body into the angry water, so near her. Instead he had helped her into the house. No, it couldn't be Charlie.

Unless he had seen the figure in the bamboos — watching. And had been afraid to do what he had planned to do.

That was wrong, too. Charlie couldn't be two persons!

Besides, there was no reason for anyone to murder her. And of course there had been, really, no attack upon her. No weapon. No shot. No hands at her throat; nothing that was physical and threatening. There had been only the strong, instinctive sense of danger.

It was still so strong that she looked at the door behind her and thought of the detective's warning and of Bill Cameron's warning. She'd get dressed quickly and go downstairs. She couldn't stay there, listening to the storm as it lashed the water of the bay, and the house and palms and everything that grew.

She snatched a dress from the wardrobe, a tailored, cream-colored dress with a red leather belt, and slid quickly into it. She brushed her hair — listening to the storm, listening, in spite of herself, for footsteps outside her room. The storm itself seemed suddenly to inhabit the house, to change it, to make it a place of shadows, of menace, of strangely frank and direct threat. She pushed her dark hair into shape. She changed her stockings and slid her feet into the red alligator pumps that went with the dress, choosing them automatically. She powdered and put on lipstick — automatically, too, but with a kind of defiance.

But where was Bill? Why had he asked her to do a thing that had proved to be so dangerous? For the danger was there. She knew it as an animal knows when a twig snaps at night below the pressure of a feral footstep. Who had been there by the bamboos? Who had known she was to be at the pier, except Bill?

Suddenly and very horribly it occurred to her that perhaps, for all their talk of motives, there was, really, no motive for the murder of Cecily and of Andre. That happened sometimes, didn't it? Something broke, some law of human behavior worn thin and the shred snapped and all at once there was murder. It could happen to people one knew. It did happen.

Tim — Judith — Winnie — Charlie — herself and Laideau.

But Laideau was out of it. The detective had said so. Laideau had no motive and, besides, Laideau was not on the island when the storm began.

She'd better go down and stay with the others. She was only working herself up to a thoroughgoing case of hysteria, standing in that room, staring at the scrubbed place on the beige rug.

In all the grisly array in the brightly lighted room across from Captain Manson's office, there had been no weapon other than Laideau's revolver. What, then, had dragged across the carpet, leaving that ugly small stain?

Blackmail, the detective had said, or revenge.

Or perhaps, Marny thought again, murder for the sake of murder.

She caught a glimpse of her own face in the mirror. Her eyes looked enormous and had faint blue shadows under them. Her face was white and her mouth looked very red by contrast.

She went downstairs, determinedly. And Tim had news for her. He was still in the drawing room and Winnie was making tea at the little table by the door. Judith was nowhere to be seen and Charlie was prowling between the porch door and the tea table, restless as a tiger, munching sandwiches between journeys.

"Oh, Marny," said Tim. "I forgot to tell you. Bill phoned. Oh, some time ago. Wanted to talk to you. I called you but you were gone. You must have just gone down to the pier."

"Down to the pier!" said Winnie sharply. "In the storm? What for?"

"She'd never have got back if I hadn't come along," said Charlie. "Damn fool thing if I ever saw one! When it storms we stay inside. Weather it out." He listened. "I say, old chap, that sounded like a tree down."

"Captain Manson phoned too," said Tim. "Told us we

could go to a hotel if we wanted to. I said we'd stay right here."

"This isn't a bad blow," said Winnie. "we're getting only the fringe of it. Tea, Father?"

Judith came in from the hall and with her a great sweep of wind that set the tea things rattling and the rugs moving on the floor. She had changed to one of the dramatic, long house gowns she liked, and the wind caught her long green skirt and swirled it close to her body. She whirled around. There was a loud bang from the hall, and she cried, "Bill Cameron! How did you get here?"

The rugs settled down. The lace cloth on the tea table fell in straight delicate folds. Judith swirled around again, her lovely body outlined in the vivid green of her dress. She cried, "Here's the Navy! Arriving in a car!" She smiled gaily and pulled her wide, gilt belt close around her small waist. She touched her dark hair. She looked beautiful and poised and smiling — and below it was a different Judith. She said, in a pretence of her usual lightness which was too bright and sharp and false, so that Marny thought everyone must know it, "Nothing can hold back our Navy. Nor rain nor wind nor hurricane . . . Come on in, Bill. You're just in time for tea."

Bill Cameron appeared in the doorway, cap in hand, raincoat shining with moisture, eyes very bright and dark, glancing swiftly around the room until he saw Marny. Relief flashed so strongly and instantly in his face that it seemed impossible for the others not to see it. He cried, "Marny . . ." and stopped and Charlie Ingram broke in, "Don't you have sense enough to stay out of the storm? How'd you get here? I thought the causeway was under water by now. Radio says there've been several tidal waves. Small, but they always affect the bay and shut us off. . . ."

"Take off your coat, Bill," said Tim. "Have a drink?"

Bill Cameron took off his glistening raincoat. He did not explain how he had reached the island and everyone seemed to accept Charlie's explanation. He said, "I thought you'd all have gone to a hotel by now."

"Oh, it's safe," said Judith and went to a deep chair and lighted a cigarette, looking old and haggard and keeping up a pretense of not being afraid, making all her graceful little gestures like a woman in a play. She smiled at Bill and at Charlie and said, "Charlie, darling, give me some tea."

Bill Cameron said, "I thought you'd better know . . ." and stopped.

Tim got up slowly, without his usual bounce and energy. His face was no longer rosy and round like a child's. It was gray and sagging, and his eyes held fear probably for the first time in all of Tim Wales' brilliant, successful, daring career. He took a long breath. He said, "Know what?"

Bill glanced at him and quite suddenly went to him and put a hand on his arm. "Laideau has escaped," he said quickly. "Nobody knows where he is. The policeman assigned to guard him was found slugged. So far they haven't traced Laideau. I thought you'd better know," he said again.

The loosened shutter somewhere upstairs banged loudly.

CHAPTER XXI

Laideau? Below that flapping, scarecrow shape? Laideau with his great shoulders and gleaming thick black hair and crafty yellow face? Laideau, whose great hands could choke out a life as quickly as they could fire a gun. Or strike in the darkness and loop a rope around a man's neck. Had it been Laideau beside the rattling, frantic bamboos?

Tim said, "*Laideau!* That's bad! He did it. Why didn't they arrest him? This — why, this proves it! Escape . . . It's a dead giveaway! An admission of guilt!"

For a moment no one spoke. Then Bill took his hand away from Tim's arm. Tim sat down and lighted another cigarette. Bill said, "I'll have tea, thanks," and took the cup from Winnie. He added coolly, "Marny, will you get me the letter I asked you to keep for me?"

It was a cheerful, perfectly open and unabashed excuse to talk to her alone. Everyone probably was aware of it. Marny got up and set down her cup with such unsteady fingers that it rattled things upon the table. "I'll get it," she said unevenly. "It's — upstairs."

No one spoke as she went out into the hall and everyone watched. Again the loosened shutter banged. Almost as if Laideau himself had pushed it against the wall to remind them of his presence. Or as if murder had taken unto itself physical sound and being and chose to warn them of its presence. Bill followed her briskly into the wide hall, took her hand and drew her across to the tiny white and coral study. It was dark and he groped for the light switch, glanced swiftly around the small, obviously empty room and then closed the door.

He had brought his tea and plate of sandwiches with him. He sat down then and began to eat hungrily. "First thing I've had to eat today, he said. "Now then. What happened? You're all right? I was scared. I tried to reach you by phone to tell you not to go down to the pier and Tim answered and couldn't find you. Said he'd give you the message. I told him to get hold of you, but fast. Apparently he didn't do it." He put down the cup, leaned across and took her hand and touched its finger tips gently, looking at them as if to be sure she was really there. "I was scared," he said again.

She swallowed hard. Tim? In the bamboos, disguised so completely yet so easily?

He went on (touching her finger tips one by one very gently, his black head lowered, his big, green-clad body looking extraordinarily solid and normal so she wanted to move closer to him, to be within that radius of the ordinary, the safe), "You see, I thought I'd find out something. For one thing I wanted to know just how much the young ensign had really seen. I had a wild idea that — oh, well, anyway, the plan failed. I saw the ensign and talked to him, and saw his commanding officer and finally talked them into letting us fly over the island again, at about the same speed and altitude of his flight over it the night Cecily was murdered. Everything was set; and then the storm didn't veer around as they thought it might, but came straight upon us and we couldn't take the plane up in the face of it. They wouldn't let us. Bad timing on my part. But it took some time, you see, to get the red tape undone. I suppose it was a silly plan. I dreamed it up last night while you . . ." He glanced at her then, with a flicker of something that wasn't laughter in his eyes, that was nothing she could identify, and yet was like some small electric spark leaping out to touch her. He said, ". . . while you weren't dreaming at all. At least you didn't so much as move all night. Or what was left of it." She didn't say anything and he added, sharply, "You did get my note?"

"Yes."

"Marny, what happened?" He got up, alarm now in his face. "You look . . . Something happened. Tell me exactly. Everything."

She told him quickly, in a low voice, for he went once to

open the door and glance quickly into the hall. "Nobody there," he said tersely. "Go on . . ."

His face grew white under its tan as she did so.

"Who was it?"

"I don't know. There was only that black, flapping shadow. I couldn't see any face. I couldn't recognize anything. I ran and stumbled and Charlie came then. It must have been Charlie in the boat."

Vines struggled and rattled against the boards outside the window like malevolent hands, trying to force their way in.

He said, stiffly, his mouth rigid, his eyes bright and hard, "Was it Laideau?"

"I don't know."

"You say the note was gone. Anybody in the house could have taken it. No one was at the gate when I came just now."

"I think they let the servants go to the mainland."

He got up and paced up and down the study. "Could it actually have been Charlie Ingram?"

She told him, "I think it was Charlie in the boat. I heard the sound of oarlocks. But then the wind came. I don't know who it was."

Bill Cameron put his hand on her suddenly as if he had to touch her, as if he had to make sure that she was there. "I was a fool. I didn't think it would be dangerous. I was full of what I thought was a bright idea. It turned out to be a dud. Look here, could Laideau be anywhere in the house?"

She thought swiftly of the loosened shutter. Or was it a shutter? Was it actually a door somewhere that had been opened, the sound of its opening drowned in the hurly-burly of the storm?

"There's something that sounds like a loosened shutter. The windows have been boarded up. . . ."

"I'm going to search the house, but first . . . Look here, Marny, I've got a funny idea. It — well, it was something — I don't know what exactly, but something that struck me wrong. It happened the night Cecily was murdered. It was some sort of inconsistency. Funny. Small. Didn't seem important at the time. But it was wrong somehow. And I can't . . .

I know this sounds dopey, but I can't remember what it was. Except it's been bothering me. As if I'd overlooked something important. As if I'd forgotten . . ."

She thought back past what seemed ages of time to the night of tropical warmth and stillness when Cecily had been murdered. His dark eyes sought urgently into her own. "Can't you think of anything? Something that struck you even faintly as being — well, wrong. Surprising, somehow, in a funny, small way?"

She shook her head wearily. Cecily dead in the starlight. And then they had come back to the house.

He said slowly, frowning, sitting on the arm of a white chair opposite her and staring down at his brown hands, turning the class ring on his finger absently, "I suppose it all comes back to motive, really. Revenge, or to stop blackmail. That's what Laideau pretended to be afraid of. His theme song was obviously that Andre had been killed by Cecily's murderer and he was afraid whoever did it would kill him too, because Laideau was in cahoots with Andre Durant, because Laideau was Durant's muscle man. Because whoever it was decided he wouldn't be blackmailed and he'd have to murder Durant to keep from being blackmailed for the rest of his life. And thus, theoretically, would have to murder Laideau, too, because Laideau would know who did it. It's a good theory, but the catch is that if Laideau is the murderer he's lying and if he isn't he doesn't know who killed Durant and who it was they attempted to blackmail, for he'd tell it to save his own skin."

But if Laideau had escaped, he could manage somehow to get into the house. There were a dozen ways to do that, with the bedroom doors opening onto the balcony, with its irregular levels and bewildering steps and halls. Again it seemed to her that the house itself felt dangerous.

And Laideau knew the house. He had stayed there a night — a horrible night, when Andre Durant had been murdered. If he had escaped the police guard he could have returned; he could have read the note from Bill; he could have followed her down to the pier.

"Why would Laideau threaten me? If it was Laideau at the pier?"

"Was it Laideau?"

"I don't know. I only saw the black thing, flapping, looking like a scarecrow, watching me . . ."

"Watching you!" cried Bill suddenly. He stood up quickly. "But that's it! Watching you. Wanting to know why you'd gone there. Why I asked you to go to the pier. Why you were wearing somebody else's dress and not your own. It isn't anything you actually know — it's what the murderer *thinks* you know that makes it dangerous for you. When I talked to Manson I asked him why he'd warned you about taking risks. He said it was only on principle. He said protecting witnesses was one of the hardest jobs a policeman had. But he said, too, that the smear of blood on the rug in your room could be another false clue. He said it was too obvious, like the other clues scattered around. He said — well, he said he didn't want another murder that might be arranged to look like suicide. And — well, confession," said Bill. "I think he believes that your finding Andre was a plant. As I do. On that basis there have been more attempts to implicate you than anyone else. And on any basis, he wants to keep all of us alive! But, Marny, think hard. Is there anything that you know? Something that could make you a potential threat to the murderer? To anybody? Tim — Judith — Winnie — Laideau — Charlie Ingram. Think, Marny."

But there wasn't anything. A medley of small facts, many of them, and nothing that was really important. The storm hurled upon the house, shaking it, rattling doors, thrusting frantically against the boarded-up windows.

"Tell me again how the thing you called a scarecrow looked. Exactly."

There was nothing to describe, a bodiless, faceless, flapping black thing. She told him again, as nearly as she could.

"All right," said Bill. "Wait . . ."

He went out and closed the door behind him. The little study was brightly lighted, white and coral, made for pleasant normal living. It seemed just then frighteningly empty and lonely. And because of the uproar of the storm, because of the wide hall and stairway between it and the drawing room, it seemed shut off and remote from the rest of the house. Nothing could happen. Even if Laideau were on the island, crouching under the swaying, frantic shubbery, making his way into the house, even Laideau would not attempt to murder her with four other people across the hall. Within the sound of her voice.

Except, of course, no one could hear her voice through the tumult of the storm. The wind was increasing in violence. The loosened shutter somewhere in the house banged and banged again.

Suppose Laideau had loosened it; suppose he had crept back into the house, with his great arms and hands and little ugly eyes. Creeping from one gloomy unlighted room to another. Waiting.

The only thing she knew that was incriminating to anybody actually was Tim's threat to Andre. "I'd like to see him hanged." But why would Tim have murdered Cecily?

The storm was a live thing, seeking to tear down, ravage, destroy. The vines beat against the window so furiously that she did not hear the door open.

But she did sense a presence or a motion. She whirled around and would have screamed, but her throat wouldn't let a sound break through. And the man standing there, in a black raincoat with a cape and a black thing like a mask on his face, whipped off the black mask and cried, "Marny, Marny, I didn't mean to frighten you! I only wanted to show you what I'd found. To see if it was the same. Forgive me, Marny. . . ."

It was Bill. He slid out of the raincoat and ran to her. Her knees were shaking and weak. She sank down into a chair. He cried, "I'm a fool! I only meant . . . Marny, forgive me! I have no sense! I . . ."

He was holding both her hands. The black mackintosh lay in a heap on the floor. She stared at the black cloth he had tied across his face like a mask. It was a large black chiffon handkerchief. He said, "I found these things in the hall closet. Anybody in the house could have worn them. It doesn't mean that anybody did wear them. I still think it's queer that Charlie

Ingram turned up, just then."

She said, whispering, "Let me see the handkerchief."

He held it toward her. It was very large with a lace "J," beautifully worked in the corner. She let it fall from her hand. Judith. With her suddenly ravaged, old-looking face, Judith.

Bill said again, "Marny, I am a fool. I never meant to . . . I only wanted to know if this mackintosh and the scarf tied around my face looked at all like whoever it was who followed you to the pier."

"Yes . . ."

"Then it means that it was somebody in the house. Somebody who had access to these things. That — or Charlie. What did he do when he came into the house with you? Did he stay right there in the drawing room, or did he leave it?"

"He left. He went into the dining room. At least I suppose he went to the dining room. He said he wanted a drink and Tim said to go to the dining room."

"Then it could have been Charlie. These black mackintoshes aren't unusual. He's got one; I saw it. Here's another. It doesn't seem to be wet, but it was hanging there in the closet. I suppose there'd have been time for it to dry. Or perhaps if someone really did wear it, whoever it was could have got to the house, just as the rain began."

"It began to rain as we went toward the house. Bill, it couldn't have been Tim."

"Who said it was?" said Bill promptly, but he eyed her rather searchingly. He said, "Why exactly did you say that?"

"Bill, suppose it is somebody we know and like."

"Suppose it is," said Bill. "You must have thought of that before now. Andre was tied up with all of them. I spent part of the day talking to Manson. He seems to be concentrating on motive and clues to Cecily's murder. He has so many clues, you see. There's a clue to Andre — his cigarette case. There are those hibiscus blossoms and you are the only person, except Andre and me, who was near the hibiscus hedge. Unless Cecily herself was there, and I don't think she'd have been picking flowers, not if she was in the state she obviously was in when she came to your room. Unless . . ." A sudden thought seemed to strike him. He stopped for a moment, frowning, thinking, and said slowly, "Unless she did come along the driveway. Unless she was the person you felt was there — felt it so strongly that you looked. If she was there . . ." Excitement came into his face. "Marny, don't you see? That could explain her coming to you. Suppose she saw you with Andre. Suppose she saw him make a fervent sort of pass at you. Suppose she loitered there and watched and pulled the flowers in case somebody was watching, for an excuse, anything to explain her standing around, watching. Suppose that's why she came to *you*. It's been bothering me, that. She had to have *some* reason to come to you. She wouldn't be likely to pull a gun on somebody — just anybody — without thinking that it was the woman Andre was in love with. Suppose she saw you and Andre; suppose she leaped to conclusions. He'd been separated from her, and obviously, some time, either that night after you and he went to the house, or before his trip to New York, he'd told her he was through with her. She saw you and Andre in a — a clinch," said Bill. "You went to the house together. She followed you. She watched — there's plenty of shrubbery around there and she could have seen both of you go along the balcony without your being aware of her. That's how she could have found your room. That bothered me, too. How would she select *your* room when she didn't even know the house, when she'd never been there before?"

"It could have been Cecily, going along the balcony. I came up to my room and left Andre there at the door. Judith came into my room and we talked for a few moments. Then there was a sort of shadow, as if someone had walked along the balcony. Yes, it could have been Cecily. . . ."

"That's when she talked to Andre! She followed him, talked to him. He was brutal with her; he would be. She came back and had seen you go into that room. But she . . ." He stopped, with a queer, inward look of intense thought. "I still think that she thought you were Judith. Tim's a very rich man and everybody knows it. Judith could have got money from him either by way of divorce from Tim and marriage to Andre. Or, if Andre could work it, and he probably could have, he may have intended, some way, to blackmail Judith. And then there's Winnie. Maybe he wanted to marry her. In any case, he was through with Cecily. He'd used her money. She was a stone around his neck. He intended to get rid of her, in any way he could."

"I'm the bread-and-butter type," Winnie had said. Marny said slowly, "But Winnie . . . I don't know . . . She's not . . ." she hesitated. "She's just not the type to . . ."

". . . to say 'all for love and the world well lost'? You don't know a thing about it. I don't suppose she's had much masculine attention. She's not like Judith and you!" His brown face with its square Scottish features had a flicker of brief amusement. "There are some women," he said unexpectedly, "who if they were in the bottom of a well, would still have some hapless male rallying around trying to get them out. Not Winnie. But if Andre was making a play for her she'd take it hard." The flicker of amusement left his face. He added somberly: "They found her earring near Cecily's body."

"If Winnie was in love with Andre she wouldn't murder him!"

Bill stared at the rug. Another furious onslaught of wind and rain surged upon the house. He said slowly, "Neither would Judith, if it came to that. If she were actually in love with Andre and wanted him. That's the flaw."

Someone knocked hard at the door and opened it. Charlie Ingram adjusted his monocle, peered in at them, said, "I say, may I come in?" and did so. Promptly, so it had a surreptitious effect of ducking out of sight in case anyone was in the hall. "Thought I saw you come in here, old chap!" His popped eyes shot nervously around the room, rested for a second on the mackintosh, and came back to Bill. "I . . . Well, you know, old chap! Honest confession and all that. I . . ." He gulped and said, "I was here last night. When you got home from dinner. Lights of the car caught me. I ducked into the shrubbery. You came after me. I sneaked around the hedge, across behind the tennis court, got to the pier and into my boat. I'd rowed over. But it was me you chased. Er — sorry, and all that. Wouldn't do to admit it to the police, you know. Don't like murder."

"*You* were here?" demanded Bill.

Charlie nodded.

"Why?"

"Well, didn't want to tell. But I . . . Fact is, I lost my hammer. I discovered it was gone last night. Couldn't sleep, you know. Knew I'd have to board up the house first thing this morning. So I went out to the little tool house to get things in shape. I'm an orderly fellow, you know, old bachelor. Hah!" He started to laugh, broke off abruptly, stared at Bill and said, "I got worried. Came over here. Intended to look for it in the garage. They keep their tools there."

"Why were you worried?"

Charlie blinked rapidly. "Just — just worried."

"Why?"

"Well, damn it all!" exploded Charlie. "Girl had been murdered. My hammer gone. Don't keep servants myself; do my own chores; keeps me in shape. Knew I hadn't lost it. Somebody had to take it. Hammers can't walk. Shadow Island nearest place. And — well, girl *had* been murdered. Didn't want my hammer to be found here."

"But Cecily was shot."

"Well, hell's bells," shouted Charlie, "how'd I know what might happen? Besides, I wanted my hammer. So I came to see if it was here."

"Why did you run from me?"

Charlie glared. "Because I knew just how this would sound," he snapped. "You don't believe it. You wouldn't have believed it then. But it's the truth."

"Did you find your hammer?"

"*No!* It's still gone. I borrowed one this afternoon but didn't see mine anywhere. It's my private opinion that Durant was knocked senseless with it. Easy thing to do. And my hammer's at the bottom of the bay. It could have been taken any time yesterday."

"Police were at the gate — police were at the pier. Nobody could have gone to your place without being seen."

Charlie blinked again, paused, sniffed angrily and said,

"Well, maybe. I didn't think of that. But that's why I was here. And now I've thought it over I'm going to tell Manson. Thought I ought to tell you, too. Didn't expect any thanks for it. Besides" — he paused, gave a sort of angry gurgle, said furiously — "besides, I've lost a gun. A revolver. Mine." He turned hurriedly to the door and left, banging it behind him.

After a long pause, Bill said slowly, "It sounds true. Muddled and scared and afraid of getting mixed up in any possible way in trouble. But is it true? Just how far do you think Charlie Ingram's devotion to Judith would carry him? I mean, well, suppose Andre was blackmailing Judith and she told Charlie. Do you think he'd drop the old-school tie, English-gentleman-in-the-tropics manner, and kill him?"

"I don't know. . . . Oh, Bill, I don't know."

"There's that clue to him. His monocle ribbon. There's a clue to everybody. Winnie's earring. Judith's handkerchief, which misfired because Winnie and not the police found it. The cigarettes with Tim's fingerprint on one of them. I've never seen him without a cigarette in his hand. He smokes without knowing that he's doing it. He'd leave cigarette ends strewn and never know it. But on the other hand they could have been planted. Even Andre's cigarette case could have been planted. The hibiscus which, if Cecily didn't pick them as she might have done, suggested you because you had been in the pool, you had gone through the hibiscus hedge twice. Anybody in the house might have known it. Laideau's revolver. The cast of the letters scrawled in the sand . . ." Bill broke off suddenly.

He looked at her, straight and hard and long and didn't apparently see her at all. He took a quick breath. His face was hard and suddenly rather grim. As if all at once, inwardly, he had conceived and passed a dreadful judgment. He looked at her and thought and the wind hurled against the house, and Bill said suddenly, "I'm going to search the house. I believe Laideau is here. I believe . . . Marny, stay here, I'll be back. . . ."

He turned swiftly, gathering up the black mackintosh and Judith's chiffon handkerchief. He glanced into the hall and apparently no one was there, for he went quickly out the door, the mackintosh and the chiffon handkerchief over his arm. He closed it behind him.

But if Charlie had killed Andre, he wouldn't have called attention to it like that, would he? Unless — unless the hammer was not, as he said, in the bay but actually somewhere on Shadow Island. Unless he knew it would be found and identified. Unless he wanted to cover himself before that discovery. Suppose out of all those clues the one real clue was the ribbon of Charlie's monocle; suppose it had been actually Charlie down at the pier with Cecily. He had worn a white dinner jacket, she remembered suddenly and sharply. Suppose the young ensign, looking down (so briefly, from so far above) had taken it to be a white dress!

Suppose Cecily had threatened Judith as she had threatened Marny. Judith had said that Andre was in her room during the time when Cecily was murdered and Andre had agreed. But he would have been quick to see the value of the alibi Judith had offered, and to take advantage of it. Suppose actually Cecily had come to Judith and Judith had turned to Charlie for help, relying on his affection for her. He could have, actually, arrived early and followed Cecily to the pier and struggled with her and taken the gun from her. And shot her with it just at the time when one of the outboard motors went past. Suppose Cecily's childish, thin white hand had snatched at him — and broken that ribbon. And it, amid all the false clues, was the real one that Charlie couldn't find; that he had to cover by hurriedly arranging others.

There was the time element to reckon with. There had to be some time for him to arrange the false clues. But, later, publicly grasping at the alibi Judith had given him, Andre had privately attempted to blackmail Judith or Charlie!

Had it been Judith on the balcony, listening, tiptoeing into Marny's room while Charlie made his escape through the shrubbery? And now, losing his nerve, tried to cover it? (Nobody apparently had remembered his white dinner jacket!)

Bill was returning already. The door was opening. He was wearing the mackintosh again and the black chiffon handkerchief across his face, and he slid silently into the room. Only it wasn't, this time, Bill Cameron!

The storm rose and screamed and tore at the house and everything in it. If she had screamed with all the force in her body no one could have heard it over the frantic wind and rain.

The shiny, caped, black mackintosh came forward, not flapping this time but quite slowly and purposefully.

CHAPTER XXII

She hadn't known that she could struggle like that. She hadn't known that she could writhe and fight and duck and squirm away from those queerly powerful arms. She hadn't known she had such strength. She hadn't known the desperate fighting courage of the cornered human animal.

She had no breath in her lungs and her hair was torn over her face and she screamed, gasping, for help and the wind and the rain and the surging, rattling house itself drowned her screams and she fought and struggled and writhed herself away and snatched a chair for a weapon only to have it wrested away from her.

She knew who it was, instinctively, by primitive, certain and horrible recognition before the shiny black cape slipped, disclosing Winnie's neat brown hair, before the chiffon handkerchief came down showing Winnie's set, blue-white face, her lipsticked mouth drawn back from her regular white teeth, her eyes bright and granite-hard like Tim's, fighting. Her arms and hands were incredibly strong — tennis and golf and swimming had done that. She was wily, determined, fighting physically as hard as Tim Wales had ever fought with his brain. Fighting for her life. She slid out of the entangling, hampering mackintosh. There were gloves on those strong, athletic hands, and she had a revolver.

"Winnie, that's a revolver! Don't . . ."

"It's Charlie's."

"They'll hear you — they're right across the hall — they'll know you did it!"

Winnie was matter-of-fact and certain. "Charlie and Father have gone out to see what damage the storm is doing to the pier. Nobody will hear. The storm's too loud."

"Winnie, you can't . . ."

"I've got to," said Winnie. And jerked the small chair out of Marny's grasp. She caught one of Marny's hands and was reaching for the other.

"You had my blue dress. I saw you. I read the letter."

"But I didn't think it was you . . ."

Winnie said, "You know now. It's my life or yours. That was the way it was with Cecily. She threatened me. She had a gun. I had to take it away from her. I didn't mean to kill her. Then it was too late."

Marny groped desperately for some weapon on the desk — a paperweight, a book, anything; there was nothing. The door was locked. She screamed and the storm was so furious and loud that the scream could scarcely have been heard on the other side of the door. There was no hatred in Winnie's face. Only her eyes blazed, like Tim's. She got Marny's free hand and dragged it down and suddenly had both her wrists, gripped in one gloved hand. "Tell me one thing," said Winnie, holding her, helpless and panting and weak from that struggle. "Does Bill Cameron know the truth?"

"Yes," said Bill Cameron in the doorway.

Winnie jerked around but held tight to Marny. Marny, straining against Winnie, felt something cold and hard against her temple.

"All right," said Winnie, "you asked for this. If you call for help I'll shoot to kill. . . . Close the door behind you."

Winnie's hold did not relax. If anything, it was tighter. The revolver pressed against Marny's temple was cold and hard. Bill came inside the room and closed the door.

The loosened shutter banged. Wind tore at the island madly. Bill said, not moving, only looking at Winnie, "You went to get flowers for the dinner table. You met Cecily when she returned. She'd realized that it was not Marny Andre meant to marry, but you. You talked to Cecily. You prevailed upon her to go back down to the pier. And there in a last burst of hysteria she turned the revolver on you. You took it away from her and she fell. You were stronger — so much stronger. The ensign, flying over the island, saw that much. He thought your dress was white; in the dusk it looked white — you were actually wearing light blue. You had the revolver in your hand and you shot her. In self-defense, I think. I think, really, you were afraid. And then — Andre decided to blackmail you. He knew somehow that you had killed her."

"He guessed," said Winnie suddenly. "I had to . . ."

Bill said very softly. "Now is your chance. Nobody's in the kitchen or the dining room. You can go that way."

It was queer, thought Marny numbly, that he was so kind. His voice was almost gentle. It was queer because it was as if he felt sorry for Winnie, who had killed Cecily and then, somehow, killed Andre. Who would kill her if Bill made a move to save her.

Bill's eyes were brilliant in a face that looked queer and rigid and gray. He said again, "You'd better go. I've just talked to Manson over the phone."

Winnie's tight, hard grip did not relax nor the cold pressure of the revolver. She said, in a matter-of-fact voice that was as queer, really, as Bill's gentleness, "What does Manson know?"

"He knows that the flowers under Cecily and your earrings were the real clues in all the false ones. You dropped those. He knows the flower bowl on the dining-room table was empty. I saw it and Marny saw it. You came to the dining room and found us there. You knew we had seen that. Yet you were known to have gone to get flowers and arrange them on the table. Cecily was at the swimming pool, yes; but she wasn't picking flowers. You were the one who got the flowers. You had them, when you killed her; you picked them, not Cecily. The flowers led straight to you. You can shoot Marny and me, too; there's nothing to stop you. But it's too late. It's no good. It's all washed up. It has been, for you, since Durant, without even telling Laideau, tried to blackmail you. After that you didn't care. I wish," said Bill honestly and bitterly, "that I'd killed Durant myself."

"Yes," said Winnie suddenly. "Yes."

She released Marny's hands. She picked up the mackintosh. Bill did not move. Winnie said, "It's all washed up. That's right. I didn't mean to kill Cecily. The gun — went off. I had

215

one of Judith's handkerchiefs — that was an accident. The maid had made a mistake and put it among mine. I tried to stop the bleeding. Then it was too late. I buried the revolver. It's queer, but I — I didn't think about throwing it in the bay. So near. I ran to the house and I thought — so fast. I had wiped off the revolver. I remembered that. I got upstairs and no one saw me. Judith and Andre were in her room. My" — her voice changed, became rough and uneven — "my father was in his room. And then I looked in the mirror and I'd lost an earring. And all at once I remembered it had slid off, down into the grass, as I struggled with Cecily. The police would find it. If I went back I might be able to find it, but if I couldn't they would later. And there wasn't much time and it was getting dark and suppose I couldn't find it. So I . . . It was then I thought of other clues. I thought, I'll place clues, lots of them, so they'll suspect everybody. I thought quickly. There was the broken ribbon from Charlie's monocle. I remembered that. I'd shoved it into a drawer of the hall table, days ago. I had Judith's handkerchief; I intended to leave that beside Cecily. Nobody would suspect my father; he didn't even know Cecily; so I gathered up some cigarette ends quickly as I passed the ash tray in the hall; I came down at once, you see. I didn't know the revolver belonged to Laideau. I didn't know he was there. Oh, yes, and Andre's cigarette case. He was safe, too, even if I left a clue to him because I knew he was with Judith. I knew he had an alibi. But if I left enough clues, you see, then everybody would be suspected. Andre's case was on the table in the hall too, beside the ash tray. There was nothing I could get that belonged to Marny. And I knew she must be in her room, dressing. I had to hurry — there was so little time."

She took an uneven breath. "I ran back to the pier, on the other side of the bamboos so nobody could see me from the house. I tried to find the earring but I couldn't. . . . I couldn't stand it! Looking for it. In the dusk. So near her. I gave up. I threw the cigarette case toward the bay; I dropped the handful of cigarette ends around; I dropped the broken ribbon. I even thought of the sand and drew letters on it with my finger — near enough for her to have reached it. C — A — M. . . . So there would be another clue to help hide the real one — my earring. But I forgot the handkerchief. I was upset, you see. I'd left it in my room on the dressing table. I had to give that up, I thought then. I got back to the house and still nobody was in the hall or the drawing room. It didn't take any time at all. It seemed so — so *strange* to me afterward, that so much could have happened in so little time. I waited so as to be sure everybody had arrived. I forgot the hibiscus flowers too — I hid the handkerchief in my room because while I was waiting I thought of a way to add to the clues. I'd tell Marny about it and show it to her and then burn it. She'd tell the police. I was sure of it. It would be better to come from her. Only you didn't tell the police, Marny. And then I began to wonder. Cecily had said so much. I hadn't had a chance to think of what she'd said. But she said she'd come to you, Marny, that she'd seen Andre kissing you, there by the pool. And I began to think and wonder and I wanted to know if he'd made love to you that week in New York. I had to know. I could tell by your face, Marny, when I asked you to tell Father that Andre had made love to you, in order, I said, to save Judith, that there was something. I began to — to change, I think." She stopped.

A mask had settled down over her face like a white layer of wax. She went on again, not looking at anyone, seeming to search for facts in her own mind. "No. Not really to change. Not then. I still loved Andre. I hadn't meant to kill Cecily. It was the revolver that did it. She aimed it at me; I had to take it away from her. And then the next day Andre came to me alone and said he thought I'd killed her. He said he wouldn't tell anybody. But he wouldn't marry me. . . . We'd planned that, you know. He hadn't told me anything about Cecily. I didn't know he was married until Cecily told me herself."

"Winnie . . ." whispered Marny, her throat tight.

"He said if I'd pay him enough he'd not tell, ever. I knew then — what he was. I — yes, of course, it was all washed up, then."

Bill said, "Don't, Winnie. You mustn't talk so much. There's not time."

217

"Time? No. No, of course there's not time," she said matter-of-factly, looking at Bill. "I traced your name, the beginning of it, there in the sand near her. It's queer. How fast I thought, I mean. But it didn't matter, any of it. He never loved me, you know. Andre . . ."

She gathered up the mackintosh and went to the door. Bill stood aside and she went out quietly, as if she were going about some errand. Bill made no effort to stop her. The door closed. The wind howled and slashed at the island and the house and everything around it.

Bill went to the window and stood there, staring at the blank boards on the outside of it.

"Bill . . ."

"It's all right. Wait."

"Manson . . ."

"Manson's not here. He's coming. But he's not here yet."

"Bill — her eyes . . ."

"I know," he said roughly. "I know. Do you think it's easy?" He sat down suddenly and put his head in his hands and held them there, over his face. For a long time. As if he were counting.

"But she has a revolver. She . . ."

"Be quiet," he said savagely behind those locked brown hands. "Wait . . ." The tone of his voice covered pain. "The Andres of the world," he'd said. "Men know what to do with them."

But women didn't. Cecily. Winnie.

Judith opened the door and came in. She said, "Where is Winnie?"

Bill lifted his head. He did nor speak and neither did Marny. Judith looked for a long moment at Bill and then at Marny. She swayed a little, dizzily, and grasped the edge of the desk, and said, "You knew."

"There'll never be a trial."

Judith said huskily, great dark eyes staring, as if hungry for reassurance. "Never?"

"Never," said Bill. "You can tell Tim that."

"Tim. Oh, yes, Tim knows, too. I saw it in his eyes. I don't know how he knows. He thought I did it. And then he thought it was Winnie. Either way, you see, it was tragedy. And I could have stopped it."

"No," said Bill. "You couldn't have stopped it. From the moment Andre met you and Winnie he was determined to get one of you. He stood to get the most money with Winnie."

"But she loved him," said Judith in a husky whisper. "It was the first time she'd ever loved anybody. I kept hoping it would be all right. I wanted her to have what she wanted. She'd never been in love before. I — that was why I sent him to Tim. I knew Andre would stand a better chance if he had a job. If he convinced Tim he wasn't a fortune hunter. But Tim thought he was my lover. Winnie . . ." She moved her beautiful head as if looking all around the little room yet seeing far beyond its white and coral walls. "Are you sure?" she whispered, her eyes coming back to Bill. "Are you sure it's better this way?"

"It's better for Tim," said Bill. "It's better for you. It's better for everybody."

"She told Charlie that Cecily had seen Marny. I asked Charlie just now. He insisted it was I on the telephone and . . ."

"Telephone?"

"Of course. Didn't he tell you? My voice is low and easy to imitate, you see. Winnie phoned him and made him think it was me; he said it wasn't a very good connection and that he couldn't hear very well but it sounded like me. He was sure it was my voice. She — she counted on the fact that sooner or later he'd tell the police. He'd tell them that I had phoned and that I had told him about Cecily."

"You'd better be the one to tell Tim," said Bill.

"Yes. Yes. I've got to do that for him. Yes . . ." She paused for a moment and pulled herself upward and seemed to gather all her strength, and went away again.

Bill said slowly, "Manson is a good guy. It'll never reach the papers."

"Tim . . ." said Marny, whispering as Judith had done.

Bill got up. "Tim's got courage. He's faced the suspicion of it. Judith will help him. He loves her. And she loves him."

She thought of Tim's pride. Bill was right. Tim could

219

conquer tragedy, even if he could never forget it. He could never have conquered public humiliation for Winnie and himself.

Bill said suddenly, "Andre Durant murdered Winnie and murdered Cecily as certainly as if he had done it with his own hands." He paused, then said wearily, "I ought to have known last night, when I saw the cast of my own name or part of it. But it only puzzled me, then, for I kept thinking about the hibiscus. It seemed to me that there was some funny inconsistency somewhere, only I couldn't think where or what. When I was going through the dining room to look for Laideau, I knew. The silver flower bowl was on the dining table and it was empty. It was empty when you and I, after Cecily's murder, went into the dining room. I remember how it reflected the flames of the candles. The candles were lighted. The table was set, but there were no flowers and somebody, some time, said that Winnie had gone to fix the flowers. And then I knew. And it hooked up everything. You had happened to wear Winnie's blue dress and would have been attacked if Charlie hadn't blundered along. Her dress, light blue, would have looked white in the dusk and from the airplane. And I ought to have seen it last night but I didn't. Winnie and you and Andre were the only people who knew I had come to Shadow Island at all. Whoever left that clue, beside Cecily, had to know my name. Andre was murdered. You hadn't done it. It had to be Winnie. I stopped to phone to Manson. They'd found Laideau, by the way, in a little hotel, hiding. He was afraid of being murdered, too. He guessed that Andre had tried blackmail once too often. But he didn't know it was Winnie. Andre apparently decided to doublecross Laideau, and didn't tell him his real plan."

"*Winnie . . .*" said Marny past a hard, painful stricture of her throat.

Bill said, "Not Winnie really. Andre Durant." Suddenly he put both arms around her. "Was it right, Marny? What I did Was it right?"

"Yes. Yes, Bill. It was right." He held her for a moment, his face against her own, and said slowly, "I think — all my life — I'm going to need you."

220

The storm passed. It was not a bad storm, really. Only the rim of the hurricane had caught at the island and the Beach and then whirled out to sea again. There was almost no damage.

One life was lost when Miss Winnie Wales, well-known tennis player, lost her life while attempting to row from Shadow Island to anther island.

The sun was brilliant, the skies blue, the sea blue and placid.

The murder case on Shadow Island dropped out of the newspapers.

Some time later Tim had a long talk with Bill Cameron. He told Marny about it, briefly — smoking, looking out across the placid blue bay. "This fellow Cameron," he said, "is all right. He wants me to string along with the others in a world conference. I've always played a lone hand, but . . ." he paused. "If there's any possible way for civil aviation to throw in its weight for peace, I'm for it. You can tell Bill that."

"Yes, Tim."

"He — Bill Cameron, you know — says it was really Durant. Durant murdered his wife and — and Winnie."

"That's right, Tim."

"Yes." He got up and stood with his back to her. A ghost of the old Tim came back into his voice. "You're a good girl, Marny. I'll miss you. But if that fellow Cameron wants to marry you, take him."

They were on the porch and Bill came, just then, through the drawing room. "Ready, Marny? We were going for a drive. . . ."

But at the curve of the driveway he stopped the car. The sun was brilliant, the banks green and thick. He said abruptly, "It hasn't been long — that you've known me, I mean. But I've loved you all my life. I . . . It was as if I recognized you there in the pool. That night I came. I — oh, hell," said Bill. "I can't talk." And took her in his arms, as if he meant to hold her there forever.